Tammy Robinson is a novelist from New Zealand. After the tragic deaths of her mother and a close friend, she sat down in 2011 to write a book and hasn't stopped since. She now has seven novels to her name and is busy working on the eighth.

She lives with her husband and three young children on a small farm in rural Waikato, and is sick of the sound of cows.

Also by Tammy Robinson

Photos of You

DIFFERENTLY
NORMAL

Tammy Robinson

piatkus

PIATKUS

First published in Great Britain in 2018 by Piatkus

3 5 7 9 10 8 6 4

A CIP catalogue record for this book
is available from the British Library.

ISBN 978-0-349-41904-6

Typeset in Garamond by M Rules
Printed and bound in Great Britain by
Clay's Ltd, Elcograf S.p.A.

Papers used by Piatkus are from well-managed forests
and other responsible sources.

Piatkus
An imprint of
Little, Brown Book Group
Carmelite House
50 Victoria Embankment
London EC4Y 0DZ

An Hachette UK Company
www.hachette.co.uk

www.littlebrown.co.uk

This book is dedicated to the beautiful Rachel Tipene,
and all the other Differently Normal folk out there.

Also to Mum and Dad, for everything.

Maddy

Photo of the week, we mutually agree, is the one that shows a life-size blow-up doll, one of those plastic ones that the manufacturers have tried really hard to make look like a real woman, propped up at a dining table. In front of her sits an untouched glass of red wine and a plate with what looks, on closer inspection, like a typical Sunday roast chicken dinner. There is even a little blue gravy jug, like the kind my nana used to keep in a cabinet.

Whoever cooked *that* is an amateur, Kyle said. The potatoes have no crisp and the chicken looks as dry as the skin on the end of Rory, our boss's, nose. We both shudder at the thought. We live in permanent fear of that skin – it has a tendency to flake off on to work surfaces and cups of coffee.

The doll's garish red mouth is wide open, like she is permanently surprised. When Kyle tells me why it's like that I make fake vomiting noises. I can't believe some people are actually that desperate, I say. It's not just some people, Kyle says, it's a booming industry, the sex toy one. He quickly backtracks when he sees my eyebrows shoot up.

'Not that I'd know from personal experience,' he adds defensively. 'I read an article somewhere.'

'Sure.'

'It's true,' he protests.

'Do you think he's named her?' I ask, turning my attention back to the photo.

'How do you know it's a he?' He grins. 'Could be a lesbian doll.'

We both ponder this.

'Do you think they make lesbian dolls different to heterosexual ones then?' I ask.

He shrugs. 'No idea. But I can look it up if you like.'

'Better not. Rory's checking the internet search history now, remember? He doesn't trust us to make efficient use of our work time,' I remind him, while we both studiously ignore a lady standing at the counter.

'Excuse me,' she calls. 'Do you think one of you could actually bother to provide me with some service?'

Kyle and I exchange a look.

'Rock, paper, scissors?'

'Rock paper scissors.'

'One, two, three, dammit.'

'Every time,' I say smugly.

'One of these days I'm going to surprise you by *not* doing rock,' he grumbles as he walks off to serve the lady.

He won't, though. Kyle is nothing if not predictable.

While he's gone I study the photo for clues as to the photographer, but there's nothing. Thanks to new age technology and smartphone apps, the photo order was sent in via the internet, so we have yet to lay eyes on them. Whoever it is will have to pick the photos up in person, though. That's one thing technology hasn't figured out.

Kyle comes back to my side.

'I bet he'll be wearing a long black trench coat,' I say. 'With lots of pockets to hide all his deviant sex toys.'

'And dark sunglasses,' Kyle agrees. 'To hide his perversion from the world.'

We snigger.

That's one of the things I like about working the weekend shift with Kyle, our minds are on a similar wavelength. That and the fact he doesn't ask me about my home life, for which I'm grateful. Sometimes I just need to talk crap and forget about things for a while.

'And he'll have a fake moustache,' I add, warming up to our theory.

'Fake? Nah. He'll have a real porn star one that twirls up at the ends. In fact, I bet he waxes it with special stuff he orders in from Europe. Or maybe just K-Y Jelly if he's cheap.'

'Gross. That's really a thing?'

'What?'

'Moustache waxing.'

'Again, I have no real experience on the subject, but I read something somewhere.'

Kyle is always reading. He has a voracious appetite for knowledge, most of it useless.

As it turns out we couldn't be more wrong. 'Mr Smith' – fake name, we both agree – arrives at 4.49 p.m. Sunday afternoon to pick up his photos. The cynic in me thinks he has timed his arrival just before closing time to avoid the crowds. But he is neither furtive nor shady, which kind of blows that theory. If I had to compare him to someone for identification purposes, he puts me in mind of a certain big fat man in a red suit, the one who drives a sleigh and says 'ho, ho, ho' a lot.

Mr Smith *does* have a moustache, or maybe it's just considered an extension of his monstrous beard, like a loft conversion. Snowy white and immaculately groomed, I can't help but stare at the opening where his lips are, although there's no sign of them. He asks for his order in a jolly voice. I look suspiciously behind him for any signs of sleighs or reindeers or giant sacks of toys.

The coast is clear.

'Sorry, what was the name again?'

'Smith. I sent the order in via the internet a few days ago. The little box at the end said it would be ready in forty-eight hours.' He fishes into a back pocket and pulls out his wallet. From this he produces a printed receipt. 'Does this help?'

'Probably.' I tap away at the computer keys. It can't be right. The guy looks like someone's grandfather. Maybe there are two orders for Smith.

Nope.

'Just a second, I'll check with the technician if it's ready,' I say.

The technician, a.k.a. Kyle, looks startled when I appear out the back wide-eyed.

'What? What happened? Did I miss something? Did Todd get fired again? Who did he hit on this time?'

'He's here.'

'Who?'

'Mr Smith.'

'Ahh. And? Were we right? Is the moustache waxed?'

'You'll have to see for yourself.'

'Intriguing,' he says, grabbing the order from the counter and following me out. He stops short when he catches sight of our customer.

'Holy shit,' he says in a stage whisper.

'I know.'

'The guy looks like fuckin' Santa Claus.'

'I know.'

'Are you sure it's him?'

'Yeah.'

'Holy shit. Just goes to show, doesn't it.'

'What?'

'You really *can't* judge a book by its cover.'

I cringe. 'Cliché.'

'Yes, but, in this case, appropriate.'

I shrug. I dislike clichés as a general rule.

Mr Smith sees us standing there, staring at him. If he is at all embarrassed that we know his most innermost secret, he doesn't show it.

'Find it?' he asks.

Kyle stands there, shaking his head. 'It's always the quiet ones,' he says. 'The ones you least suspect.' More clichés. I take the photo wallet from his hand and complete the transaction. We watch Mr Smith leave.

'Is it just me, or has the world become a little bit more jaded,' Kyle says sadly.

'You expect too much from people.'

'I know.'

'It's not healthy.'

'I know.' He shakes himself from his melancholy. 'I need a shower.'

'Luckily for you—' I check my watch '—it's knock-off time.'

'Are you coming for a drink?'

I imagine the luxury of sitting in a pub nursing a cold beer, no responsibilities. 'Better not. My mother has book club tonight.'

'You mean the one where they sit around drinking wine and discuss the meaning of life?'

'Yeah.'

'Well then, my dear, I shall catch you on the next drift,' he says. Kyle is on a mission to create new slang. So far it's spectacularly failed to catch on.

Albert

The old bastard is on to me.

I know this because when I hear the front door slam and saunter out to the kitchen, confidently expecting the place to be empty, he is standing there, arms folded and face expressionless.

'What time do you call this?' he asks.

'Hammer time?'

My wit, as so often happens with my father, goes unappreciated.

'Are you planning on living at home for ever? Eating my food and watching TV I pay for?'

'And using your Wi-Fi. Don't forget using all your Wi-Fi.'

His lips roll in on each other, expressing his displeasure. I watch him limber up to deliver a sermon.

'Your friends might think you're funny, Albert—'

He's wrong there.

'—but in this house I expect you to show the appropriate amount of respect.'

Ah, it's that speech. The respect speech. I lean back against the kitchen counter and cross my arms across my chest, settled in for the ride.

'I work bloody hard,' he continues.

I know this one off by heart. *To put a roof over your head and food on the table.*

'To put a roof over your head and food on the table. When I was your age—'

I didn't ask my parents to support me. Why, I was working in the quarry at the mere age of fourteen and I'd get as filthy as anything.

'I didn't sit around the house, expecting my parents to support me. I was only fourteen when I got my first job. Ball-busting physical work it was too, in the quarry. I'd come home covered in grime but proud, and—'

I earned my father's respect by paying my own way. You could do well to learn from that.

'—my father respected me because I paid my own way. I certainly wasn't a burden.'

Wait, what? That's new.

'I'm a burden?'

'I owned my own car by the age of – what?' He blinks, disturbed from the script.

'You think I'm a burden?'

'Of course not. Wrong choice of word. You know what I mean.' He looks shifty though, like he knew full well what he was saying. He checks his watch. 'Right, I'm off. Shift starts at oh-eight-hundred-hours. Tell your mother I've gone but I'll be home in time for dinner.'

He leaves, banging the front door shut behind him. My mother emerges from the laundry carrying an empty washing basket.

'Oh, he's gone already, has he?' she says, pretending she's disappointed. I don't know why she's bothering because her audience is me, and I couldn't care less if she's avoiding him or not. Plus, the laundry sits off one side of the kitchen – there's no way she couldn't hear us from in there.

I must look rattled because she puts the basket down on the counter and sighs.

'You know he didn't mean it like that, love,' she says.

'Yes he did.'

'He didn't. He's just old school, your father. You know that. It's a generational thing.'

'No, it's an asshole thing.'

'Hey, don't call your father an asshole.' She says it half-heartedly though.

'Sorry.'

'He loves you, really he does.'

'He's got a funny way of showing it.'

'You don't need to tell me,' she mutters. 'Aren't you working today? You better get your skates on or you'll be late.'

Shit, I check my watch. I was so busy trying to avoid my father I let time get away on me. Being late wasn't exactly a good look, especially not with what I had planned today.

'Yeah, I better get going.' I grab a piece of bread from the cupboard and slap some Marmite on it. As I leave I call back through the door, 'Dad says he'll be home for tea.'

'Great, I'll lay out the best china and shave my legs.'

I'm fairly sure she's being sarcastic.

After fetching my bike from the shed, I jam the piece of bread in my mouth and take off down the street. I love my bike, now. But as far as learning to ride a bike goes I was a late starter. I don't know what it was but there was something about the whole look of the thing that scared the hell out of me, much to my father's disgust. His method of teaching involved plonking a helmet on my head and taping my feet to the pedals with black insulation tape. Then he'd push me off and stand there yelling, 'Pedal your feet, pedal your feet, PEDAL YOUR GODDAMN FEET, YOU IDIOT!' I would just sit there, terrified, eventually wobbling to a stop and falling sideways to the ground. He would sigh and remove the tape, then dust off my knees and spit on the grazes to clean away the blood.

'Let's not tell your mother about this, eh?' he'd say on the way home.

It was the fear of being left out that got me on a bike in the end. All my friends would boast of the freedom to go wherever they wanted, usually the local swimming pool to ogle girls, and I didn't want to miss out. Of course most of my friends have cars now. And as much as I'd love a car of my own so I could take off to the beach whenever I feel like it instead of having to beg to borrow my parents' car, I'm saving my money for something I deem far more important: getting out of here. My plan is to get enough money to head back to the coast where I spent the majority of my childhood, and where I learned to surf. I still know a few people there and I'm sure someone will hook me up with a job. From there, with breathing space away from my father, I'll save even more, eventually heading to Bali where I've heard they're always looking for surf instructors.

The bike I'm riding was a gift from my mother last year for my eighteenth birthday. She was worried that my old one was more rust than metal and had nightmare visions of it disintegrating and toppling me in front of the wheels of a car. As crappy as it was, I'd still been sad to see it go. That bike had been my ticket to freedom for over seven years.

At this time of the morning there is hardly any traffic about so I make good time. The sky is grey but it doesn't feel like it's going to rain. More like it will burn off and we'll be left with a nice sunny day. I feel the familiar sense of pleasure I get whenever I am outdoors. I feel more at home outside than I ever do inside four walls. At the stables only Deborah is about. I wave hello. She ignores me as usual because I am clearly below her social circle. I park my bike behind the barn and say hello to Freckles, my favourite pony. She nuzzles my hand affectionately.

'How ya going, old girl?' I ask her, rubbing her on the soft spot between her eyes, which I know she loves so much.

Before I started at the stables my experience with all animals equine had been limited to a ride on an aged donkey at a fair when I was four years old. According to my mother I held on to its ears and cried the whole way around the ring. She has a photo that backs up her story and likes to wheel it out on occasion when she's feeling nostalgic for my childhood, especially after a few wines.

In our last year of high school, we seniors were encouraged to volunteer our weekends for a whole term as part of an internal awards system they set up to encourage us to Strive for Excellence, and to become Well Rounded Members of Society instead of the selfish misfits they feared some of us were destined to become. While most ended up nursing kittens at the local RSPCA or playing card games with lonely elderly people, my friend Connor and I were lucky enough to get spots here at the stables. In a classic case of 'it's not what you know it's *who* you know', his mum knew the lady, Francine, who runs the place. I don't think she was particularly pleased to be lumbered with a pair of teenage boys who barely knew one end of a horse from the other, but she owed Connor's mum a favour and Connor's mum called it in.

After the term finished and we could legitimately leave, Connor did, without a backward glance, but I stayed on. To everyone's surprise, I turned out to have a natural affinity with the horses. I often knew what they needed before they did, or sensed if one was a little under the weather or out of sorts. And I liked working with them. They didn't expect too much from me, and they never judged. After graduation Francine offered me a paid job, not many hours working for a pittance really, but I jumped at the chance to earn some regular money. My savings aren't growing as quickly as I'd like though, so I've decided to ask Francine for more hours.

'Wish me luck, girl,' I say to Freckles. She whinnies and stomps one foot, then turns her attention back to her food.

Taking a deep breath, I knock on Francine's office door.

'Come in,' she calls. Some of the staff call her Fat Francine because she's almost as wide as her desk. She's been pretty good to me though so I don't. Todd and Matt the stable boys give me shit over beers, saying she has a crush on me, but I doubt that.

When I enter she is looking pretty chuffed with herself. The bouquet of cheerfully coloured flowers with a yellow bobbing balloon gives me a clue.

'Birthday?'

She nods.

'Aw lovely,' I say.

'Guess how old I am,' she asks coyly.

I freeze, instantly on alert. I'm wary of this game. It seldom ends well, yet for some reason women still initiate it.

'No idea,' I say.

'Guess, go on,' she prompts.

I pull a few faces while I scramble to think. If I had to hazard a guess, I'd say somewhere between forty and sixty.

'Happy fortieth!' I say, erring on the cautious side.

Her face falls. 'I'm thirty-eight.'

Aw shit. Which is exactly why I don't guess stuff like that.

'I was joking.' I grin manically. 'Haha. I thought you were only, like, thirty or so. Haha. Haha.'

Neither of us believes me.

'Did you want something?' She has turned her attention to her phone and I think maybe I should come back later. But no, I'm here. I grab my confidence by the metaphoric balls.

'I was wondering if there was any chance of picking up a few more hours?'

It's her turn to pull a face.

'Please?'

She sighs. 'I don't know, funding is pretty tight.'

This would normally be the point where I'd apologise for breathing and back out of the room. But I need this.

'Pretty please?' I give her the most charming smile I can muster.

She sighs. Her chins wobble. 'Leave it with me. I'll crunch a few numbers and see what I can do.'

'Thank you!'

'I can't promise full time,' she warns.

'That's fine. I'll take anything.'

'All right. Come and see me on your way out at the end of the day and I'll have a new contract for you to look over.'

'Ah, you're brilliant. Thanks, Francine, you won't regret it,' I say, beaming as I back out of the room. Her face looks unconvinced.

Maddy

When I walk into the kitchen my mother is sitting cross-legged in a yoga pose in front of the French doors facing what she thinks is east but which is actually west. The fact the sun doesn't rise from that direction should be her first clue. Embarrassingly, it's not.

Bee has her nose pressed to the window, watching the clouds. She has her headphones on and is flapping her hands, conducting music only she can hear.

'Do you have everything ready for riding today?' I ask, opening the fridge and surveying its meagre contents. Nothing appeals so I nudge the door shut and start making the coffee I need in order to function without ripping anyone's head off.

'Um, about that,' Mum says.

I can tell by her tone I'm not going to like what comes next so I add an extra spoonful of coffee powder.

'First of all, I've been thinking maybe we try somewhere different?' she says. 'Like that place across town. What's it called? Greener Pastures?'

'No. Bee's settled. You know how important her routine is.'

I put my coffee down and walk over to my sister. 'Have you had breakfast?' I ask her.

She ignores me.

I tap her on the shoulder. 'Bee, look at me. Have you had breakfast?' I ask again when she does, signing eating with my fingers to my mouth. She looks over my shoulder.

'Pocahontas,' she says.

'She's had toast. The thing is,' Mum says, 'we're not welcome there any more. Well, I'm not. They tried to ban me from the premises so I told them where they could stick their riding. We don't need their charity.'

'What did you do?'

'Nothing! Nothing, honestly. Storm in a teacup.'

I pick up my coffee and drink, staring at her, waiting.

'OK, OK, I *might* have maybe defaced one of the political placards on their front fence.'

I sigh while she carries on quickly in an effort to justify her vandalism.

'They shouldn't have them there in the first place,' she said. 'They're supposed to be impartial, aren't they? Government agencies?'

'It's not a government agency, it's a privately run charity.'

'Oh. Are you sure? Well anyway, they had that tosser Trevor Ballard's sign on the fence. That man should eat one of his own carrots. Pest control my foot. His 1080 poison is decimating our native wildlife.'

I close my eyes and take a huge mouthful of coffee. It tastes good. It tastes *really* good. 'Do you think we could keep the Greenpeace speeches till after I've finished my coffee. Besides, I don't care if he sells drugs to pensioners.' I say. 'This was about Bee, not you. You couldn't just stay out of trouble.'

She untangles her legs and comes into the kitchen where she puts a green tea bag in a cup. 'Don't be cross, darling.' She pouts. 'It's not like I meant to get banned. What happened to freedom of speech? Not my fault they can't handle a little passive activism.'

'At least you weren't arrested this time, I guess. We can be grateful for that.'

I finish my coffee. Bee is at the window, cloud watching. She knows she has riding today because I got her jodhpurs out of the wardrobe last night. If she doesn't go now it will throw her routine out, and the last thing I fancy doing is upsetting my sister.

'Have you at least rung the new place? Booked her in?'

'Of course. I called and spoke to the manager. She said we could pop out and have a look before we commit. Make sure that Bee likes it there.'

'What time are you going?'

'The lady said around ten would be a good time. There's a class then so we can see what they do.'

I check the clock on the microwave. Eight thirty. 'You're cutting it fine.'

'Well, that's the other thing. Can you take her?'

I stare at her. 'I can't, I have work today, you know that.'

My mother and I sync our rosters at the start of every fortnight so that one of us is always home when Bee is. My mother works as a care nurse in a retirement home and obviously earns a higher hourly rate than I do, so her job takes priority.

'I know. But Sonia asked if I could cover her shift while she goes to some fortune-telling fair up north. I need to be at work by nine.'

'Since when can Sonia tell fortunes?'

'She can't, she wants to see what they have to say about the whole Adam situation.'

'Didn't he run off with her sister?'

'Yes, the bastard. But she thinks maybe it was just because he was feeling neglected.' She drains the last of her green tea and plonks the cup down on the bench, from where she thinks it will magically find its way into the dishwasher.

'Then she doesn't need to see a fortune-teller, she needs to drink a cup of concrete and harden the hell up. Why would she even want him back? She should thank her—' I stop and take a deep breath, counting to ten. It's one of my biggest pet peeves, weak women who let men give them the runaround and go begging back for more. I've been around that behaviour my whole life, courtesy of my mother.

'Whatever.' I pick up her cup and make a point of putting it in the dishwasher. 'Fine. You go to work. I'll call in sick and take her.'

'Thanks, sweetheart, you're a gem.'

I eat a piece of toast and watch the news until my mother leaves for work. I can't relax when she's here and I'm pissed off with her. I know she's not doing it on purpose and that she'll be feeling pretty rotten about it herself, but it bugs the shit out of me when she does something that screws with Bee's routine.

'Come on, Bee, shower time.'

I wait while she finishes arranging her cassette tapes in a straight line across the dining room floor. She can, and often does, spend entire days arranging her tapes. But today we have things to do, so I tell her again.

'Shower, Bee, horse riding.'

'Oh cheese, Gromit,' she says. 'We need cheese.'

I lead her to the bathroom where I help her take off her pyjamas. As each item is removed she throws it on the floor.

'Washing,' she says.

'Yes, Bee, washing.'

We have our shower routine down pat. She refuses to touch soap so I lather it up on my hands and wash her body while she regales me with nursery rhymes. She lifts her face up to the water and licks at it like a cat. Her hair we leave for last. It is wild, unruly hair, courtesy of her Maori father, and it takes me a while to comb the conditioner through. She closes her eyes and pretends to be asleep while I do it, snoring.

Miraculously, we are dressed and ready to go in good time. I'm about to start the car when I realise I have no idea where I'm going, so I get out my phone and use a search engine to bring up a map to the stable.

'I don't suppose you have any idea where we're going?' I say to Bee conversably while I wait.

'Oh I will never sleep if I don't have cheese,' she says unhelpfully.

When I turn left out of the driveway instead of the usual right she points and says, 'Which way.' She's noticed the change in direction immediately and looks worried, so I reassure her. My sister can't tell me how she likes her eggs cooked or what day of the week it is, but she knows if you take a wrong turn.

'Horse riding, which way,' she says again.

'Yes, Bee, horse riding.'

'Horse riding, which way.'

'Look, Bee, fire engine.' I point as we drive past the station in an effort to distract her. It doesn't work though, as I knew it wouldn't.

'Horse riding.'

'Yes, Bee, horse riding.'

We're only ten minutes late by the time I pull into the stable parking lot, which is not a bad effort on my part.

'Horse riding.'

'Yes, horse riding.'

I get out of the car and immediately step into a muddy puddle.

'Fuck,' I mutter under my breath.

I get the bag of her riding gear out of the boot and open her door, then take her headphones off and place them on the dashboard.

'Later, Bee,' I tell her. She swings her legs around and giggles while I remove her sneakers and leave them in the passenger footwell. Her pink boots obviously got wet the last time she wore them because they have dried stiffly, and it takes some effort on my part to get them on her feet.

'Push,' I say while she giggles and I end up with something on my hands that looks strongly like dried horse manure. I wipe it on my jeans, then put her gloves and hat on.

'Horse riding,' she says.

'Yes, horse riding.'

A gate separates the car park from the buildings, and a heavy rusted bell hangs beside it. There is also a hand-painted sign that says, ring for attention.

I give it an experimental shake and it dongs loudly.

Bee immediately pushes past me to seize it gleefully and gives it a few energetic shakes.

Dong dong dong.

'Bee, stop.'

Dong dong.

She is strong, my sister, and I struggle with her arm while she holds on determinedly.

A whippet-thin blonde carrying a bucket of horse manure comes out of the stables and glares at us.

'Stop ringing that damn bell before you frighten all the horses,' she snaps.

'Sorry.' I finally manage to wrestle Bee's arms down to her side. 'Where's the office?'

She looks me up and down disdainfully, which is a bit rich

considering she's the one carrying a bucket of shit, and idly points to the smallest building sitting to our right.

'There,' she says. 'Where there's a sign saying "Office".'

'Oh right. Thanks.'

'Whatever.' She whirls on one foot with her nose in the air and I flip my middle finger at her back. Someone snorts with laughter behind me and I flinch, hoping it's not the manager.

It's not though. Not unless the manager is a young guy with messy blond hair. I give him a wary look.

'Sorry,' he says. 'It's just that you did something I've always wanted to do but have never been brave enough.'

I have to think for a minute to realise what he's talking about.

'You mean give someone the finger?'

'Not just someone – Deborah. She kind of thinks she's better than the rest of us.'

'Yeah, I got that impression.'

He puts down the bucket of water he's carrying and strides towards me energetically. I take a step back, unnerved by his enthusiasm.

'I'm Albert,' he says, thrusting out a hand.

I smirk.

'I saw that,' he says.

'What?'

'You smirked.'

'Sorry. I've never met anyone under the age of seventy named Albert before.'

He sighs. 'I know. Although technically it's *Al-bear*. My mother wanted it pronounced the French way.'

'You don't look French.'

'What do you mean I don't look French? Why, because I'm not wearing a beret and carrying a baguette? That's stereotyping.'

'You have to admit it's a bit stupid.'

'What is?'

'Well, your mother named you Albert, but wanted it pronounced *Al-bear*, right?'

'Right?'

'Was she planning on following you around for the rest of your life, correcting everyone?'

He opens his mouth and closes it a few times. Then he sighs. 'Yeah, she didn't really think it through.'

'No kidding.'

'That's why I just say Albert. It's easier.'

'Why not shorten it to Bert. Easier again.'

'Because I get enough grief as it is without sharing a name with a *Sesame Street* character.'

'Fair enough.'

He looks behind me. 'Why is she doing that?'

I turn around, expecting anything. As far as things my sister *could* be doing, it's relatively tame.

'She's giving you the finger.'

'Yes, I can see that, but why?'

I shrug. 'Mimicking my behaviour.'

'Ah. Like a game of Simon Says.' He nods, as if he understands perfectly.

'Not really. Bee, come here.'

She walks to my side and looks out of the side of her eye at Albert.

'Hi,' he greets her, smiling.

I try not to be a judgemental person, as a general rule, but when it comes to how people greet my sister I can't help it. Some people almost fear her, or pity her, and it shines through in their eyes even if they try to hide it. Some people treat her as if she's almost an inanimate object, like she's a pot plant. Some can't even look her in the eye, as if they're worried about how she might react.

But then there are the ones, like Albert, who look at her directly and greet her as if she were just like them.

I trust these people.

Bee curls her top lip up in a gummy smile and flashes her teeth at him. 'I'm a loudmouth schmuck,' she says.

He looks from her to me and back again. 'I'm sure that's not true.'

'It's a line from *Looney Tunes*. She only speaks echolalic.'

'What's that?'

'She repeats stuff she hears from movies or cartoons etc. It's her way of trying to join in on the conversation. You get used to it.'

'I see.' Something occurs to him. 'Did you just call her Bee?'

'Yes.'

'So that must make you, wait, don't tell me, let me guess.' He screws his face up playfully. Is he flirting? He's not bad looking, if you're into the whole 'healthy outdoor' kind of look. 'Butterfly? Caterpillar?'

'Close. Maddy.'

'Maddy. Short for ... Madison? Madeline?'

'Maddy.'

A door slams behind me and I hear footsteps stomp across the gravel. A tall, very thin lady wearing jodhpurs that have seen better days stops beside Albert and looks at Bee.

'Hello there,' she says cheerfully. 'Newbies are you? I'm Carolyn.'

'Rubbish,' Bee says.

'Ah.' Carolyn consults her clipboard. 'You must be ...' She pauses, squints, looks up at me quizzically. 'Madonna and Beyoncé?'

Albert snorts with laughter.

'Maddy and Bee will do just fine,' I say through gritted teeth.

Albert

I'm not sure if she heard me laugh or not. I did cough afterwards in an attempt to disguise it.

Madonna and Beyoncé. And I thought *I* had it bad.

'This way, please,' Carolyn says, leading them off in the direction of the office. 'We'll just go inside and sort out the paperwork. Your mother already filled us in on Bee's disabilities, so you just need to read over the forms and sign them. After that I can give you a tour and Bee can have a ride. Did you bring her list of medications with you? We need it for insurance purposes.'

'Yes. Got it. Everything is right here.' Maddy pats a green backpack she's carrying.

'See you around,' I call after her as they walk away.

She flicks me a quick look over her shoulder. 'Yeah maybe.'

I do see her a few times throughout the morning. They've given her sister a horse called Teddy to ride. He's a sturdy old fella, white with a black spot on his head and another on his chest that looks like a map of Africa. He plods along, never frisky or letting anything faze him. Of course, when you're a horse with pretty much nothing to do but eat, shit and let someone sit on your back for brief periods of the day, life's grand.

'I hear you scored yourself more hours,' Matt says when we're mucking out one of the stalls.

'Yeah. Only a few, but it's a start. It'll keep the old man off my back anyway.'

'So how was it?' he asks.

'How was what?'

He pauses from turning the hay to wipe his brow and give me a sneaky look. 'Well I assume you screwed Fat Francine to get more money out of her.'

'Fuck off.' I throw a spade full of horse shit at him but he ducks out of the way and it splats on the wall behind him.

'You're cleaning that up,' he says.

'Fine, but mention me and screwing and Francine in the same sentence again and I'll shove your head up your ass.'

'Ooh struck a sore spot did I?'

'You're an idiot, Matt, seriously. An actual fucking idiot, you know that?'

'I've been called worse.' He checks to make sure the coast is clear and pulls a cigarette from his pocket which he clenches between his teeth. 'Cover for me will you?'

I don't really want to, partly because of his smart comment but mainly because I don't fancy getting fired before I can start earning proper money. But it's a bloke code thing. You look out for each other, even if you don't particularly like the guy.

'All right. But hurry up. And if anyone sees you you're on your own.'

'Wimp.'

He slinks like a wraith around the corner and is gone. The hay isn't going to shovel itself so I set to it. Before long I have sweat dripping down between my shoulder blades and off my forehead. I take off my shirt and use it to wipe my face, then sling it on to a hook by the door.

It's physical work, this job, but that's one of the things I like most about it. Beats sitting behind a desk answering calls and emails all day, that's for sure. When I finish and bike home at the end of the day, I *feel* like I've done a proper day's work. The only downside, apart from being paid peanuts, is that it gives me too much time to think.

Normally being alone with my own thoughts wouldn't bother me. Apart from being a monumental disappointment to my father, I've not much to be ungrateful for or unhappy about. But meeting Maddy has reminded me of someone I've been trying really hard to forget. I don't know what it is, because she looks nothing like her apart from maybe a similar dark hair colour. Maybe it was a certain cynicism, or air of I-couldn't-care-less, but she reminds me a bit of Kate.

Kate.

My girlfriend, or at least she was, till she dumped me seven months ago.

While I was cruising along happily thinking we were doing

just fine, she was bored, apparently. She fixed that by sleeping with Jamie-fuckin'-slimeball-wanker-Hunt, which is of course not his actual name but which should be. The devious bastard sensed her dissatisfaction and made his move. Or several moves, from what I observed when I busted them shagging on the back deck of my friend Connor's house. It was supposed to be a surprise birthday party for me. It was certainly a surprise all right.

To make matters worse, I'd drunk so many beers I cried, *I actually cried*, in front of everyone. This turned out to be not the way to win back Kate's affections.

'Sorry,' she'd said, disgust clear on her face. 'But we just grew apart. I'm not the same person I was at fifteen, Albert, and neither are you.'

'But ... I ... don't ... understand ...' I snivelled like the broken-hearted drunk I was. 'You ... said ... you ... loved ... me.'

'Christ, Albert,' she hissed, leaning forward so only I could hear her. 'Get a grip, will you? You're embarrassing yourself.'

I spent the rest of the night on Connor's couch alternating between crying and vomiting. He, being the good mate he is, kicked everyone out and keyed Jamie's car as he and Kate drove off. Or so he says. He's more of a lover than a fighter though, so I have a feeling he just said it to cheer me up.

Kate.

We'd been together since we were fifteen. I'd watched her develop from a girl to a woman. Physically this had been the most impressive, especially when her boobs came in. But it

29

was more the fact that she *got* me. She of all people knew just how complicated the relationship between my father and I really is.

Connor reckons my hurt is more of an injured pride thing than a legitimate broken heart. He reckons Kate and I had outgrown each other, that we were more friends than anything towards the end, and that we wanted different things from life but were stuck in a comfortable rut that neither of us wanted to be the first to break out of. He says Kate did us both a favour and that although I might not see it yet, I will.

I reckon Connor needs to get a job and not watch so many *Oprah* repeats.

It was after we broke up that I hatched my plan to travel while teaching surfing. Bali is first on the agenda because I've heard they'll take on anyone who can ride a few waves, even though I'm significantly better than that. From there I'll see where things take me. I don't mind really, because anywhere is better than here.

'Dude, put your shirt back on, you make the rest of us look bad,' Matt whines as he comes back.

'You should quit that stuff,' I tell him, trying not to breathe in too deeply. He reeks of smoke and in this confined space it's making me feel queasy. 'You know it stunts your growth right?'

He makes a crude gesture towards his crotch. 'Nothing to worry about in that department, if you know what I'm saying, mate.'

'Yeah, *mate*, you're not exactly subtle.'

'Subtlety's overrated.'

Between his yellow-toothed sniggering and the stink of smoke wafting off him I feel the sudden urge for fresh air.

'I'm off for a leak,' I say. 'Don't slack off while I'm gone.'

Outside, in the circular driveway, I'm just in time to see Maddy buckle Bee into her seat before driving away. She goes straight past me without a glance.

Maddy

Mum walks in a little after ten. I can tell straight away she's been drinking, and not only because she reeks of cheap wine and second-hand smoke. At least I hope it's second-hand; we have enough trouble paying the bills as it is without her adding an addiction into the mix.

'Darling,' she slurs cheerfully, as if I am some long-lost bosom buddy. I glance at Bee, who is sitting beside me on the couch watching a Disney movie on her laptop, to make sure she is wearing her headphones. She is curled up against my side like a cat, her curls tickly against my arm. If she has noticed Mum come in she doesn't show it.

'Where have you been?' I ask, trying to keep my tone from being too confrontational.

'Work, of course.' She laughs, but it's forced.

'And in the five hours since?'

She waves a hand and sighs exaggeratedly like our roles are

reversed and she is my daughter and I am giving *her* the third degree.

'Out.' She pouts.

'With?'

'Friends. God what are you, the fun police?'

I give this the answer it deserves. Silence. She cracks within five seconds.

'I'm sorry,' she sighs, flopping down on to the armchair opposite and kicking her shoes off, her relief evident on her face. 'But I am allowed to have some fun. It's not easy working and being a full-time mum.'

I open my mouth to say something sarcastic when an alarm sounds in the kitchen.

'I'll get it,' Mum says, scrambling to her feet ungracefully and exposing the massive hole in the tights she is wearing under her uniform that extends from just above her knee to her crotch.

'Did you know your tights are ripped?'

She flushes and nods, unable to meet my eye 'I can't afford new ones until payday,' she says quietly. 'Besides, you can't tell when I'm standing.'

Any anger I feel flees and leaves me feeling deflated and heartbroken at the pathetic sight of my mother making do with holey tights because she can't afford a new pair, at the ridiculous price of $5.99 or whatever they cost.

She's right. She works hard in an often thankless job and frequently goes without to make sure Bee and I have a roof over our heads and food on the table, so I shouldn't begrudge her a night out here and there. Although it's not actually the night out that worries me. It's the fear she'll meet a new man.

I watch her leave the room to switch the alarm off and get Bee's tablets. She looks good for her age, my mother, like a younger version of Goldie Hawn. She has the same fluffy blonde hair and trim figure. I know from old photos that she was a stunning teenager. You can still see that beauty, it's just a little faded and smudged around the edges.

'I could have lent you the money for tights, Mum, if you'd asked,' I tell her when she walks back into the room.

'Oh I know you would, love,' she says, coming over to sit beside Bee. She puts a glass of water down on the coffee table and taps Bee on the shoulder, signing for her attention. Bee climbs on to her lap and smiles at her mother.

'*Pocahontas* now available to own on Disney home video,' she says.

Mum kisses her on the forehead. 'Hello, beautiful girl.' She passes her the glass of water and the first of the five tablets Bee takes every night before bed.

'I can't take any more of your money though,' Mum continues. 'You already contribute more than someone your age should have to.'

'I don't mind. Besides, six bucks isn't exactly going to break the bank.'

'Six bucks here, seven there, where will it end? No. You already contribute to the bills more than I'd like.'

'I'm not going to have this argument again.'

'Who's arguing? I'm grateful. But keep your money. Don't

go giving it out willy-nilly to any old charity case with ripped tights.'

'You're not a charity case, Mum.'

'I know. Sorry. A moment of self-pity.' She passes Bee her last pill then closes her eyes and says a yoga chant. 'Hmmm, ommm, ummm.' Then she opens her eyes and smiles. 'There. Moment over. Normal programme resumed. Bedtime I think.'

'I'll get Bee ready if you want to take a quick shower.'

'Thanks, love.' She smiles gratefully. 'I'd love one.'

'Bedtime, Bee,' I tell my sister when Mum has gone. She shows no sign of having heard me while I turn the TV off and check the doors are locked.

'Bee, bedtime,' I repeat as I walk back into the lounge. 'Turn the laptop off now, please.'

She does as she's told this time and follows me down the hallway to the bedroom she shares with Mum. She turns her MP3 player off and watches as I plug it into the charger and make sure it's switched on at the wall. I've only made the mistake of not checking once, and it's not a mistake I'd care to repeat. Her headphones go on the bedside cabinet.

I help her pull off her top and she wiggles out of her jeans by herself. Then I pass her a pyjama top with the tag at the back so she just needs to pull it over her head. She sits on the bed to put the bottoms on, but accidentally puts both legs into the one hole.

'Oops,' she giggles.

'Come on, you silly sausage.' I help her put them on properly. We only have one bathroom and it's a cramped affair, so while Mum showers, Bee goes to the toilet and then after flushing, closes it and sits on the lid so I can brush her teeth.

'Open your mouth,' I tell her.

'Hello, Paddington.'

'Open your mouth, please, Bee.'

This time she obliges.

'How was riding today?' Mum calls over the shower curtain.

'Yeah, not bad.' Bee pulls away from my brushing to wipe at the toothpaste that has leaked out of her mouth. She doesn't like it on her skin and holds a towel ready while I brush so she can immediately clean any spillage.

'Open your mouth. She seemed to like it. They gave her a nice gentle horse.'

'Oh good. There you go, silver linings. It was obviously meant to be.'

It's too late and I'm too tired to argue, so I just roll my eyes. Bee giggles, causing more toothpaste to spill. She dabs it away quickly. When I've finished cleaning she wipes her mouth one last time, swallowing the toothpaste foam because she won't spit it into the sink. Then she opens her mouth wide for my inspection.

'What lovely clean teeth,' I say, and she rewards me with a big grin.

The shower gets turned off and Mum pulls back the shower curtain. 'Pass me my towel will you.'

'Jesus, Mum.' I avert my eyes and pass it to her. 'Ever heard of boundaries?'

'Yeah, yeah. Nothing you haven't seen before.'

'That doesn't mean I want to see it again.'

She wraps the towel around herself and laughs.

'I'm not joking,' I mutter. 'I'm fully serious.'

'No secrets in this house. It's the three Baxter girls against the world, remember?' She links arms with Bee and I and smiles toothily like we're on the cover of some Hallmark card. I pretend to vomit.

Bee, who has no idea but who has an impeccable sense of timing, chimes up. 'Nonsense,' she declares.

Back in their room, while Mum gets her nightgown on, Bee goes to the window and pushes apart the curtains to have one last look at the night sky. She presses her nose up against the window glass, her breath causing steam circles that bloom and disappear just as quickly with the cold.

'Bed, Bee,' I tell her. It's late and I am weary. I want to sink into my own bed, my own pillow, and check out on the day.

She smoothes a tiny wrinkle from the bottom sheet before she is satisfied enough to lie down. I lean over and kiss her forehead.

'Good night,' I say. 'I love you.'

She smiles at me and starts reciting the scene from *The Lion King* where Mufasa is telling Simba he basically needs to grow up and take his responsibilities seriously. My mother slides into the bed beside Bee and pulls the duvet up. She kisses her lovingly on the forehead before she rolls on to her side, with her back to Bee.

'Go to sleep, Bee,' she says. 'I love you.'

'No, no, no, no, not the stick,' Bee says, still re-enacting *The Lion King*.

'Night, Mum.' I flick the light switch off on my way out.

'Night, love.'

I head to my own room where I barely pause to strip off my jeans and unhook my bra before climbing into bed still wearing my T-shirt. I can hear the murmur of Bee's voice through the walls, but I know if she doesn't fall asleep soon Mum will help her.

It's a routine we've been following for years.

Albert

My mood, already low from the unintended trip down memory lane, dips even lower when I turn into my street and see my brother's car parked hard against the kerb outside our house.

I'm tempted to do a U-turn, head to Connor's and hide out until the coast is clear, but then I'd be leaving my mother to deal with my father and brother alone, and she's done nothing to deserve that. My brother isn't a bad person, depending on your definition of bad. Opinionated, outspoken, a touch racist and ever so slightly a bit on the sexist side, he's like a younger model of my father. The two of them share the kind of relationship I could never hope to be a part of, one I resigned myself to being without a long time ago.

There's also a small part of me that can't wait to tell them that I now have almost full-time hours at the stables. I'm kind of hoping Dad will be impressed by this news, but past experience is stabbing me repetitively in the ear telling me I'm ridiculous to get my hopes up.

Sure enough, the windbag himself is holding court from my father's La-Z-Boy, a beer in one hand, the remote in the other. His various offspring, four of them, are lolled about on the couch absorbed in their phones and tablets.

'Say hello to Uncle Albert,' Miranda, their mother, says when I walk into the room.

'Mumble deadbeat mumble loser,' they say, or at least it sounds like it. They don't even bother to look up.

My brother, Louis (pronounced the French way of course, *Louie*) looks me up and down condescendingly, even though he's not much to look at himself. In fact, he could quite comfortably rest his beer can on the mountainous stomach that sits proudly before him.

'Y'all right?' he says.

'Yeah fine, thanks. You?'

'Fucking fantastic, mate.'

'Don't swear,' his wife scolds him, checking the 'children' to make sure they haven't been traumatised by their father's vulgarity. I'm willing to bet they've heard, and said, much worse.

'Got another pay rise,' he carries on proudly. 'Second one this year. Only guy in the company to get one.' He drains the rest of his can and crushes it like tissue paper in his meaty hand. Then he throws it at my head. Luckily, it's not the first time, so I'm prepared.

'Good catch.' He nods. 'Get me another one would you.'

Then he lets out a huge burp.

'*Louis,*' Miranda scolds.

'What? Better out than in.'

'Where's Mum?' I ask.

'Dunno. Around. She was here before.' But his attention is fixed on the TV, where I can see the All Blacks are currently playing Ireland.

'Run, run, RUN FASTER, YOU COCONUT!' He smiles, satisfied, when a try is scored.

'Louis,' Miranda hisses.

'What?'

'You can't go around saying racist things like that.'

'It's not racist,' he says. 'I work with a bunch of bloody islanders remember?'

I try, and fail, to understand how this statement justifies his racism. It's nothing new though. If you don't look like my brother thinks you should look, he'll have a special word just for you, guaranteed, and you won't like it.

'Where's that beer?' he asks.

I've just opened the fridge to get him one when I hear muffled voices from the laundry. I sidle over to press my ear against the door.

'Don't pretend you don't want this,' a husky voice says. 'You want me just as much as I want you, I can see it in your eyes and the way your breasts are heaving against my hot, naked chest.'

My eyebrows shoot up. *Say what?*

'Quick,' the voice continues. It is male, but it is not the voice of my father. 'Give me your hand. Here, feel my desire for you.'

Then the tone changes. 'Katherine gasps as she touches the taut skin of his—'

I decide I've heard enough and throw open the door. It bangs heavily against the wall and my mother screams, clutching at her chest.

'Jesus, Albert, you scared me half to death.'

I look around the laundry, confused. There's no one else here.

'Ever heard of knocking?' she mutters.

'Whose voice was that?'

'Voice? Oh.' She turns and picks up a CD player from the top of the washing machine. 'I was listening to an audio book while I did the, er ...'

She looks around wildly and then opens the door of the dryer before closing it again.

' . . . washing.'

I look pointedly at the half-empty bottle of wine that is sitting on the lid of the washing machine.

'What?' she says defensively. 'It's thirsty work.'

'Relax, Mum. Your secret's safe with me.'

'Good boy.'

'You do know Louis is here right?'

'Why do you think I'm hiding in here?'

'How long does it take to get a bloody beer,' my brother's voice complains from the lounge. 'I could have brewed my own in the time you've taken.'

My mother rolls her eyes. 'Tell him to fetch his own.'

'Yeah, I quite fancy my face the way it is, thanks.'

She gives me a sympathetic look. My brother is a carbon copy of my father in so many ways.

We hear the back door open. Mum quickly stands in front of the wine.

'What are you two doing in here?' Dad asks, popping his head around the door frame, frowning.

'I was just asking Mum for advice on how to get horse muck out of my clothes.' The lie comes out smoothly.

'Give her a break,' he says. 'You're big enough and ugly enough to figure it out for yourself. She's not your slave.' He sniffs the air. 'Is dinner ready, love? I'm starving. A hard day's work will do that.'

The last comment is, of course, for my benefit. I take it as my cue and straighten my shoulders proudly.

'Actually, Dad, you'll be pleased to know that as of—'

'I'll just have a quick splash in the shower,' he says, as if I hadn't spoken. 'Won't be long.'

Then he disappears.

My shoulders sag.

'Sorry, love,' Mum says quietly. 'He doesn't mean to be so rude.'

'Yeah he does.'

'Actually speaking of stains.' My father reappears and squints at his uniformed shoulder. 'Do you think you could get this blood out of my sleeve?'

He mistakes my mother's expression for one of concern.

'Oh don't worry, it's not mine. Idiot perp tried to headbutt me while resisting arrest. I ducked my head though,' he says smugly. 'Broke his nose on my forehead. That'll teach him.'

He disappears again.

'What were you going to say?' Mum asks.

I tell her about the job and my increased hours and she's happy for me, of course. She fetches another glass and we have a toast in front of the washing machine.

'Here's to your bright future,' she says proudly.

'Thanks, Mum.'

'No I mean it. You're destined for good things, Albert. I've known it since the moment I clapped eyes on you.'

She's lying of course. Or the wine is. But I'm grateful anyway.

I try again to broach the subject when we're all seated around the table eating dinner. My audience is hardly the most receptive. Louis's kids are sulking because they've been made to leave their electronic devices in the lounge. Their faces look like their hands have been cut off, so I could probably announce I'd been abducted by aliens and they wouldn't care less. My brother and father are on the whiskey, which means I have a small window while they still feel jolly and goodwill towards mankind, before one too many glasses tips them over the edge and they become brooding and spoiling for a fight.

'Ahem.' I clear my throat, and wait for someone's, anyone's, attention.

Mum looks from me to Dad and gives me a wink. 'Yes, love?' she says unnaturally slowly. A stage actress she is not. 'Do you have something exciting to announce?'

'Speaking of announcements,' Louis says. Some mashed potato escapes through his teeth as he talks and does a kamikaze leap to the tablecloth. I don't blame it. Of the two fates I know which I'd prefer. 'You're going to need to buy another chair in a few months.'

I lean back in my chair. As far as announcements go, he's just trumped me.

Miranda flushes and lowers her cutlery to the table. 'I thought we'd agreed not to tell anyone yet.'

My brother looks genuinely surprised, which is a clear sign he most likely wasn't listening when that particular conversation took place. 'Did we? Oh well. Doesn't matter whether we tell them now or in six months. We're screwed regardless.' He sees her crestfallen look. 'Sorry, you know I'm just joking.' He pats her on one drooped shoulder.

'We'll be fine,' he says unconvincingly. 'They already outnumber us. One more isn't going to make much difference.'

My mother, maybe because of the unknown quantity of laundry wines already consumed, is slow on the uptake.

'Why do we need another chair?' She looks blankly from Louis to Miranda.

'I guess congratulations are in order,' I say. 'Congratulations.'

Louis narrows his eyes at me. 'What's that supposed to mean.'

'Congratulations? It's a term people use when someone shares good news. Means well done. Good on ya, mate.'

'Don't be a smart-arse.'

'Can someone tell me what's going on?' Mum asks.

'Why did you say it like that?' Louis growls at me. The whiskey window has closed and Louis the Hulk is here. Normally

45

it's my cue to keep my mouth shut, but I'm resentful that no one is interested in hearing my news. So I prod the bear instead.

'Like what?'

'Like the way you said it.'

'How did I say it?'

'Like you were having a go.'

'Well I wasn't.'

'Sounded like it.'

'I wasn't.'

'Better not have been.'

'Or what?'

'Wouldn't you like to know?'

'That's why I asked.'

Our father is watching the exchange with amusement. Growing up, he always pitted us against each other. 'Competition is healthy,' he would say. 'A little confrontation is what separates the men from the boys.' Which was all very well in theory, but what it meant in practice was that I frequently got my arse walloped at the hands of my older, much bigger, brother, whether I was in the right or not. Who needs to be right when you have brute strength on your side?

'Keep going and you'll find out,' he says menacingly.

But I'm not twelve any more, and since my heartbreak I've had a small streak of a death wish anyway. If he wants to wallop me at the dinner table because of some misconceived slight, he's welcome to.

I stare at him, waiting until I know he thinks he's won and

I've shut up, then just as he's lifting a piece of steak up to his mouth I fire the kill shot.

'Not my fault you can't keep it in your pants,' I say.

With an angry roar, he drops the fork to the table and shoves his chair back violently.

'Outside, now,' he bellows. He is panting with fury and ready to rip my head off. To an outsider this would probably be an alarming sight. For us it's just a regular family dinner.

Miranda grabs an arm that is pointing an angry finger at me and tries to pull him back down on to his seat.

'Louis, please,' she says. 'Stop being silly. He didn't mean anything, did you, Albert?' She looks at me desperately. She looks exhausted, and for the first time I notice she has wrinkles that don't go away any more when she smiles, instead they are carved into her skin in a permanent reminder of a frown. It's not easy living with my brother 24/7, I know first-hand. And she also has his offspring and now a bun in the oven to deal with. I take pity on her.

'No.' I smile charmingly. 'Of course I didn't. I'm really happy for you guys.'

She smiles at me gratefully. 'See?'

Louis grumbles, unconvinced. But he relents and lets her push him back down into his seat.

'It's early days yet,' Miranda says. 'So please don't tell anyone. And no, before anyone asks, it wasn't planned.'

'Oh!' My mother claps her hands together and squeals. 'You mean you're having another baby?'

Maddy

Photo of the week, *not* mutually agreed upon, is a stunning night shot of the moon, framed by clouds and dotted around by stars. It is the blue of midnight, of dark denim, of the ocean right at that point where the bottom drops off. Whoever took it clearly fancies themselves as somewhat of a nature photographer. Based on their photos, I'd be inclined to agree. There are photos of flowers, trees, birds and even a small lake that has Kyle and I mystified. Neither of us is aware of the existence of any lakes around these parts. But it's the moon photo that captivates me.

It is not Kyle's first choice, or even second, but it beat his choices by way of a round of rock, paper, scissors.

It's not often we disagree over our photo of the week choice, but occasionally it happens. We keep our selection pinned to a board in the back room. Depending on what we've chosen, they're either there to inspire or entertain us.

Kyle went all soppy on me on Tuesday when he processed

an order from an old couple's sixtieth wedding anniversary. Misty-eyed as he flicked through the shots – 'Just *look* at the love on their faces when they look at each other, have you ever seen anything so sweet?' – he nominated a photo of the two of them sitting at a table with a big cake in front, bearing the words 'Happy 60th Wedding Anniversary Edith and Pete!!!' (with two extra exclamation marks needed to get the point across apparently). They are leaning in towards each other, their heads touching, smiling for the camera.

'So romantic,' he sighed dreamily. 'Can you imagine spending sixty years of your life with someone?'

'Yeah, in my nightmares maybe.'

'God, you're so cynical. I suppose you don't believe in love at first sight either.'

'Not unless you're talking about between me and a pizza,' I say, grinning.

He shakes his head sadly.

The second photo he puts forward for nomination is less the romantic side of him and more the rampant horny bastard.

'Holy shit,' I hear him whistle on Thursday. Sensing excitement, something the last five hours of my shift has lacked, I'm out the back immediately.

'What? What?'

'Check this out.'

I peer over his shoulder at the screen, then groan. 'I should have known.'

'I bags being there when she picks these photos up,' Kyle says. 'I don't care if I'm rostered on or not.'

'You don't think she might be a touch out of your league?'

We study the screen. The photo is a selfie taken on a stick by a drop dead gorgeous brunette who could easily give the Kardashians a run for their money in the lips and buttock department.

'Do you think they're natural?' I ask, touching my fingers to my own inadequate lips.

'Probably not. Who cares? I bet they feel great when she goes dow—' he remembers his audience. 'I mean when you kiss her.'

'Nice save.'

'Thanks.'

'You could rest a beer on her butt.'

'It does look a little like a shelf, doesn't it?'

'Do guys seriously get turned on by that kind of body?'

'I can only speak for myself, of course, and normally as you know I'm more of a boob man, although she has a pretty spectacular pair of those too. But yes, there is something about her body that makes me want to—'

I put my hands over my ears. 'Stop. TMI.'

'Sorry.'

'I don't care what you want to do to her, it's not going on the board.'

'Oh come on, you have to admit she's pretty spectacular.'

'Compared to what?'

He looks me up and down.

'I'd think twice before you say what you're going to say,' I warn him.

'Compared to your crappy moon shot, is what I was about to say,' he lies. 'Give me a chance.'

'It's not crappy. You loved it too when you saw it.'

'That was before I saw *this*.'

'Rock, paper, scissors?'

'Rock, paper, scissors.'

'One, two, three, go.'

'Dammit.'

It's not that I crave that obvious, high-maintenance, glamorous look, because I don't. For the record, I'm perfectly happy the way I am. I *like* being low maintenance.

I'm crouched down with my back to the counter, doing a quick stocktake of supplies in the cupboard later that afternoon because I am *that* bored, when I hear my name.

'Maddy?'

It's a feminine voice, slightly familiar, but not enough for me to immediately identify its owner.

'Madonna Baxter, is that you?'

Ah. I cringe, as the voice recognition slots into place. I stand up and turn, coming face to face with the glistening white smile of Casey Smith, the most popular girl in our high school. She's one of those girls you'd love to hate, but can't, because despite being painfully beautiful she's actually a fairly decent person as well.

'Oh my God,' she squeals. 'What are the chances of running into you here?'

'Pretty good, considering I work here.'

'You do?' She blinks and looks down at the shop logo that is embroidered on to my shirt, just above my left breast.

I nod.

'Full-time?'

'Yes.'

'On the photo desk?'

'Yes.'

'Oh. Well, good on you.'

'Thanks, I think.'

'Don't be embarrassed,' she says. 'A job is a job.'

'I'm not.'

'So does this mean you didn't go to university?'

'It does.'

'Why not?'

'Oh you know,' I say, 'few reasons.'

She gives me a questioning look and tilts her head as if she's waiting for further explanation, but she's out of luck. I'm not discussing my life choices with her or anyone.

'How about you?' I reflect the question back to her. 'How's life treating you?'

She nods enthusiastically. 'Great. Almost finished my second year of Veterinary Science studies. It's tough but I love it. Few more years left till I graduate and then I think I'll take a couple of years off and do some travel. Europe maybe, or Asia. Or both. So many places I want to see.' She laughs.

I manage a semi-smile.

'Well, I better get back to work,' I say, thumbing over my shoulder. 'Those staples won't count themselves.'

'OK. Well it was really nice to see you again.'

'You too.'

'And next time I'm in town we'll do lunch or something.'

'Sure,' I lie. 'Sounds good.'

I watch her leave.

'Kyle,' I call.

His head pops around the door. 'What?'

'I need a break. Cover for me.'

Something in my expression causes him to frown. 'Are you OK?'

'Grand. Back soon.'

I walk away quickly, out the front doors even though we're supposed to use the staff exit, and I don't stop until I'm at a bench seat a block away. On a small patch of grass on a street corner that the council has tried to 'pretty up' in an effort to make the town more appealing. I sink down on to it and exhale slowly.

I try not to dwell, generally. And most of the time I do a damn good job of it. But occasionally, like now, life likes to rub my face in the fact that while everyone else is caught in the fast lane that is life, whizzing past me and racking up achievements and milestones and generally going from success to success, I am stuck on the shoulder, not even in the slow lane. I am, in fact, stationary. Broken down with hazard lights flashing. Working the same job I have for the past six years, after school and the odd weekend at first and then full-time since graduation. Living in the same house. It's not like I don't have aspirations, because I do. There are other, equally as dead-end jobs as the one I do available. But I took the job on the photo desk because I love photography.

And I'm good at it, at least I like to think so. I even have this vague idea at the back of my mind that maybe I could make something of it, one day. But the realist in me doesn't see how, or when. Even though it's my passion, it has to take a back seat to my obligations.

When I get home after my shift finishes the house is quiet. Too quiet.

'Mum? Bee?' I check the lounge. It's empty.

'In here,' Mum calls from their bedroom.

They are lying on the bed, Bee watching something on her MP3 player. Mum has her arms around her and is smoothing fine tendrils of hair away from her forehead.

'Everything OK?' I ask, sitting on the end of the bed and wriggling my sister's big toe. She doesn't look up at me.

'She had a fit.'

'For how long?'

'About forty minutes. Then she slept for an hour. She's just woken up.'

Apart from being a bit pale, Bee looks her usual self. She usually does though, after a fit. Just quieter. She is transfixed on the small screen in her hand, her other hand flapping near her face in a self-soothing gesture.

'I'd like a three-minute egg,' she says. 'Woah! Steady on! Oww!'

'It's my fault,' Mum says guiltily. 'The change in routine, changing stables. I should have known it would upset her.'

'That's not true. You know her fits are completely random. Don't blame yourself.'

She sighs. 'I know. It's hard not to. After all these years they still terrify me.'

Mum looks pale too, and tired. Her eyes are red-rimmed like she's been crying, which she probably has. It's not like her to blame herself or go down the self-pity route, not for a long time anyway. I know she's kicking herself. I also know that anything that happens with my sister's health is not her fault or my fault or indeed anyone's fault. It's just the way things are.

When Bee was born Mum was already the proud owner of another bastard child, namely me, product of father unknown. Well, she has some hazy details. A good-looking stranger, she says, that she met in a bar after a Madonna concert (hence the name). She didn't even catch his name, and the mechanics of their meeting were brief as she tells it. A drunken fumble in a back alley, forgotten until she fainted at work four months later and learnt he'd left her with more than the imprint of a brick wall on her arse.

Bee's father was at least in the picture slightly longer. I was eight when she was born, the result of a brief fling my mother had. Her father was nice enough, harmless, good-natured. He was also jobless and transient, grateful for the warm bed my mother provided him. He took for the hills when my mother told him about his impending fatherhood. We woke up one morning and he was gone, and we've neither seen nor heard from him since.

She was the most beautiful little baby, my sister. Tiny, like a baby bird, with delicate features. Her skin hung off her and she had very little muscle tone.

I fell in love with her fast and deep.

She's like a little doll, people would exclaim.

The doctors suspected something was wrong from day one, and we went for appointment after appointment while they ran tests.

'She's just not growing,' Mum insisted. 'She doesn't even have enough energy to drink her milk properly.'

There were other things we noticed too. Her eyes wouldn't focus, they flicked from side to side and her head measurement was too big compared to her tiny body. The doctors thought she had hydrocephalus, and scans showed the ventricles in her brain were enlarged, which most likely indicated fluid on the brain. A cerebral shunt to bypass the obstruction was discussed. I was only eight, playing on the floor of the waiting room with my doll, and the big words the doctors threw at my mother went over my head more often than not, but the intention and the worry on my mother's face were clear enough. Then one day not long after, when she was just shy of five months old, she stopped flicking her eyes from side to side and focused, and the doctors said the fluid in her brain had found its own drain. I remember my mother celebrating with a small glass of wine that night, saying that everything was going to be OK now.

But at eight months we were back in for more investigation. She still wasn't growing as she should, or meeting her milestones. Cerebral palsy was mentioned. Again, I didn't know what that meant, but I heard my mother cry at night and I knew it wasn't good. At a year old, Bee weighed less than the

Jack Russell puppy next door, although her head was that of a much larger toddler. It was so big she couldn't hold it up, or crawl or roll over, and she was floppy, like a rag doll. We were told she would never walk or talk, but Mum was determined to prove them wrong. She did the special physio exercises she'd been shown religiously at every nappy change and was rewarded when Bee took her first steps at the age of two and a half. It took her much longer to learn how to balance properly without falling flat on her face.

We tried hard, Mum and I, to teach her words, but she remained non-verbal despite our best efforts, so we learned Makaton, the signing language. It was a turning point; at least now we could communicate with her.

When she was six my mother requested an appointment with a new doctor. The autism diagnosis came as no surprise to us really. We knew something was different, and now we had a label for it. I was fourteen then, and more aware. There had been an autistic boy in one of my classes a couple of years prior. He wore nappies and once masturbated in the cloakroom and we avoided him like the plague. I remembered the other boys teasing him when the teacher wasn't around. If he understood the words they called him he never showed it.

Bee was toilet trained, thanks to my mother's determination, and always happy. She went to a school for children with special educational needs where she did intense speech therapy and physio. We learnt to ignore the stares and the snide comments from people who really should know better. I never stopped wanting to hurt or maim anyone who looked at her like she was a freak, but I did learn not to act on it. Bee taught us tolerance and patience. If she didn't feel sorry for herself, what right did we have?

Puberty brought with it another diagnosis, epilepsy. It was hard not to feel bitter and think, *Hasn't she been through enough?*

But we learned to live with it. What choice did we have?

Still, at night when I would lie in bed and listen to Mum comfort her after yet another epileptic fit, I would cry silent tears into my pillow. I was terrified for what the future held for my little sister, but I knew that as long as she had me and Mum she would be OK.

Albert

The next time I see Maddy she makes my heart stop, not for a long time, just enough for the tick of a clock hand. I catch a glimpse of her from behind, you see, and her resemblance to Kate is uncanny enough to leave me stricken, caught up in momentary fantasy that it *is* Kate, here now, looking for me, to tell me she made a huge mistake and to beg for my forgiveness.

It's not of course.

The world is generally not that kind, not to me anyway.

I'm on a break so I follow her and her sister to the indoor arena and loiter in the shadows of the doorway from where I can watch them unseen. She's attentive to her sister, helping her on to the horse, standing just close enough to be there should she be needed, but she doesn't mollycoddle. She lets Bee take the reins, literally and figuratively, and watches on proudly as Bee smiles broadly from the back of the horse.

She's quite pretty, Maddy, with her long dark hair. I'm not

one of those guys with a preference for one female body part over another, but still, I can't help but notice and be appreciative that Maddy goes in and out in all the right places. Her eyes are an intense green that remind me of the ocean just after a storm.

Somewhat guarded at our first meeting, it's here when she's unaware she is being observed that she lets that guard down. Her features have relaxed as she smiles and calls out words of encouragement. She isn't wearing any make-up, or if she is it's subtle, but she doesn't need it.

Maybe it's the weight of my inquisitiveness, but something tips her off and she stiffens and tilts her face to the side. I quickly draw out of sight, aware the situation could come across a little on the creepy side. Checking my watch, I realise my break is over anyway so I head to the stable to finish polishing the leather with a cream preserver. I'm lost in thought when Todd comes up behind me.

'Payslips are out,' he says, flourishing a piece of paper at me. 'Let's see what pittance we've earned this week, eh?'

I take mine from him and watch as he rips along the dotted lines of his own, his forehead furrowed as he mouths out the figures he sees.

'Aw damn,' he says. 'I'm short this week. Mustn't have any sick days left.'

'When were you sick?'

'Monday.'

'What was wrong?'

He leans forward and looks both ways as if he's about to

cross the road. 'Between you and me and that saddle,' he says, 'I had a case of can'tbefuckeditis'.'

'Never heard of it.'

He looks at me like I'm thick. He's not the first.

'Dude, it's a joke. Get it? Can't-be-fucked-itis?' He says it slower.

'Is that anything like appendicitis?'

He's lost for words, and his eyes search my face as if he can't believe what he's hearing. I can't hold my smirk in any longer.

'You fuckwit,' he says, laughing. 'Jeez, you had me going. I thought Matt was the dumb one around here.'

'I heard my name.' Matt sticks his head around the door and looks confused when we erupt with laughter.

Later, when they're gone, I rip open my own payslip and smile with satisfaction at the black numbers on the bottom. Almost double what I was earning before, and if I bank the majority of the extra straight into my savings I could be out of here by the end of the year. The thought is hugely exhilarating and I look around for someone to share it with, but there's no one nearby. I feel melancholic for a moment then shake it off. This is a good thing. Plus, I've decided to pay my father board so he doesn't carry on thinking of me as a burden.

I stay up that night until my pay goes into my account just after midnight, and then bike to an ATM to draw out fifty dollars cash, which I hand to him over the breakfast bar the next morning.

'What's that?' he asks.

'Money.'

'No shit, Sherlock, I can see that. Why are you giving it to me?'

'For board.' I shrug. 'I asked Francine for more hours and she said yes. So I'm earning more now, and I want to pay my own way.'

He looks at it and then looks at me. I don't realise I am holding my breath, waiting for some kind of recognition or praise that I swore black and blue I neither needed nor wanted, until he speaks.

'You think fifty bucks covers the food you eat?' He opens his wallet and slides the note inside. 'Hell, it barely covers the toilet paper you wipe your arse with.'

'It's plenty,' Mum says. I hadn't realised she was standing behind me, observing the exchange.

'I can get you more,' I say stiffly.

Dad opens his mouth and looks over my shoulder at Mum. 'No it's OK,' he says. 'Fifty is fine.'

No 'congratulations' or 'well done'. I wasn't really expecting it, but at the same time it would have been nice.

Maddy

I don't recognise the guy standing on the other side of the counter at first, although he grins at me like we're long-lost twins.

'Can I help you?' I ask, wishing not for the first time that Tony had taken some of my suggestions in the suggestion box more seriously. As far as he's concerned, a panic button for dodgy-acting weirdos is 'unnecessary', and a baseball bat for just plain old weirdos 'illegal'. As far as I'm concerned this is all very well and good for him sitting up high in his office on the second floor, safely out of harm's way.

'Maddy, it's me.' The guy standing on the other side of the counter throws his hands wide as if this should help with the identification.

It doesn't.

Kyle is standing beside me, amused. I know what he's thinking, but unlike him I don't make a habit of sleeping with and then forgetting people's names or faces.

'You're going to have to give me another clue,' I say.

The guy clicks his tongue. '*Bonjour, mademoiselle, comment allez-vous?*'

Kyle leans closer. 'I didn't know you speak French,' he whispers.

'I don't.'

The guy looks dejected. 'Shit, I know I'm no great looker, but I didn't realise I was *that* easily forgotten.'

Somewhere in my brain the connection is made, and the correct file slots into place.

'Albert.'

He brightens. 'Al-*bear*. You *do* remember me.'

'To be fair, we have only met once, for like five seconds.'

'Twice,' he says. 'Although the second time I don't think you noticed me.'

'Is there something I can help you with? Only I'm due a break.'

'Oh yes, I'm here to pick up some photos for Francine.' He rummages in a pocket and pulls out a receipt which he slaps on the counter.

'No problem, won't be long.' I pick up the receipt and head out the back. Kyle follows me and hovers while I flick through the photos waiting for collection.

He clears his throat pointedly.

I ignore him.

He sighs.

I ignore him some more.

'Madonna Baxter,' he says finally. 'You've been holding out on me.'

'No I haven't, and if you call me that again I'll chop your nuts off.'

He puts a hand protectively over his crotch. 'No need for threats. Now dish, who is he?'

'You do realise you're sounding gayer every day right?'

He waves a hand dismissively. 'My sexuality is fluid, and irrelevant. If you don't want to tell me who he is I'll go and ask him myself.'

'Go ahead. He's just some guy from Bee's new riding stable. I've barely said three words to him.'

'Oh,' he says disappointedly. Then he brightens. 'Well you obviously made an impression.'

'Why?'

'He remembers you.'

'So?'

'So you must have done something right.'

'Don't do that.'

'What?'

'Read things into situations that aren't there.'

'I'm not.'

'You are.'

He slaps a hand to his chest indignantly. 'Is it bad of me to want to see you happy?'

'I am happy.' I find the photo wallet I'm looking for and nudge the drawer shut with my hip.

'Maddy, in the whole time I've known you you've never even been on a date. I'm starting to think there's something wrong with you.'

'Why? Because I don't jump into bed with anyone who might look twice at me?'

'Are you insinuating I do?'

I roll my eyes. 'Kyle, I'm fine. I don't have the time or energy for a relationship. Anyway, I don't need a guy in my life to be happy. I'm perfectly capable of creating my own happiness.' I walk back out the front and he follows me.

'Ah,' he says, 'you're talking about masturbation.'

As he says it the music that pipes from overhead speakers trails off as a song finishes and his voice comes out unnaturally loud. I see Albert's eyebrows shoot up and his cheeks redden. My own start to feel warm too as I whirl to glare at Kyle.

'Sorry,' he mouths.

I can't meet Albert's eyes as I bag the photos and ring the purchase up on the till. 'Eighteen dollars, thanks,' I mumble.

He passes over a twenty and I hand him his change.

He doesn't walk away.

We both stand there awkwardly, me wishing there was a fire alarm button close enough so that I could set off the alarms and end the torture. He's better-looking than I remembered, but maybe I was just too busy making sure Bee was OK the other day to notice. His honey-blond hair looks like it's kissed by the sun and bathed in the sea, and his smile stretches from ear to ear, almost too wide for his face, but it suits him. He is wearing a white T-shirt that shows off his deep tan and toned arms. I know without looking my own arms are like snow in comparison, thanks to being confined to artificial lighting.

'Um,' he finally says. 'So I was wondering if you'd like to come out for dinner or a coffee some time?'

'No thanks.'

'Could you at least pretend to think about it?'

'Sure.' I squint over his left shoulder and count to ten in my head. 'No thanks.'

'Maddy,' Kyle hisses from behind me. 'Don't be so rude.' He steps forward and gives Albert his smoothest smile. 'She'd love to.'

'No I wouldn't.'

'Yes, you *would*. It won't kill you to go out and act your age for once.' Kyle takes over the negotiations. 'Does tonight suit?' he asks Albert.

'Tonight would be great,' Albert answers, looking from me to Kyle uncertainly.

'That's sorted then.' Kyle picks up a pen and scribbles my number on a piece of paper, which he hands to Albert. 'Text her the name of the restaurant and she'll meet you there.'

'I can't,' I say. 'Mum's on a late shift so I have Bee.'

'Bring her with you.'

'She's not a fan of noisy places.'

'As luck would have it I know a quiet one, hardly any people.' Albert beams.

'If there are hardly any people then it can't be very good,' I grumble.

He holds out a finger. 'I can see how you might think that, however, you'll just have to trust me. Do you like spicy food?'

Albert

She's not coming, I've been stood up.

My paper serviette is torn to shreds on the tablecloth in front of me. I wasn't even aware I was doing it, a sure sign of my nervousness.

My fault, I suppose, for accepting a date that the other party was effectively bullied into.

'You want another beer?' Boonsri asks.

I say no, because another beer coupled with the sympathy that is thick in her voice just might be enough to make me cry again, something I'm trying to avoid.

'Just the bill, Boonsri,' I say. 'Thanks.'

She clicks her tongue and shakes her head. 'Silly girl who no come. You handsome man. I twenty years younger I marry you.'

'You're just being nice,' I say, chuffed nonetheless.

'Yes, I paid to be nice remember.' Then she laughs. 'No, no, you are nice boy. She no know what she missing.'

'Hi.'

Boonsri turns to where Maddy and Bee are standing behind her and promptly falls in love. I see it on her face. Some people have a natural affinity for the crippled ducks and lonesome amongst us, she is clearly one of them. Maddy is wearing the same clothes she had on earlier, and I'm not sure whether that means she doesn't care enough to make an effort, or she feels comfortable enough not to bother. I hope it's the latter. She has a backpack slung over her shoulder. Bee is wearing her headphones and watching something on her MP3 player.

'*Sawasdee ka*,' Boonsri bows. 'Welcome. Sit, sit.' She bustles to pull out their chairs.

'Thanks,' Maddy says. 'But if you don't mind can we move to that table over there?'

She points to a table in the back corner. It's probably my imagination, but it looks dark and dingy and far away from anyone and everything.

'Ashamed to be seen with me?' I joke.

She doesn't laugh. 'If it's too much hassle we can always leave.'

'No, don't.' I jump up. 'I was kidding. I'm sure it's fine. Boonsri?'

'Yes yes, is OK.' Boonsri gestures. 'You sit anywhere you like.'

'Bee has no concept of personal space,' Maddy explains. 'So unless you want her grabbing other diners, stealing their food or twerking in their faces while they eat, it's best we sit in the corner.'

I stand back like a gentleman and let Maddy and Bee lead the way. She settles Bee into the chair closest to the wall and sits beside her. I take the chair facing Maddy and watch as she starts moving all the cutlery and napkins that are in front of Bee, pushing them to the empty space opposite. I take the opportunity to check Maddy out without her knowledge. Her long dark hair falls around her face like curtains, straight except for the ends which flick and curl in every which direction rebelliously. Her skin is pale, and I wonder if she even spends any time outdoors. If she does she must go through a heck of a lot of sunscreen. She finishes sorting out Bee and looks at me, arms crossed, her guard up. I'm on to her though. She might exude toughness but there is an underlying vulnerability in her eyes.

'Hi, Bee,' I say. She doesn't look up. 'Can she hear me over her headphones?' I ask Maddy.

'Yes. She has incredible hearing.' Maddy turns and lifts them from Bee's ears. 'Say hello, Bee,' she says.

'Say hello Bee,' Bee echoes.

Maddy smiles. 'Bee, this is Albert.'

Bee looks at me. 'Bert. Bert, Bert. Oh, Ernie, go to sleep.'

'*Sesame*—' Maddy starts to say.

I cut her off. 'Yeah, I know that one. Hi.' I give Bee the thumbs-up signal for 'hello' as I say it.

'You know Makaton?' Maddy asks, surprised.

'No, well, a little. I've picked a bit up from working around the stables.'

'Hm.'

I'm not one hundred per cent sure, because her expression hasn't changed, but I think I just impressed her a little.

'Isn't this nice,' I say, smiling broadly to overcompensate for the nerves I'm feeling. I've just realised this is my first proper date. Ever. Kate and I started going out when we were barely in our teens. By the time we started dining out at restaurants I knew everything about her.

This is new territory. I asked Maddy out on a complete spur of the moment. It wasn't planned. I didn't even know she worked behind the photo counter until I saw her there and when the words came out of my mouth they surprised me as much as they did her. Now we're here, and I have no idea what I'm supposed to talk about.

'Do you like Thai?' I ask.

'Too bad if I don't, seeing as we're already here.'

My face falls. 'I guess I probably should have checked first.'

Then I notice her faint smile.

'You're teasing,' I say.

'I am.'

'You had me worried there.'

'Relax. I like Thai.'

She opens up the backpack and starts taking things out and I watch with interest. Out comes a colouring-in book and some pencils. For the moment, Bee is busy watching cartoons and ignores them.

'It's all new to me, sorry,' I say.

'What is?'

'This. Dating.'

'This isn't a date.'

'It's not?'

'No.'

'What is it then?'

'Dinner. One that I was bullied into coming to, by the way.'

'Sorry about that.'

'It's fine. I only really came to shut Kyle up.'

'Wow.' I wince. 'That's really flattering.'

She shrugs. 'Sorry. That came out harsher than I meant it.'

Boonsri comes to the table and interrupts before things get too awkward. 'Here your menu,' she says.

Maddy intercepts the one for Bee. 'She doesn't need one, but thank you.'

Bee suddenly reaches over and grabs Boonsri's hand. She thrusts her MP3 player at her.

'Wash your face,' she says.

Boonsri, quite rightly, looks confused. 'My face?'

'It's a line from *Looney Tunes*,' Maddy explains, in a voice that says she's explained the same thing a thousand times. 'She's watching it.'

'Ah OK.' Boonsri nods, although it's clear she doesn't understand at all. 'You funny girl, I go wash.'

'No that's not what she mea—'

But Boonsri is already gone. Maddy sighs.

'So. Madonna eh? Interesting name.'

'"Interesting" is open to interpretation,' she says dryly. 'When you've spent your childhood being teased and having

"Like a Virgin" sung at you every time you walk into a classroom, it loses any interest pretty fast, believe me.'

'I can see why you'd shorten it.'

She leans back in her chair and smirks. 'You're hardly in a position to make fun of someone else's name, *Al-bear*.'

I shake a finger at her. 'Exactly. From one tragically monikered soul to another, I'm merely sympathising.'

'If you say so.'

'Is there a story behind it?'

'There is, but it's not one I tend to relay on first dates.'

'Ah, so this *is* a date?'

'No, it's not – that's not wh—I meant go out for dinner.' She flushes attractively when she corrects herself. 'Can we talk about something else?'

'Of course.'

I watch her while she looks at the table, then the wall, over my shoulder and finally at Bee. I try desperately to think of something, *anything* else to talk about that doesn't involve her name. I fail.

'For the record, I don't think it's *that* bad.'

She starts to stand up.

'Sorry! Don't go. I'll talk about something else.'

She lowers herself back into her chair and gives me a cautious look. 'Promise?' she says.

'Promise.'

'Good.'

'So, Beyoncé,' I say. 'What's the story behind that on—'

'Oh for—' Her chair scrapes back.

73

'You ready to order?' Boonsri has arrived just in the nick of time. I'm left guessing whether Maddy would have actually walked out or not, and decide not to mention names again just to be safe. 'Yes. I'll have the usual.' I smile gratefully, trying to look cool and sophisticated.

'Sure, sure.' She stands there, waiting, her pen poised. 'Which is?'

Maddy snorts, but sinks back into her chair and shuffles it back in towards the table.

'The red curry. With chicken.'

Boonsri scribbles it down. 'How hot you want?'

'Fairly hot. I don't mind a bit of a kick.' I smile at Maddy and pat my stomach. 'Iron constitution.'

'No handle Thai hot.' Boonsri shakes her head. 'I make you medium.'

'Pfft,' I scoff. 'Don't worry about me. Make it as hot as you like, I can take it.'

Boonsri scribbles something down on her pad. 'And you?' Boonsri asks Maddy.

'I'll have the same. But medium heat, please. I know my limitations. My sister will just have a bowl of rice.'

'Bread?' Bee suddenly asks, looking up from her screen.

'No Bee, no bread. Rice.'

'Bread?'

'No bread.'

'Just rice?' Boonsri frowns.

'Yes please.'

'No sauce?'

74

'No. No sauce.'

'You sure?'

'Very,' Maddy says firmly. 'Thank you.'

While we wait for our food and Maddy stares at a poster of Phuket on the wall, I search desperately for something to say. This isn't going how I thought it would. Not at all.

'I'm sorry, about before,' I say finally. 'I won't mention it again.'

'Mention what?'

'Your nam— oh.' I notice she's holding back a smile. 'That was a test?'

'Which you nearly failed.'

'Sorry.'

'Stop apologising.'

'Sorry.'

'You did it again.'

'I know, sorry. Oh for the love of …' I shake my head ruefully

'It's like a disease.'

'It really is. Courtesy of my middle-class upbringing.'

'We're from the bottom,' she says. 'We don't apologise for anything.'

I don't know what to say to that, so I just look a bit like a possum in headlights until she takes pity on me and laughs. When she does it transforms her face, and I feel myself relax.

'I'm kidding,' she says.

I smile ruefully. 'Like I may have mentioned once or twice, this is all new to me.'

She shrugs. 'It's just dinner. People eat dinner every night. Nothing to get worked up over.'

'I guess when you put it like that.'

She gets distracted by Bee making signs at her.

'Excuse us,' Maddy says. 'Bee needs the bathroom.'

'Of course.'

I watch them walk away, Maddy holding tightly on to the back of Bee's elbow to steer her in the right direction. Breathe, I tell myself, aware that I'm not making a great impression. The opposite, in fact. Boonsri brings our food over just as Maddy and Bee come back.

'Can I have a spoon for her, please?' Maddy asks.

'Spoon?'

'Yes.'

'No fork?'

'No.'

'Just spoon.'

'Yes.'

'OK. I get spoon.'

'Does she always repeat everything you say?' Maddy asks me, sliding back into her chair. She pushes Bee's rice on to the opposite side of the table. 'It needs to cool down before she can eat it,' she explains, when she sees my questioning look.

'I can't say I've noticed.'

'Maybe it's just me then.'

'Maybe.'

'Do you come here often? And have your "usual"?' She snorts with laughter again at the memory.

'Yes, OK,' I concede, laughing with her. 'That was me trying to show off.'

'It didn't work.'

'Clearly.'

'Why would you want to show off to me anyway?'

I shrug my shoulders, unsure whether to say something clever or just go for honesty. 'I don't know. I just thought that's what you do, on dates. Or non-dates, as you pointed out this is.'

She chews thoughtfully on a piece of broccoli while she watches me. 'Why did you ask me out?'

There's no way I'm going to tell her it's because she reminded me a little of my ex, or that she has a piece of broccoli stuck between her two front teeth for that matter. I take a mouthful of my own curry to buy myself some time. 'Why not?' I say when I've finished chewing. 'You seem like a nice person.'

'Until tonight we'd barely exchanged five words. How can you tell if someone is nice from that brief an impression?'

'I don't know. You just can.'

She thinks about what I've said while she polishes off her curry. I'm impressed with how quickly she eats. I become aware that my tongue is starting to tingle. Suddenly Bee stands up and starts singing 'Mary Had a Little Lamb' at the top of her voice. Maddy busies herself calming her down, and while she's distracted I take the opportunity to drink both my own water and hers. Shit. Shit shit shit. My mouth is burning.

'Everything OK here?' Boonsri has appeared beside the table seemingly from nowhere.

'Mm,' I mumble, because I'm worried that if I open my mouth I might breathe actual fire.

'Everything is fine, thanks,' Maddy answers. She has got Bee sitting again and has started to feed her the rice. She catches sight of me and stops spooning to give me a funny look.

'What?' I ask, thinking maybe I have a piece of broccoli caught in my own teeth.

'Are you OK? You're sweating an awful lot.'

'Am I?' I wipe my forehead with my napkin and it comes away drenched.

'Sir?' Boonsri says.

'Mm?'

'You OK, sir?'

I clear my throat. 'Just grand. Although, could we have some more water, please. For the table.'

'Have mine, oh. That's weird.' Maddy picks up her glass and realises it's empty.

'Food too hot? You want I take away?'

'What? No.' I wave my hand airily. 'The food is—' I cough a few times '—absolutely delicious.'

It seems to take an eternity for her to come back with a fresh jug of water, during which I smile through my agony and try hard not to combust in my seat. I gulp three glasses of water, none of which seem to make a bit of difference.

'Why don't you just admit it?' Maddy asks, clearly amused.

'Hmm?' I swallow. Is it just my imagination or is my throat closing up? 'Sorry?'

'You can't handle the heat. There's no shame in admitting it.'

'Heat? Oh you mean this?' I gesture at my bowl. Now that I look closely I can actually see the chilli seeds floating on the top. Like a thousand small eyes, they mock me. 'Is it spicy? I barely noticed.'

'Really? You're going to keep up the pretence?'

'I don't know what you mean.' I spoon up another mouthful of curry, carefully trying to dodge as many seeds as I can. It's like trying to take a dump on a public toilet without touching the seat. I close my eyes and open my mouth. The spoon hovers. I open one eye to see if she's still watching. She is.

'Waiting for something?' she asks.

'No.'

I eat the curry.

Fuck.

I spit the curry back out.

My mouth, already inflamed, reacts like I've just prodded an angry wasp nest, and a thousand stings stab at every corner of my tongue.

I forgo the glass and gulp straight from the jug.

Maddy laughs.

'I'm ... glad ... I ... amuse ... you,' I manage to splutter.

'I thought you had an iron constitution?'

'I thought I did!'

'Everything OK here?' Boonsri has appeared again.

Maddy is laughing too hard to answer her. Boonsri fetches me a glass of milk which goes some way to putting out the fire in my mouth but sets me off on a coughing fit.

'No Thai hot next time,' she says. 'You silly boy. No listen to Boonsri.'

'Sorry,' I say through tears while she bashes me on the back.

'The stunk he smells pee you!'

We all look at Bee who is grinning.

'She means skunk,' Maddy says, as if that explains everything.

Maddy

'So?'

'Whar.'

'How was it?'

'How was what?'

'Duh, the date.'

'None of your business.'

Kyle pouts. 'Fine, don't tell me then.' He flounces off out the back, hoping reverse psychology will work. He's back thirty seconds later.

'Please please please tell me,' he pleads, kneeling at my feet and wrapping his arms around my legs.

'Get off.'

'Not until you give me all the juicy details. Come on, I have no life of my own so let me live vicariously through you, please?' I look at his pathetic face and cave.

'Ugh. Fine.'

He climbs to his feet and claps his hands together. 'So?'

'So what?'

'How was it?'

'It was . . .' I shrug. 'It was fine.'

'Just fine?'

'What do you want me to say? I went. We ate. It was fine.'

'I want you to tell me you felt the earth move. I want you to tell me that you fell madly in love with him and he carried you off into the sunset and shagged you senseless over a bottle of bubbly wine back at his place.'

'You read too many Mills & Boons.'

'I know, blame my grandmother.'

'Anyway, I had Bee with me, remember?'

'Oh yeah. So no carrying off then?'

'No.'

'And no shagging?'

'Definitely not.'

'Well, that sucks. Still, I suppose there's always next time.'

'There won't be a next time.'

'Why not?'

I shrug. 'I'm just not interested in anything. I have enough going on.'

This isn't strictly accurate, but Kyle doesn't need to know that. It *is* true that I have a lot going on already, with little time left over for anything else. And up until now I've been OK with this. I've never felt like I was missing out on anything. But after our date I can't help but wonder. Is this how it feels? For normal people? I get this kind of shiver of something in my chest when I think of Albert. It's not unpleasant. I enjoyed my night out with him, and not only because it made a welcome change to have company other than my mother or Bee. Most people my age, they have wide social circles. Friends. Romantic interests. Extended family. Fellow students, co-workers.

There's just Mum, Bee and I. It's always been that way.

He snorts. 'If you ask me it's sad. Here you are in the prime of your life, probably as good-looking as you're ever going to be, and look at you. Single.'

'You're single too,' I point out. 'I don't see you dashing off home to someone every night.'

'Yeah, but there's a difference.'

'What?'

'I don't choose to be single, but you do. You're single because you just can't be bothered.'

He's wrong, but I don't bother explaining it to him. Unless someone has someone else who is so dependent on them for everything like my sister is on me, they can't understand. They might think they do, but they don't. Everything I do, every single decision I make, has to be weighed up carefully to decide how it will affect my sister. I have to consider things we may encounter that will upset her. Whether there will be loud music (most shops these days), or flashing lights that could trigger a fit. If she gets too tired, it can trigger a fit. She isn't a huge fan of either babies or dogs, both can easily upset her. And then there's her little routines, her quirks. Like the fact that she wants to eat the same thing for lunch every day. Peanut butter sandwiches. If, on the rare occasion we go out and she eats something else, she will still ask over and over for her peanut butter sandwiches. So we plan ahead and take them with us. There are a million things that will either make my sister happy or upset, and only two people in this whole world who know what those things are. It's a heavy responsibility.

But I wouldn't have it any other way, because every single day she makes me laugh. With her own laughter, loud, raucous and unforgiving, and with the funny things she repeats, often with devastatingly brilliant comic timing. Of which, of course, she is blissfully unaware. She's taught me to not take myself so seriously, and that embarrassment is a waste of time. I've lost count of how many times she's twerked her bottom in someone's face, or opened the toilet door on me in public when I've been perched over the bowl, knickers around my ankles. She's poked, prodded and grabbed strangers. Sat on people's laps, insisting they kiss her hand like she is the queen and they are her subjects.

I've learnt the art of patience, and that judgement is for the insecure. But most of all, I've learnt about unconditional love.

She is locked inside her own world and innocent, heart-breakingly so. All I want to do is protect her. Not because I *have* to, but because when she wraps her arms around my neck and breathes her hot breath on to my skin, the love I feel for her threatens to explode in my expanding chest.

Albert

Three days.

Three whole days and something like sixteen hours. That's how long it's been since I last thought about Kate. Apart from when I realised I hadn't thought about her and tried to calculate how long it had been. But that doesn't count.

My date with Maddy may not have gone as well as one would generally hope a first date would, but I learned at least two things from it.

The first: that I can't handle chilli as well as I thought I could. (And that I shouldn't try and show off on first dates.)

And the second is that Maddy, even though she may have spent the first half of our 'date' a little resentful about being there, underneath it all is actually quite a nice girl.

When the usual staffroom morning tea banter kicked up about the weekend and 'What We'd Got Up To', it was nice not to be the pathetic one who'd sat at home by himself watching old *Terminator* films on rerun like usual. With his parents in the next room.

'Did you shag her?' Matt wanted to know.

'None of your business.'

'That's a no then.'

'A gentleman never kisses and tells.'

'Still a big fat no.'

'Fuck off.'

After our 'non date', I'd stood awkwardly on the pavement while Maddy buckled Bee into her car, trying desperately to recall anything the boys might have mentioned about acceptable sexual advances on a first date. I didn't want to move so fast I ended up with a slap and a police caution, but on the other hand I didn't want to offend her by not trying anything, whereby she might think I wasn't interested. To kiss or not? Shake hands and move in for a hug? What the hell was protocol?

In the end I spent so long dithering she was already around her side of the car by the time I'd decided I would just go for the shake and see where it led.

'Good night,' she said over the roof of the car.

'Good night.'

'Thanks for dinner.'

'You're welcome.'

Bee banged on her window loudly, causing me to jump.

'You are a pig!' she shouted.

'*The Lion King*,' said Maddy.

'Do you know all her cartoons off by heart?'

She shrugged. 'Pretty much.'

'Impressive.'

'It's all she watches. Day in, day out.'

'I can think of worse things, I suppose.'

'You didn't have to pay for her dinner too, you know.'

'I don't think a bowl of rice will break the bank.'

She smiled.

'I hope it wasn't too unbearable in the end, going out with me.'

'Let's just say it wasn't as horrible as I expected it to be.'

I nodded, smiling. 'I'll take that.'

'Good night, Al-*bear*.'

'Good night, Madonna.'

It was only after her car lights had disappeared around the corner that I realised we hadn't made plans to see each other again. Was there like a cooling-off period that I was supposed to observe between the date and a follow-up phone call to request another date? I couldn't ask Connor. He made a point of *never* calling a girl, preferring to let them do all the chasing. This actually meant he sat at home watching *Terminator* reruns and texting me most Friday nights.

I wait in my room until Dad has left for work the next morning then seek out Mum for advice.

'Oh hello, love,' she says when I open the laundry door. She is sitting on a foldable camp chair watching *The Ellen Show* on a small TV that is perched on top of the washing machine. A coffee machine is plugged in on the laundry bench and brewing; the smell rich in the confined space.

'Hey, Mum, I was hoping you could help me with something.'

'Of course, hang on a sec.' She gets up and turns the volume on the TV down. She opens a cupboard, takes out a cup and pours herself a coffee. 'Would you like one?'

'No, thanks.'

She sits down again. 'Fire away.'

'How long should a guy wait after a date before he calls a girl to ask her out again.'

She takes a sip of coffee and muses upon my question. 'Wait,' she says. 'This is missing something.' She gets up and opens another cupboard to reveal a bottle of Baileys. After unscrewing the lid, she tips a bit into her mug.

'What?' she asks defensively when she sees my concerned face. 'Your grandfather was one-eighth Irish, didn't you know? It's medicinal. It's like taking a daily multivitamin over there.' She sits back down. 'OK, so back to your question. I've heard that you should wait a day or two before you call, so as not to appear too keen. But who are we talking about here? Are you "the guy"?'

'Maybe.'

'Then don't wait. Don't. Call her now, have a date, fall in love, get married and escape from this house. There's no hope for me but you can still get out. Run. RUN WHILE YOU STILL CAN.'

I stare at her. 'What?'

'I'm joking of course, darling, ha ha. Ignore me, it's the Baileys talking.' She takes another gulp of coffee and mumbles something under her breath. 'No look, seriously. If you want to go out with her again just call her. I don't see the point in waiting around. You might wait too long and she'll lose interest.'

'Do you really think that might happen?' I ask, alarmed.

'It's possible. But how should I know? I married the first man who asked. Which obviously I'm grateful for because otherwise I wouldn't have you,' she adds quickly. 'Look, is she nice? Do you like her?'

'Yes and yes.'

'Then call her. Now if you don't mind Ellen's about to interview Tom Hanks. I like him, very talented man.'

'OK. I'll leave you to it.'

'Turn it back up on your way out, please.'

I ignore my mother's advice, and the fact she seems to be slowly moving into the laundry, and I wait a couple of days so as not to appear overly desperate before I call Maddy. It rings five times then goes to voicemail. I panic and hang up, because in all the fantasies I have had about how this conversation might go, I haven't allowed for that. Then I realise she'll see she has missed a call from me and might think it's weird that I haven't left a message, so I call back, this time with a bright and breezy, slightly comedic message rehearsed and ready.

She answers. 'Hello?'

'Oh shit, you're there.' I nearly drop the phone.

'Excuse me?'

'Sorry for swearing, I wasn't expecting you to answer.'

'It's what people generally do when you ring them.'

'Yes, I know, I just mean because you didn't answer the *first* time, so I wasn't expecting you to answer *this* time.'

'I can hang up if you like.'

'No don't, I just meant ... Look, any chance we can start again?'

'Oh fine, go on then.'

'Hi,' I say brightly.

'Hi.'

'How are you?'

'I'm good, thanks. Yourself?'

'Also good, thanks. In fact, I'm wonderful. Everything's good. Life is, well, life is ...'

'Good?'

'Well yeah. Um, so I was wondering ...'

She says nothing but I hear her breathing softly so I know she's still there, waiting.

'Would you maybe like to, if you're not too busy I mean, and didn't have a horrible time the other night, would you maybe like to go out again?'

'That depends.'

'On?'

'Are you going to eat spicy food and sweat all over the table all night again?'

'Oh ha ha. No, no way. Christ, that was awful.'

'Look, Al-*bert*, I'm flattered. And I think you're a really nice guy.'

I sense a 'but' coming and dive in quickly. 'I think you're nice too.'

'I'm just not interested in a relationship right now. It's not personal.'

'Oh.'

'Sorry.'

'Are you sure?'

'Yes.'

'Oh.'

'Sorry.'

'For the record though,' I rally, 'who said anything about a relationship? I was only talking about dinner.'

'I know, but—'

'Dinner. A meal.'

'Yes but—'

'Between friends.'

'Friends? We barely know each other.'

'And that's not going to change is it? Unless you come out with me again.'

'Like I said—'

'Come on,' I wheedle. 'A meal. Just one. You have to eat don't you?'

She's weakening I can tell. I give it one more push. 'Please?'

She sighs. 'You're not going to give up are you?'

'It's not in my nature.'

'Fine. Just one meal though.'

'I knew you couldn't resist me.'

'Don't push it.'

Maddy

'Please?'

'No.'

'Yes?'

'No.'

'Aw please?'

'No.'

'If I hadn't just bought these jeans I'd get down on my knees and beg.'

I sigh. 'Give me one good reason why I should.'

Kyle swings his chair around in a circle while he bites his lower lip and tries to think of an answer. I see the moment he comes up with one. His eyes widen and his mouth forms an O shape as he gives a little gasp. He plants his feet on the floor to stop the chair from spinning.

'You should come,' he says. 'Because, well not *only* because it's for me and you love me and you should feel duty bound to help me celebrate the day of my birth ...'

He can see this argument is failing to sway me and carries on quickly.

'But *also* you should come because it's a chance for you to invite Albert as your "plus one" and, as I am practically a parental unit to you, it's only right that I should meet him properly and decide whether he's good enough.'

I narrow my eyes. 'Parental unit?'

'Yes. I *was* almost your new stepfather,' he says.

'Ugh.' I shudder. 'No, you weren't. And we agreed never to speak of that night again, remember?'

'You mean the night I "romanced" your mother?' He does finger quotation marks in the air when he says 'romanced', just in case I'm in any doubt as to what he means.

I know exactly what he means. Unfortunately, some memories can't be erased. The night of my eighteenth birthday was memorable for all the wrong reasons. My mother threw me a party, after a flash of guilt that I was socially stunted by my responsibilities and because my sum total of friends was one, namely Kyle, and even he sat more under the umbrella of co-worker. She upgraded him to friend status purely because he was the only other person in the world I spoke more than cursory greetings with. It was excruciating, because if anything it brought home just how pitiful my life was, as I sat in the lounge under a few half-hearted balloons and streamers and made polite conversation with the ladies from Mum's work, Kyle and a few of the electronic geeks from work that he'd coerced into coming, the neighbours from one side who couldn't have looked more uncomfortable if they'd tried, and the lovely man and his wife from the corner shop. I feigned a headache just after ten, and lay in bed shedding a few tears as I listened to them all gratefully depart. When I thought the coast was clear and got up for a glass of water I found my mother and Kyle in the lounge, in flagrante. It was horrendous, and I've done my very best to try to forget it ever happened. Kyle, on the other hand, has not.

'Shut up,' I say.

'Shut up about what? The night your mother and I entwined ou—'

I cover my ears and close my eyes. 'Shut up, shut up, SHUT UP.'

He grins smugly. 'I'll stop talking about it as long as you agree to come.'

'Fine.' I scowl. 'But I'm not inviting Albert.'

Even though I agreed two weeks ago to go out with Albert for another meal, I haven't. Instead I've been screening my calls and not answering any from him or numbers unknown, in case he's sneakily tried to call me from work. I feel bad, but it's just easier this way. There are too many unknown variables, but anything that started would end painfully; of this I have no doubt. Because there's someone in my life who would always be my first priority and not many guys could handle that. I'm not letting my sister down for anyone, even if it means I have to forgo love. I'd rather spare myself the hurt to begin with. Besides, if he'd taken the hint when I said I wasn't interested the first time, he'd have saved himself the effort.

'If you don't call him,' Kyle warns, 'I will.'

'You don't have his number.'

He holds up his phone. 'You mean this one? That I copied from your phone when you were on an extended ladies' room break?'

'Did you seriously go through my phone?'

I'm outraged but he is unrepentant. 'Maddy, if you won't take control of your own destiny then somebody else has to. May as well be me.'

Someone rings the bell on the counter, wanting service. Usually I'd let them ring it a few more times before bothering to go out, but the big boss is somewhere on the floor today 'making observations' and I need this job.

'This isn't over and you're not forgiven,' I say to Kyle.

'Just make sure you call him, or I will.' He has the smug expression of someone who knows he holds all the cards. 'Party starts at eight. Just an informal gathering, nothing major. If your mother feels like coming, with Bee of course, she'd be more than welcome.'

I ignore his last comment, but have a suspicious thought. 'It's not a theme party is it? I'm not coming if it is.'

He places a hand on his chest in indignation. 'Of course it's not. Hello, I'm not a child.'

I walk through his front door just after eight and immediately I'm assailed by *Star Wars* memorabilia. There are black sheets stapled to the walls, with pinned posters and bunting all over them. Lightsabers dangle from hooks on the ceilings, along with silver balls and plastic stars. The pièce de résistance is a full-size cardboard cut-out of a stormtrooper looming in the corner. I shake my head as Kyle emerges to greet me. He is wearing a full-length black cloak, black T-shirt, black jeans and boots and is carrying a Darth Vader mask.

'Let me guess,' I say, looking him up and down. 'Yoda?'

He rolls his eyes. 'So witty. No wonder you don't have a boyfriend.'

'Neither do you.'

'Is your mother here?' He cranes to look behind me.

'Why?'

'No reason. Is she?'

'No. She's looking after Bee.'

'Oh.' He looks crestfallen for a second before rallying. 'Where's Albert?'

'He couldn't make it, sorry,' I lie smoothly.

'Really?'

'Yeah, he had something else on already.'

'Did he?'

His tone says he doesn't believe me. He stares me down for a few seconds then tuts and puts a hand on one hip. 'You didn't call, did you?' he says.

'I did,' I protest. 'I did. But it was such short notice, you know. He already had other plans. Some family gathering, I think it was his father's birthday? Or his grandparents' wedding anniversary? Something like that. To be honest I think

96

he's just not interested in me and that was his polite way of letting me down.' I try to look sad.

Kyle clears his throat and steps to one side. Standing sheepishly behind him, carrying a beer and clearly having heard the entire conversation, is Albert.

'Oh, hello,' I say, wondering if it's too late to make a run for it.

'Hi,' he says.

'You heard all that?'

He nods.

'Right.' I nod. 'Right.'

'I've *told* you lying will get you in the shit one day,' Kyle says, sweeping past, his cloak smacking me lightly in the face. 'Now be nice. I have other guests to greet.'

After he leaves, Albert and I stand awkwardly in front of each other for a minute or so while people flow around us like we are a rock in a river. I am unable to look him in the eye and can't think of a single thing to say that might rectify the situation.

'Beer?' Albert asks, leaning forward to be heard over the music.

'Yes please,' I say gratefully.

With bottles in hand, we head for a two-seater couch in a dark corner of the lounge. Albert gestures for me to sit, a gentlemanly gesture I rather intriguingly find sweet, rather than irritating like I would have if anyone else had done it.

'So Kyle called you, huh?' I grimace, my eyes firmly on my knees.

'He did. Maddy, I'm curious.'

I take a swig from the bottle and wipe my lips. 'About what?'

'Why you made up that whole, rather elaborate story instead of just saying you didn't want to call me.'

I shrug. 'It's complicated and hard to explain.'

'Try me.'

Where to start though? It's not as easy as he thinks. It takes time for people to understand my world. Time for them to get to know Bee and her needs. It's all very well to tell someone that your sister needs round-the-clock care, but from past experience people don't grasp what that fully entails.

'Enough about me,' I say, changing the subject. 'How long have you been working at the stables?'

He gives me a shrewd look that indicates he's not ready to let go of our conversation but he'll play along and come back to it later.

'Officially? Not long. But I was volunteering there for almost a year before I joined the payroll.'

'Volunteer? As in no pay?'

'No pay,' he confirms.

'Really.' I smile. The knowledge that he worked at the stables and with people like my sister voluntarily just made him a whole lot more interesting.

Albert

I'm confused.

I don't get the impression I repulse Maddy, which is always a positive of course, but for some reason she seems insistent on keeping me at arm's length. Obviously I don't want to be one of those pushy guys who won't take no for an answer, so if I felt for a second she was feeling harassed I would back off, no question.

But there's something in the way she looks at me occasionally that says she just *might* be attracted to me. That she might *ever so slightly* find me interesting.

'How about you?' I ask. 'How long have you been working at the photo desk?'

She groans and sinks back into the couch. 'Too long.'

'Not your dream job I take it?'

'Not so much, no.'

'So what is?'

She shrugs, takes a drink from her beer. 'It doesn't matter.'

'Yes it does. Tell me.'

I watch her weigh it up, whether she trusts me enough to tell me or not. She reaches her decision. I have to do a double take, when she starts talking, because it is like someone just turned a switch on inside her. She becomes luminous.

'Photography. I'd love to be a photographer.'

'Ah, so working on the photo desk was not a completely random decision then.'

She shakes her head. 'No. For various reasons, mostly lack of money and family commitments, I couldn't go away and study after high school. At least in this job I can kind of self-teach, if you know what I mean.'

'I'm not sure.'

She waves her hands about as she searches for the words to explain. 'Like, I study the photos that come through, for what works and what doesn't. Sure, the majority are family shots, candid, everyday life. But there are plenty of others too. I use them to learn about settings and lighting and composition. They give me ideas and then when I get some time, I go out and practise myself.'

'Where?'

'Anywhere. Parks, playgrounds. Depends what I'm photographing. I don't get to go out enough, though.'

'Can I come with you some time?'

Her hands drop and she looks guarded again. I sense she is worried she has revealed too much.

'Why?' she asks.

I shrug. 'It sounds fun. I could be your assistant. Every good photographer has one. To carry your bags or fetch you drinks. Or I could be your model. I've been told I'm pretty photogenic.' I give a big toothy smile and wink and she laughs.

'I'll think about it,' she says.

'Is that a yes?'

'You don't give up, do you?'

'Not when it comes to something I want.' I stare intently into her eyes.

She holds my look, and I wonder if I should kiss her, but then she blinks and pulls back. 'Anyway. What about you?'

'Me?'

'Yes. What was your dream job when you were a child?'

I consider the question. 'Pilot. Well, that was when I was ten. Before that I wanted to be a cowboy, but there's not much call for them around these parts.'

She laughs. 'I guess you're halfway there, working with horses.'

'Hey that's true, I never thought about that.' I grin.

'And now? Are you planning on staying at the stables long term?'

I take a mouthful of beer to buy myself some time. If she knew I was planning on moving away as soon as I have enough money saved, she might wonder why I'm bothering to try and get to know her. In all fairness, and now that I actually think about it, I probably shouldn't. But I can't back off now. Not when she's just starting to open up to me.

'Not sure. Is your friend always like this?' I point and she turns her head to see what I'm pointing at.

We watch as Kyle and another guy dressed in a brown towel with a belt around the waist have a mock fight with lightsabers. It ends when Kyle falls backwards on to the table and spills chips all over the floor.

'Yes,' she sighs. 'He is. Hey, I'm sorry about before. When I lied about inviting you. Not my finest moment.'

'It's OK. But I need you to promise me something.'

'It's a little early for promises, don't you think?'

'That's my point. Look, I'm just going to lay my cards out on the table because the last few weeks have been kind of frustrating and if I'm wasting my time – and yours – I'd really rather just know now. Maddy, I like you. I'd like to get to know you. I thought we had a really good time that night at the restaurant, all things considered.'

'You mean the chilli incident.'

'Yes.' I wince at the memory. 'The chilli incident. How is Bee by the way?'

'She's fine, thanks.'

'Good. She's quite a character.'

'That's one way of putting it.'

The whole time we've been talking we've been sitting side by side, facing outwards, occasionally turning to smile nervously at each other. But I am emboldened by the beer and the fact she hasn't told me to get lost outright. I turn sideways as much as I can on the couch and regard her seriously.

'Maddy, I want to get to know you better. Spend time

together. Maybe, you know, go on some dates or something.'
Any boldness I feel abandons me when she turns and looks
straight into my eyes. In that one instant, I can see the faint
freckles on her nose, her individual eyelashes that curl like
waves. I watch as her lips part, and her tongue comes out to
lick at the top one, leaving a glossy slick of moisture behind.
A single tooth comes out to bite at her bottom lip and then
disappears before she swallows, nervous.

I can smell the sweet scent of her hair.

See the glow of youth on her skin.

She is beautiful.

I want to kiss her. I lean forward imperceptibly; she doesn't
back away. I summon every ounce of courage I have in me and
decide I will do it. What's the worst that can happen?

Apart from rejection and total humiliation, of course.

I close my eyes.

'Oh, aren't you two just the cutest,' Kyle coos.

I blink and turn my head. He is standing over us like some
benevolent uncle, hands clasped in front of him, beaming
proudly. He turns and calls over his shoulder. 'Aren't these two
just perfect for each other.'

'Get a room,' someone says.

Maddy

'What on earth is it?'

He walks in circles around it a few times, at one point reaching out with a toe to prod experimentally at one of the tyres.

'It's called a Duet Wheelchair bike.'

He crouches down to study the mechanism where the chair attaches to the bike more closely. 'Amazing,' he says. 'Absolutely bloody amazing. I've never seen one of these before.'

'I think there's only a handful in the country.'

'How much was it, if you don't mind me asking? I'd imagine thousands?'

'We didn't pay for it. It was gifted to us, second-hand, by a charity organisation.'

'Amazing.'

'Yes. As fascinating as this is, we really need to get going,' I say, checking the time on my phone.

'Of course.' He straightens up and grins at me. 'Your assistant is ready and awaiting instructions.'

When Albert dropped me home after Kyle's party the night before we'd sat in the car for a while talking, and when he mentioned that it was his mother's car and normally he biked most places, I'd found myself, in a weak moment, inviting him to join Bee and I on our planned excursion today. It's something we often do, on Saturdays when Mum is at work.

'If you want to be helpful, you can carry this backpack,' I tell him, passing it over. He takes it and pulls a face.

'Heavy,' he says. 'What's in it?'

'Wait and see.'

I get Bee from the house. As soon as she sees the wheelchair bike she gets excited.

'Let's go, yellow bike,' she shouts.

'Yes, Bee.'

She calls it yellow bike because of the yellow plastic moulded seat. I help her in and make sure all the harnesses are secure. I take her headphones off, which she insists on keeping firmly in her lap, while I fasten her helmet. It is hard to squash down her abundance of curls but I manage. Because she feels the cold in the wind, I wrap a blanket around her legs and tuck it underneath her securely.

'Let's go, yellow bike,' she shouts again, rocking her whole body back and forward in the seat and flapping her hands as if that will get the bike started.

I fasten my own helmet, trying to ignore the fact it makes me look completely uncool in front of Albert.

'Safety first,' he says intuitively. 'Lead the way.'

I push off and as usual it takes me to the corner to build up any real momentum, with the added weight of Bee and the wheelchair up front. I love these excursions, but having Albert with us on this one is bringing an extra element of excitement I'm not used to.

My mother didn't tell me when she applied to a local foundation for the chair because she knew how I'd feel about it. I have a hang-up about accepting charity, preferring to get by on our own. But when the chair arrived, already a done deal, I got over my annoyance pretty quickly. Bee can only walk so far before she becomes tired, but the chair opened up areas and possibilities previously unexplored. It quickly became a favourite thing for us both to get on the bike and head out and about. It also meant I could practise my photography outdoors.

I lead the way through town, the bike attracting its normal share of attention. Occasionally someone beeps and waves and Bee waves excitedly back.

'Fast, fast,' she shouts.

We pass through town and then into more industrial streets. I flick a quick glance over my shoulder to make sure we haven't lost Albert and he holds one hand up and gives a questioning glance, as if to ask where we're going. I smile but keep pedalling. He'll find out soon enough. We bike up a small incline and then down a long slope.

'Weeeeeeeee!' Bee squeals, flapping her hands excitedly. At the bottom, just before the gate to where we are going, there is a small speed bump, there to stop boy racers from speeding through the area. I normally slow down to a crawl but today I am distracted and it's not until the last moment I remember its presence. I quickly brake and the bike slams to a stop.

'Crash! Oh shit!' Bee yells.

I hear a snort of laughter from behind me and turn to see Albert has also stopped and is standing, feet aside the bike on the ground.

'Did she just say what I think she just said?' he asks.

'She did,' I confirm. 'But she didn't learn it from me if that's what you're thinking.'

'Of course not,' he says with a smirk.

'It's true,' I protest. 'She heard it on *Postman Pat*.'

'Postman Pat swears? News to me.'

'No, he doesn't, but you find all sorts of weird stuff on YouTube. People dub over shows with their own narrative and that's one of the examples you'll find. She watched it without us realising.'

'Funny.'

'Anyway, we're here,' I tell him, gesturing to the gate. He reads the sign on the fence.

'Tree Trust?' he asks. 'What's that?'

'Come and look.' I bike gently through the gate and he follows. Immediately, a sense of calm washes over me. I like it here. It's serene. Peaceful. Now that we're off public roads Albert bikes alongside me, and I watch as he looks around, taking in the area.

We make our way along a fine gravel path that weaves around large, developed and newly planted trees. At the bottom of some of them are plaques, like little headstones. The grass is in some places neatly clipped, and in others long and unruly.

We bike past some toilets and I pull up next to a picnic table that is beside some coin-operated BBQs. Albert stops beside me and leans his bike up against the table. I immediately remove my helmet and do the best I can to fix my flattened hair. He sees what I'm doing and smiles.

'It's not for your benefit,' I mutter defensively.

'I didn't say anything.' He turns in a circle, taking in our surroundings. 'I can't believe I had no idea this place was even here.'

'Not many people do. In some ways it's a shame, but mostly I'm grateful. Means it's quieter when we come.'

'Is this a cemetery?' he asks.

I detect a note of trepidation in his voice and look at him curiously. 'No. It's a memorial park. People can dedicate trees to deceased family members.'

'But they're not actually buried here?'

'No.'

He shudders. 'Good.'

'You don't like cemeteries?'

'Does anyone?'

'Good point,' I concede.

'It just gives me the heebie-jeebies,' he says. 'The thought of being buried for all eternity in the ground.'

'I don't think it'd bother you if you were dead.'

'It would,' he insists. 'Wouldn't it bother you?'

'I've never really thought about it.'

'You're lucky. When my nana died, my mother dragged me along to her grave every weekend for a year. It was awful. Imagining her sweet little face down there, under all that dirt, rotting.' He shudders again.

'How old were you?'

'Eight.'

'I can see how that would be terrifying.'

'Yeah.' He lifts the small backpack that I gave him off his shoulders and drops it on to the picnic table with a thud. 'Argh,' he groans. 'That was heavy. Are you going to tell me what's in it now?'

'Sure.' I unzip and tip it carefully over. Rocks roll out. Some the size of spoons, others the size of eggs and bigger.

He frowns and picks one up. 'Seriously? You made me carry rocks here? What, was it some kind of a test?'

'No. Look closer.' I roll the rocks over so he can see they are painted on one side. He studies the one in his hand. It is green and has a small painting of Humpty Dumpty on it. On the back, in black marker pen, is written 'Have an eggs-cellent day!'

His eyebrows shoot up. 'Have an eggs-cellent day?'

'I know it's a little corny. That's one of my mother's ones.'

'OK you might need to start at the beginning because I'm kind of lost right now.'

'If I tell you, you have to promise not to laugh.'

'Why would I laugh?'

'Because it's kind of a little bit kooky.'

'OK, I promise.'

'Bee paints. And draws. She's very artistic actually. A few years ago she got really sick and for a while we thought she might not make it. Her immune system is not the greatest anyway, so something as simple as flu can really knock her around. She developed pneumonia and wound up in hospital. In the children's ward they try and do things to entertain them, and one day they brought in a whole bunch of rocks for the kids to paint. Bee really got into it, so we've kept it up with her ever since. After a while we had so many at home we were running out of room to store them, so my mother had this idea to write little notes to people on the back and then hide them around town. Kind of like a little random act of kindness thing, but more with compliments and cheerful inspiring messages.'

He nods understandingly. 'Like "Have an eggs-cellent day"?'

'Yes.'

'I think it's cute.'

'Really?'

'Yeah. I really do.'

I smile at him gratefully. He has no idea how much it means to me that he understands. That he likes what we do, instead of mocking it. It's a massive deal for me to let someone who is still effectively a stranger in on something that is so personal to our little family.

'Now what do we do with them?' he asks.

'Put them back in the bag and I'll show you.'

While he does, I disconnect the wheelchair from the bike. The two front wheels drop forward.

110

'Bump!' says Bee.

'That's the other handy thing about this bike,' I tell Albert. 'I can lock the bike part up once we reach our destination and push Bee around in her chair.'

'Amazing,' he declares. 'Bloody amazing.'

I sling the backpack holding the rocks over the chair handle and unzip the bag I was wearing to pull out my camera. I suddenly feel shy doing this in front of Albert. Photography has always been very personal to me. Until last night, I could count on three fingers the number of people in this world who even knew I was into it. Now, of course, there are four.

'I don't know anything about cameras,' Albert says. 'Is it a good one?'

I shrug. 'It does its job.'

In truth I saved for a year to buy this camera, and even then I felt guilty splurging so much money on it. My mother convinced me to do it. She thinks I have 'talent'. Of course she would say that. It's in her job description.

I lift it to my eye and make a few adjustments. As soon as I feel the cool sensation of the camera against my cheek I relax. It has a soothing familiarity.

'This way,' I say, pulling the strap over my head and resting the camera against my chest. Albert walks along beside me as we meander along the path, in and around trees.

'Do you want me to push?' Albert asks.

'No, Bee wouldn't like it, but thanks for the offer. OK, keep an eye out for places to hide the rocks.'

'Like where?'

I point out holes in tree trunks where branches once were, or crevices where the tree has split into two while growing. Sometimes the trees roots have grown out of the ground and twist around the base of the tree leaving little pockets of hidey-holes.

'There.'

After a while he warms to it and frequently darts off the path to hide the rocks in more inventive places. I fire off a few shots when he's unaware, or pretend I'm photographing the tree when actually I'm framing him against it.

Click.

'What if no one finds them?' he frets.

I smile. 'They will. Eventually. I've been hiding them here for years. A lot of families come here for walks. I think the kids have actually started to look for them now, like a treasure hunt.'

When the rocks run out, he takes over pushing the chair so I can click away happily. I make a big of fuss of him pushing, which encourages Bee to think of it as an adventure. She giggles as we roll along and pretends to smack his hands playfully. We come across a large silver fern and he lifts the leaves to admire the contrast of colour between the green on top and the silver underneath.

'You can see why it's our national plant,' he says.

Click.

'Is it?'

He rolls his eyes. 'Are you serious? Have you never watched an All Black game?'

'Rugby isn't really my thing.'

Click.

'And you call yourself a Kiwi.' He reaches into the middle of the plant and pulls apart the leaves.

'Look.' He smiles. 'A new frond. I always thought these looked like monkey tails when I was growing up.'

'Hold it steady,' I say, lifting my camera to my face. 'And up a bit.'

The fern frond is beautiful, no doubt about that. But it's *his* face in the background that captivates me. He's so good-looking with his sun-kissed hair and skin, and a broad smile that curves openly with his delight at being here with me.

Click.

He looks up and blinks, then smiles even wider. 'I'm going to need a copy of that.'

After an hour or so we end up back at the picnic table and I unpack sandwiches for Bee, and some extras I made for us.

'Nothing flash, sorry,' I apologise, flushing a little. 'Just peanut butter.'

He takes a big bite and smiles at me. 'My favourite.'

We eat. A couple of women wander past us at one point, wearing exercise clothes. The area attracts a lot of walkers so I don't pay them any attention at first, but then they're back, five minutes later, walking the other way. I hear giggling and look at them, my heart sinking, but they're not looking at Bee as I expected. They're staring openly at Albert, like they want to devour him, and nudging each other. We hear them giggling even as they disappear off in the distance.

'Get that a lot do you?' I ask Albert dryly.

'Get what?' he replies innocently.

I tilt my head. 'Women drooling all over you.'

He runs a hand through his hair and laughs. 'I'd hardly say drooling. Look how hard I had to work to get *you* to come out with me.'

He watches me fuss over Bee, making sure she is warm and eats enough.

'What's it like?'

'What's what like?'

'Living with someone like Bee.'

'Someone with autism?'

'Yeah.'

'That's a big question.' I try to think about how I can answer him. 'It's hard, sometimes. And then other times it's not. We have good days, and bad days, just like anybody. It's just a different kind of bad. We're limited in what we can do and where we can go. Anything can upset her and she can't tell us what or why. I think that's the hardest part. Not being able to understand what's going on in her head. I'd love to know what she's thinking. I get sad when I think about how I'll never have a conversation with my own sister.'

'I've never had a conversation with my brother either, but that's just because we have nothing in common. And he's a bit of a dick.'

'You might not get on with him but at least he has a regular life. I'll never see Bee walk down the aisle, or hold her own baby. She'll always need full-time care, like an eternal toddler.'

A tear makes its way down my cheek and I wipe it away quickly before he can notice. I hate thinking about the future my sister should have had but never will.

'Sorry. I wasn't trying to trivialise your situation.'

'I know.'

'Do you ever wish she was, you know, normal?'

I shrug. 'What's normal?'

'Not autistic, I suppose.'

'Who's to say they're not the normal ones and it's the rest of us with variations of dysfunction?'

'I never thought about it like that.'

'I'm kidding.' I nudge him with my shoulder. 'I'm well aware Bee is not what people consider "normal". But to me she's just the way she's always been and the way she was obviously meant to be. If that's not the definition of normal, what is?'

'We're all different.'

'Exactly.'

'Differently normal.'

I smile at him. 'That's perfect.'

'I can't take all the credit. I read it somewhere.'

'Sorry if I sounded defensive before. I know every family has differing degrees of dysfunction, I do. Most people we meet are still ignorant as to what autism actually is. And people tend to fear the unknown. There are varying levels of functionality, but unless you live with someone with autism it's hard to understand how each one works. They're all different, just like you and I. Anyway.' I clear my throat. 'There's no point dwelling on it. It is what it is.'

115

He reaches over and puts a hand on top of mine. 'Thank you for sharing this place with me.'

'You're welcome,' I say, hoping that the heat I suddenly feel isn't reflected in my cheeks.

'I hope I can return the favour one day soon.'

Albert

I can see how much of a big deal it was for Maddy to share this with me. Not just this place, but the ritual of the painted rocks and her photography. I feel flattered that she has, and grateful that she allowed me to come along for the day, not only because it gets me out of the house.

I trail around behind her, watching her take photos. It is clearly her passion and she is in her element once she is behind the lens. She is wearing a pair of black jeans, ripped at the knee, and a long-sleeved white top. Her hair has gone a bit wild from the helmet and the wind on the ride over, and she spends some time huffing it out of her eyes impatiently while she lines up photos, before giving up and using an elastic band off her wrist to put it up. Doing this exposes her long, slender neck and I have visions of leaning forward to kiss it.

She turns and catches me staring at it.

'What?' she asks. Her eyes widen. 'Is there a spider on me?'

I pretend to check. 'Nope, you're good.'

'OK.' She flicks through the digital screen on the back of her camera and changes a few settings. 'You're up.'

'Sorry?'

She puts one hand on a hip and stares pointedly at me. 'Remember? Last night? You volunteered to be my model.'

My words come back to haunt me. 'Ah yes, this is true. But I was only joking.'

'No, no way.' She shakes her head. 'You're not backing out now.'

'You don't want me ruining your shots.'

She rolls her eyes. 'You don't strike me as the modest type.'

'What type do I strike you as then?' I grin.

She tilts her head while she considers the question. 'Confident. Self-assured. Unafraid of anyone or anything.'

At her words, my smile slips then recovers. I hear the camera click. If only she knew.

'What's wrong?' she asks.

'Nothing.'

'I saw that.'

'What.'

'That look.'

'This one?' I pull a *Zoolander* face in an effort to lighten the mood again, sucking in my cheekbones and pouting my lips. It has the desired effect of making her laugh.

'Or this one?' I turn away from her and peer sexily back over one shoulder, winking.

She lifts the camera and starts clicking away. 'That's it, work it, baby, work it.'

I contort myself into a variety of positions like I'm a super-model while she snaps away. After my grand finale, where I end up with one leg wrapped around a tree, pretending to lasso like a cowboy, we collapse into laughter as she reviews the shots she's taken.

'Delete them,' I say.

'Never.'

'What are you going to save them for, blackmail?'

'Maybe, should the occasion ever arise.'

I pretend to look wounded. 'I didn't figure you for that kind of person.'

'You don't have to do that, you know,' she says, shrewdly.

'What?'

'Put on an act around me. In fact, I'd prefer you didn't.'

'I don't know what you're talking about.'

She walks closer until she's close enough for me to smell the scent of her hair and admire the slight dusting of tiny freckles across the top of her nose. Less than ten, only visible from a close distance. I find them endearing.

'I want to get to know the real you, Al-*bear*. I don't have time to waste on someone who is not being authentic.'

I take a deep breath and sigh it out. 'I'm not being inauthentic. Really, I'm not. But your words struck a nerve before. When you said I was unafraid of anyone or anything.'

She waits expectantly.

'It's hard to explain,' I say, because it is.

'Try.'

'You know how you said every family has their different degrees of dysfunction?'

'Yes.'

'Let's just say mine hasn't escaped unscathed.'

'Care to elaborate?'

'Not really. At least, not yet.'

She studies my face for a moment and I hold my breath, worried she'll decide I'm not worth the hassle.

'OK,' she says finally. 'I'm not going to pressure you.'

'I appreciate that.'

'Just know that I'm a pretty good listener, if you ever need someone to, you know, listen.'

I smile. 'Thanks. I'll keep that in mind.'

'Good,' she says.

She looks down for a moment, and when she looks back up, I feel my breath catch in my throat. Maybe it's because she has seen my weakness behind the jokes, but she is looking at me like I just got a whole lot more interesting. I step forward until I am so close we are almost touching.

'I'm going to kiss you now,' I say. 'If that's OK.'

She nods, vulnerability in her eyes but bravado in the lift of her jaw.

I close my eyes and lower my head. The world explodes.

Or at least that's how it feels when our lips touch.

'Wow,' I whisper when we pull apart again.

'Wow,' she repeats.

'Was it just me or was that pretty amazing?'

'No, that was pretty amazing.'

'I think we should do it again, don't you?'

She nods.

'Burrowing bounders! They must be breeding like, well, rabbits.'

We blink, and swivel our heads to look at Bee who is beaming at us from her wheelchair.

'*Wallace and Gromit*,' says Maddy.

Maddy

'Where are you taking me?' I have to speak loudly to be heard over the music blaring from the car stereo.

Albert takes his eyes off the road for a second to look at me and shake his head, his smile teasing.

'You're not very good with surprises, are you?'

'Yes I am,' I say, although I'm really not.

'Like I said five times already, you'll have to wait and see.'

I pretend to sulk.

'It'll be worth it, I promise.'

'It had better be.'

'You're cute when you sulk, you know that?'

'Shut up.' I smile out the side window so he can't see.

It's going to be a beautiful day. The sky is clear of clouds and stretches cornflower blue in every direction. I have no idea what the temperature is but the haze coming off the road tells me it's already up there and it's only just gone eight. We have the windows down and a cool breeze weaves through the car, teasing my hair and causing goosebumps to spring up on my arms. I haven't felt this relaxed in a long time. I rest my head back against the seat and close my eyes, enjoying the feeling of having no responsibility for the day. In a rare event, both Mum and I had the same day off work, so she's taking Bee out for a walk in the wheelchair and to do the grocery shopping, and I have the whole day to myself. Well, myself and Albert. Despite everything I said about not wanting a relationship, I think it's just possible I'm in the first buds of one.

Just maybe.

Even though we've been out for a few meals and back to the Tree Trust a couple of times, this will be the first time we've spent an entire day together. I'm surprised by how relaxed I feel.

'In the back,' Albert says.

'Sorry?'

'There's a green bag behind my chair. Can you reach it?'

I pull my seat belt to the side and crane my arm, my hand connecting with a canvas backpack. It's stuck on something but I give it a few tugs and it finally comes free. I notice another bag behind it that looks familiar.

'What's in the other bag?'

'Other bag?' His voice is all mock innocence.

'Yes, other bag. The blue and white one. It looks familiar.'

'You'll see.'

'Another surprise.'

'More like a component of the first surprise.' He risks a look at me. 'Don't worry, you don't have long to wait. Open it.' He gestures with his eyes towards the green bag that I now have in my lap.

I unzip it and immediately an amazing smell is released. 'Ohh,' I moan. 'I know that smell.'

He beams, proud of himself. 'You might have mentioned once or twice how much you need coffee in the morning in order to function, so I took the liberty of preparing a Thermos. Least I could do to say sorry for dragging you out of bed so early.'

I say nothing, because I'm feeling all sorts of weird and soppy emotions that he's done this for me, and reach into the bag to pull out a silver Thermos.

'I hope it's OK,' he says, sounding worried. 'I don't drink a lot of coffee myself so I just went for the brand that cost the most.'

I unscrew the lid and inhale the released steam deeply to buy myself some time. It is rich and dark and exotic, and I swear my mouth starts watering. 'Cups?'

'In the bag.'

I find two plastic travel mugs. Underneath them is a brown paper bag. It rustles when I touch it.

'Oh yes.' Albert flicks his eyes sideways for a second. 'There's a couple of pastries as well. The French are a big fan of pastries in the morning.'

'You're not French.'

'Maybe not by birth, no. But I have that certain va va voom allure that only the French have mastered. Don't say you haven't noticed.'

I snort. 'I'm sorry, but you're about as alluring as Kyle in his Darth Vader dressing gown.'

'Ouch,' he winces.

'I'm kidding.'

'Just as well. My ego couldn't take many more of those compliments.'

I pour coffee into one of the mugs and pass it to him, then fill the other one and hold it awkwardly between my knees while I screw the lid of the Thermos back on. The car swerves to the left sharply and I nearly drop it.

'Hey,' I protest.

'Sorry. Pothole.'

I watch as he takes a tentative sip from his cup and screws up his face.

'You don't like it?' I ask.

'I wouldn't say it's the best thing I've ever tasted, no.'

'I'm not sure we can be friends.'

'How about if I let you have all the coffee and I have most of the pastries?'

'I'd say you have a deal.'

Kicking off my sandals, I lift my legs up to rest my feet on the open car window frame. The wind tickles my toes as Albert cruises down a winding road. It's years since I've been anywhere beyond town limits, and it's not until we pass a big green sign that I realise where we are headed.

'We're going to the beach?'

He smiles playfully. 'Yes, Miss Impatient. We're going to the beach.'

'Oh.' I digest the news. Then a thought occurs to me. 'But I don't have anything, togs or sunscreen etc.'

'Ah see, that's where the mystery of the other bag gets solved.'

I twist to look at it again. No wonder it looked so familiar, it is my mother's bag. I give him a questioning look.

'I got your mum's number off Kyle. Called and asked her to pack a few things. She was more than happy to oblige. Said, and I quote, "I'm glad Maddy is finally having a social life."'

I cringe. We carry on in silence for a few minutes.

'You're not upset, are you?'

He sounds worried.

'No, not at all.' I can't explain to him what I'm feeling, because I'm not sure myself. 'I haven't been to the beach since I was a kid.'

He does a double take and reaches to turn the stereo down a fraction. 'You're kidding right. It's only a forty-minute drive; it's practically on our doorstep. I'm there every chance I get in summer.'

'Bee doesn't like the beach.' I shrug. 'After she was born we stopped coming.'

'She doesn't like to swim?'

'No, she loves swimming. Proper little dolphin in the water, although a polar bear is probably more of a fitting description. It's the sand she can't stand, along with grass and dirt. It's a sensory thing.'

'I think it's great that you help your mum look after her. A lot of people our age wouldn't be so selfless.'

'It's not selfless, she's my sister. We're family.' I say it as if it explains everything, and to me it does.

'I'm sorry if I upset you,' he says.

'You didn't,' I reassure him.

We carry on in silence for a few minutes. I know his intentions were good, and he hasn't upset me, not really. I like that he asks me questions about Bee instead of acting like she doesn't exist like some people do, or, worse, like she's some inanimate object in the corner of the room that can be ignored.

I'm trying to think of something to say to break the silence when we both hear it.

Woop woop.

I look in my side mirror and see the blue and red flashing lights of a police car indicating for us to pull over.

'Were you speeding?' I ask Albert as he pulls on to the gravel shoulder and cuts the engine.

'No.'

His face and voice have tensed up.

'It's probably just a random breath test,' I say to reassure him, but he doesn't answer.

We listen to the crunch of gravel as the policeman does a slow circuit around the car, looking for what I'm not sure, before he stops beside Albert's window and leans down, lifting his sunglasses off his face.

'You got any idea why I pulled you over?' he asks sternly.

'No, Dad,' says Albert. 'But I'm sure you're going to tell me.'

'Damn straight. Who said you could borrow my car?'

'Mum did.'

'Last time I checked it's my name on the registration papers.'

Albert stares straight ahead, his jaw clenched. Apart from his vague hint that day at the Tree Trust that his family is dysfunctional he hasn't talked about them much, just the basics. I've kept to my word and not pressured him, waiting for him to open up when he's comfortable enough with me to do so. Now, meeting his father, I get an inkling as to the problem.

'Fine. Is it OK if I borrow the car, *Dad*?'

The last word is loaded with tension.

'It's a bit late asking me now, isn't it?'

'Do you want me to beg?' Albert snaps, finally twisting his head to glare at his father. 'If you're trying to embarrass me then congratulations, you've succeeded.'

'Embarrass you?' His father pretends to notice me for the first time. 'Well, well, so it's true. You do have a new lady friend.'

'Dad, this is Maddy. Maddy, meet my father, Colin.'

'Morning, sir,' I say, noticing that there is a vague physical similarity about them, in the shape of the eyes and nose.

'Sir?' He smiles, but there's little warmth in it. 'Listen to those manners. You could learn something from that, Albert.'

I notice his father doesn't use the French pronunciation.

'No offence,' Colin carries on, 'but you look far too nice to be hanging out with the likes of this joker.' He thumbs towards Albert. 'Oh wait, I get it.' He puts his serious cop voice back on. 'Is this man taking you somewhere under duress? Blink twice if you require assistance.' Then he stands up and chuckles loudly at his own perceived wit.

I have no idea what to say, so I just give a little half-smile, even though he can no longer see me and apparently requires no participation in his joke anyway.

'Sorry about this,' Albert says, staring dead ahead. 'My father can be a bit of an asshole.'

I flinch hearing him use the word towards a member of his family, but it's been obvious from the moment his dad pulled us over that there is some serious tension between them. It's not my place to judge.

His father leans back down and frowns at him. 'Have it back at a decent hour. And not a mark on her, you hear? If your surfboard damages the paintwork you'll be forking out for a new paint job. A proper one, not from one of your idiot mates.'

'Yes, *Dad.*'

'And lose the tone. You're lucky I'm not making you walk home from here, or hauling your ass into the station and charging it with car theft.'

Albert bites his lower lip, and I wonder if it's to stop himself from saying something that might inflame the situation.

'Nice to meet you, Maddy,' his dad says, tapping on the car door. 'You two enjoy the beach. But next time you ask *me* if you want to use my car, not your mother. You only asked her because she's a soft touch and you knew she wouldn't say no.'

'You got me.'

'Keep to the speed limit.'

'I will.'

'And don't take my car on the beach. I don't want sand in the undercarriage.'

'I won't.'

'And make sure you put it back in the garage with a full tank of gas.'

'Of course.'

Colin runs his eyes up and down his car as if he's worried he'll never see it again.

'Relax, Dad,' Albert says. 'I won't damage your precious car.'

'I hope not. She's worth more than you.'

My jaw drops.

'I'm only kidding. Weird sense of humour in our family, isn't there, Albert?'

He doesn't sound like he's kidding though.

'You could say that,' Albert agrees quietly.

We watch as he walks back to his car and gets in. He flashes his lights twice then does a U-turn and goes back the way we came from. Albert clenches and unclenches his hands on the steering wheel a few times. His knuckles are white.

'Do you still want to go to the beach?' he finally asks, and his voice is sad like he thinks now I have had such an intimate glimpse into where he comes from I will run screaming for the nearest exit.

'Why wouldn't I?'

'The old man can come across a little . . .' He tilts his head while he searches for the word he's looking for. 'A bit of an asshole, I guess, is what I'm trying to say.'

I reach across and lightly lay my hand on top of his leg. I hear him suck in his breath and his thigh muscle contracts underneath my fingers. 'It's lucky I'm not dating *him*, then, isn't it?' I say softly.

He looks at me, his eyes roaming across my face as a smile tugs at his lips. 'Last chance,' he says. 'If you want to escape tell me now, because I promise you, once you meet the rest of my family it's only going to get crazier.'

I squeeze his leg in answer. 'Ha. Crazy and I go way back,' I say. 'Wait till you meet my mother.'

'I have met her; just now when I picked you up. She gave me the bag while you were in the toilet and seems perfectly lovely.'

'Anyone can seem perfectly lovely for a few minutes. Wait till you meet her properly.'

He smiles and reaches to turn the key in the ignition. The engine purrs back into life.

'All right then,' he says. 'Let's do this.'

Albert

The road down to the beach is narrow and bumpy, mostly made up of sand with the odd gravel patch. I wince a couple of times when I hear the car connect with the ground, my father's words echoing in my ears, but I'm not turning back.

There's only a small Ute in the car park when we turn the last corner. It's not really a car park, more a flat area of ground worn down by tyres over the years to resemble one. There are much more popular swimming beaches both up and down the coast, but this one is a little gem shared mainly by fishermen and surfers, though not always amicably.

'Place is deserted,' Maddy remarks.

'Aren't you glad I made you get up early now?' I tease.

She pulls a face. 'Jury's still out on that.'

I get out of the car and stretch my legs, breathing in a deep lungful of salty air. The stress that settled on me after our encounter with my father dissolves away, replaced by a sense of wonderment and freedom, like I always feel on a beach.

From the moment I first paddled in the waves as a chubby-legged baby I've felt an affinity towards the ocean. It's hard to explain, so I've never tried, but if I were pushed I would say it's where I feel at home. There's a kind of serenity that washes over me when I'm in the water, a sense of enlightenment. In the water, I know exactly who I am and where I'm supposed to be. It's only back on land that I flounder.

I haven't been out in a while, mainly because of the aggro I get from Dad every time I ask to borrow the car. With the door open, I stand on the side of the car to reach up and un-strap my ocean-blue surfboard. It might not be the flashiest board in the world, but we've been through some pretty big waters and it's never let me down yet. Laying it on the dry grass behind the car I run my fingers up and down its length lovingly, checking it survived the ride OK.

'Am I interrupting a moment?' Maddy asks dryly.

I hadn't noticed her get out of the car and come around to stand near the exhaust.

I laugh. 'You sound jealous.'

'Of a surfboard? No, I do have some dignity.'

'It's not just a surfboard,' I say indignantly. 'It's a vessel to a special kind of nirvana.'

She stares at me. 'Sorry, did you get stoned in the thirty seconds since we've been here?'

I shake my head and pat my board tenderly. 'I don't need drugs when I've got this baby right here.'

'Seriously, you've started speaking this weird kind of hippy language.'

'I can't help it. Put me near the ocean and my inner beach dude comes out.'

She nods her head. 'I see. Well that explains the messy blond hair.'

'My hair is messy?'

'A little.'

'In a bad way?'

'No. Some girls probably find that kind of look sexy.'

'You think I'm sexy?'

'I said *some* girls. I didn't say I was one of them.'

She frowns to cover her blush and I resist the urge to tease her further. After our first date I thought she was a bit of a tough nut to crack, but, as I'm learning, it's more of an act.

'Did you grab your bag?' I ask.

She nods, lifting up one arm to show the blue and white striped backpack she was trailing near her feet. 'Right here.'

'Then let's go.'

She follows me down the narrowing path as it weaves up and over a small dune. I hear her sigh gently as we crest the top and the beach and ocean come into view and I can tell right away it's a sigh of appreciation. It makes me like her even more. We pick our way along the beach a hundred metres in the opposite direction of the only other person in sight for miles. A fisherman with a long line out in the water, he waves a friendly greeting then turns his attention back to rolling himself a cigarette.

'How about here?' I ask, because really any spot is as good as another.

'Here is good,' Maddy answers, dropping her bag to the sand and stretching her arms up over her head. When she does her short T-shirt rides up and a sliver of her stomach is exposed. It's creamy, in contrast to her arms and legs which have a light golden colour. Not all of her legs though I notice, while trying hard to make it look like I am not looking. Today she's wearing white shorts that come down to her mid thigh, and a navy T-shirt that hangs lower on one shoulder. With her dark hair loose, curls forming in the salt spray and wrapping themselves around her face, she looks amazing. More than amazing.

'Are you going to be OK on your own if I hit the waves?' I pull my T-shirt over my head and kick off my sandals.

She gives the question the gravity it deserves and rolls her eyes. 'I think I'll survive.' She looks around with a frown.

'What's up?' I ask.

'If I'd known I was coming to the beach I could have worn my togs underneath my clothes. There's a distinct lack of changing facilities around here.'

'That would have put a crimp on the whole "surprise" aspect of the day though. How about I promise to look the other way and you can strip off here.'

'Yeah, I almost believe you. But I think I'll find somewhere up in the dunes all the same.'

I watch her walk up the beach, and don't realise how big my grin is until she turns and catches me staring. She puts one hand on her hip.

'Thought you were going surfing, *dude*,' she admonishes.

'Forgot which way the view was for a second.'

The water is cold but refreshing. It feels damn good against my skin so I just stand for a moment in the shallows, with the foamy breakers swirling around my thighs. I shut my eyes and breathe in deep. I smell the ocean and adventures waiting to be had. Other countries hide just over the horizon, and although I can't see them, the promise of them is there. My board is tucked safely under my left armpit, and it fits there like I was carved to accept its shape. I trail my right hand at my side, letting the water eddy around my fingers. It checks me out like a puppy does a stranger, curious at first and then embracing as it recognises I am a friend.

I have missed this, and I cannot keep the grin from my face.

Maddy

I find a discreet spot in the dunes behind an aged and twisted pohutukawa tree, and open the bag. Knowing my mother, there's a fair chance it could contain all of the things I might need today, or none at all.

Thankfully it's a little of both.

I pull out a large beach towel and a bottle of sunscreen she's dredged up from the depths of the bathroom cabinet. I shake it experimentally; might be enough to cover a leg if I'm lucky. There's a spare pair of shorts, my camera case, a baseball cap and a water bottle. At the bottom of the bag I see a flash of hot pink and my stomach drops.

She didn't.

With trepidation I reach in and pull it out slowly.

She did.

Instead of packing my barely worn, *perfectly proportioned to cover as much of my torso as possible* bathing suit that I wear to the indoor pool in town when I take Bee swimming, my mother has packed a bikini. More specifically, a hot pink bikini that I last wore when I was approximately fourteen. I hold it up in front of me and stare aghast at the tiny scraps of material. There's no way my butt is fitting in that, but it's all I have. The sun is warming up the air nicely and, dammit, I'm at the beach for the first time in a long time and there's no way I'm missing out on a swim.

I try it on.

Without mirrors, I can only guess at the amount of flesh left uncovered by the tickles of breeze on my skin. One particular tickle in the buttock region nearly has me changing my mind, but after popping my head around the tree I confirm that Albert and I and the fisherman are still the only inhabitants on the beach, so I decide screw it, and I wrap the towel around myself and head back down to the beach.

At first glance I can't see Albert anywhere on the water, but then he pops up on the other side of a wave and I realise he is dolphin diving beneath them as he heads out to deeper water. His wet blond hair curls around the nape of his neck, stark against the skin on his back which is a deep brown and evenly tanned. I wonder how it is he can spend so much time with his shirt off, as he so clearly does. Taking advantage of a lull between swelling waves, he sits astride his board and turns to scan the beach, checking for me, I presume, and, when he sees me, he waves. Even from a hundred or so metres away I can see the white of his teeth as he smiles. He lays back down on his board and paddles until he meets a wave, this time going over the top in one graceful move. I see the tip of the board point up to the sky and it pauses there for a full second as the wave curls, before plunging down the other side of the wave. He disappears from sight for a moment. I don't realise I'm holding my breath until he pops back up and I release it again.

I bash the bottle of sunscreen against my palm a few times to dislodge as much of the cream as possible. It's enough to cover one and a half legs. As I'm putting the bottle back in the bag I notice the expiry date on the bottom; two years previous. I may as well not have bothered. I put my T-shirt back on, at least it will offer some protection. My legs are white, and I struggle to remember the last time they saw the sun. Between work and home, I've not spent much time outdoors recently, not unless you count the riding stables.

Now what? I'm not feeling warm enough for a swim yet, and I'm not one for sunbathing, so I just sit and watch Albert. After a while I remember my camera and take it out, firing off a few beach shots and a fair few more of him.

I watch him for over an hour, almost two, but it feels more like five minutes. Not once do I feel bored or restless. I can't take my eyes off him in fact. He is a natural out there, and the way he rides the waves it's as if he can read the water. He dips and dives and coasts along the tops as if he's dancing, making it look effortless. When he's had enough, he catches a big wave that deposits him just on the other side of the shallows. I try to look like I'm not watching him walk up the beach, but it's a bit hard considering there's nothing else to look at.

'Oh man, you should feel the water.' He grins, dropping the

board gently on to the sand beside me and shaking his head like a retriever dog. His hair flies in all directions and water splashes me on the face.

'Hey,' I protest.

'Sorry,' he says, looking anything but. He flops to the sand beside me and leans back on his elbows, looking out over the water with a look of deep satisfaction on his face.

'You love it out there, don't you.' I quietly state the obvious.

He nods. 'I do.'

'When did you learn to surf?'

'When I was about five we moved to the east coast, a small seaside settlement on the Mahia Peninsula. Back then my father used to accept any small town police position offered, so we transferred a lot. He preferred to work alone rather than with others, and still does, but my mother made him move to a big city when my brother and I hit high school to give us a better education. He's probably regretting that now.' He laughs, but without real mirth.

It's not in my nature to pry into other people's relationships. Plus, I have enough to worry about with my own complicated family to give time or thought to anyone else's. But when he talks about his father he's in pain, I can feel it. It bothers me because he's starting to grow on me, and I don't like it when people I care about are hurt. 'Did you teach yourself?' I ask in an attempt to change the subject.

'Sorry?'

'To surf.'

'Yeah mostly. School holidays I would leave the house before the sun was up and head for the beach. I wouldn't go back home again until the sun went down. My mother bought me a second-hand board for my seventh birthday and I just spent my days in the water, watching the big boys and copying their moves.'

'Sounds idyllic.'

'It was.'

'You must miss it now, being back in the city.'

He sits up and hangs his arms over his knees, staring out to sea broodingly. 'Hell yes, I do. As close as it is I don't get here anywhere near as much as I'd like. Now that I'm officially working at the stables it'll be even less.'

'You're like some kind of outdoorsy boy wonder,' I joke, trying to lighten his mood.

'You can't tell me you enjoy your job stuck inside all day.'

'Of course not. But it pays the bills.'

He looks down at where he's burrowed his feet into the sand. 'Speaking of, I have a question I've been trying to think of a way to ask you without sounding like a stalker or jealous and obsessive.'

'Sounds ominous.'

'Promise you won't think bad of me?'

'No. I can't promise that until I hear the question.'

'OK.' He takes a deep breath. 'Has there ever been something between you and that guy you work with? Kyle?'

I snort. 'Me and Kyle? No.'

'Never?'

I shake my head. 'No. Never. Never, ever, ever, *ever*. Ever.'

'That's definitive.'

'I can't be any more so.'

'Right. OK then.'

'Why are you asking?'

'I'm just a bit confused.'

'Because?'

'Well, the first time I asked you out, in the shop, he practically forced you on me.'

'I wouldn't say it happened quite like that.'

'You know what I mean. You wouldn't have come to dinner with me if he hadn't persuaded you to, would you?'

'No, probably not.'

'But yesterday when I called him to ask for your mum's number he was all weird and demanded to know why I wanted it.'

'Really?'

'Yeah, he gave me the total third degree.'

'That's weird.' A thought occurs to me. 'How was he *after* you explained why you needed my mother's number?'

He shrugs. 'I don't know. Maybe slightly nicer now that you mention it, why?'

'Kyle and my mother had a thing. Well, not really a thing. They had a one-night stand after my eighteenth birthday.'

Albert's eyebrows shoot up. 'Are you serious?'

'Unfortunately.'

'How old is he?'

'Almost thirty.'

'And your mum is?'

'Forty-five.'

'Woah.'

'Tell me about it.' I trace circles in the sand with one finger. 'Not exactly the memory I wanted to take forth from the night I officially became an adult, but there you have it.'

'So you think he was weird on the phone because he was jealous? Because he thought I was after your mother?'

'It's the only explanation I can think of. He certainly wasn't jealous about me.'

'I must say I'm relieved. I thought I was going to have to compete for your affections against him, and there's no way I can compete against someone who wears black nail polish.'

I laugh. 'Yeah he's trying out a slight gothic look at the moment.'

'He tries out different looks?'

'He's harmless. Confused, eccentric and a little mental, but totally harmless. He's pretty much my only friend.' I don't know why I said the last bit and I regret the words as soon as they're out of my mouth, aware it makes me sound like a total loser.

'I find that hard to believe.'

I look out to sea. 'It's true. It's hard to make friends when you can't do things normal friends can.'

'Like what?'

I try to think of how to explain it to him. 'Like drop everything at a moment's notice to go to the mall, or movies. I can't take Bee with me because she doesn't like crowds or loud noises. Or go to a sleepover, because Mum would have to leave early to go to work in the morning and I'd need to be there to look after Bee.'

'It must have been tough.'

I shrug. 'It is what it is. When it's all you're used to you don't really know any different. I mean, sure, there were times I felt sorry for myself, or got angry or cried because everyone else seemed to be carefree and having so much fun and there I was wiping my sister's bum and making sure she didn't miss her meds because if she did there's a high chance she could die.'

'That's a lot for a teenager to deal with.'

I give a hollow laugh. 'Teenager? I've been doing it since I was a kid. My mum stopped hiring babysitters because for one, we couldn't afford them, and two, they had no idea how to look after my sister. I'd end up having to babysit the babysitter.'

He doesn't say anything for a while, but I can feel his eyes on me as I stare resolutely out to sea.

I am not going to cry, I tell myself, blinking furiously to banish the tears that are welling. I don't even know why, because I'm not in the habit of feeling sorry for myself.

'I'd really like to be your friend too,' he says finally. 'If you'll let me.'

I flick him a quick smile. 'I'm pretty crappy at it, remember. You'd never be first on the priority list.'

He shuffles sideways in the sand until his leg is mere centimetres away from my own. I'm acutely aware of the warmth coming off it. He reaches out his hand and lifts mine, weaving our fingers together. The simple act of holding hands makes my heart beat faster.

'I can accept that, if it means being with you.'

I duck my head, letting my hair fall like a curtain to cover my face so he can't see the brief panic that flits across it. I like him. I *really* like him. I don't know what to say or do and I'm worried about saying or doing the wrong thing and making a fool of myself.

I'm not a blushing virgin. I've had boyfriends before. Two, in fact. I wasn't particularly attached to either of them, and when the relationships ended I was more relieved than anything. I was already stretched thin with Bee and helping Mum make sure we didn't end up without a roof over our heads, so devoting time stroking some guy's ego into thinking I couldn't live without him just didn't interest me. They ended up resenting me for it. Worse, they resented Bee. And I could never be with anyone who resented an innocent soul such as my sister.

Albert is different to any boy I've ever met. I want to let him in, but at the same time I am scared.

'Last one in the water is a rotten egg,' I say, dropping his hand and climbing to my feet. I lift my T-shirt off over my head and let it fall to the sand, and it's not until I hear his sharp intake of breath that I remember the bikini.

Albert

Considering two seconds ago she went all shy on me after I held her hand and mentioned being together, it surprises the hell out of me when she jumps to her feet and takes off her T-shirt, revealing a tiny pink bikini that barely covers anything it was designed to cover. I can't help it, my mouth drops open and my eyes nearly bulge out of my head. I give a low, appreciative whistle.

'Don't stare,' she squeals, trying to cover her boobs with both hands. It just draws more attention to them.

'I'm not.'

I try to look away, at the sea, the sky, the sand; anywhere except her. But she's like a magnet and my eyes keep getting dragged back against my will.

'For your information this is *not* my normal bathing suit. My idiot mother packed this instead of my proper one. Which is your fault, of course. If you'd just told me where we were going I could have packed my own bag.'

'Sorry.' I'm not though.

'You're still looking.'

'Sorry.'

'This is so typical of my mother. She doesn't think.'

'Mm.'

'What?'

'I didn't say anything.'

'I just want you to understand that I don't normally make a habit of walking around with this much flesh exposed.'

'I'm not complaining if you do.'

She scowls, but smiles at the same time. 'You go first. I'll walk behind you.'

'I thought the last one into the water was a rotten egg?'

'I'd rather be a rotten egg than be ogled, thank you very much.'

When the foamy water is churning around my knees, I stop. 'Now what? It's going to be awkward to swim if I can't look at you.'

There's a blur by my right side as she runs past me through the water and dives, leaving only ripples that linger on the surface. I'm glad she's not one of those girls who take for ever to get in the water, inch by inch, squealing as the cold touches each new section of skin.

Maddy's head pops up a few metres in front of me and she takes a deep breath, turning to grin as water streams off her head down her face.

'Shit that's cold,' she laughs.

I follow suit, diving underneath a small wave and aiming

for where I think she is, but when I pop up she has moved and she laughs, splashing water at my face.

'Gotcha,' she says.

I narrow my eyes. 'Going to be like that is it?'

She pouts. 'What's the matter? You can't handle a little splashing?'

'If it's war you want, you asked for it.' I cup my hands and splash back at her.

She laughs and lies on her back in the water, using her feet to kick large quantities of water in my direction.

'Hey, that's cheating,' I protest as it goes in my mouth and my eyes. There's only one thing for it. I dive beneath the water and swim like an eel, streamlined and fast, and she is caught unaware by my speed. I see her legs kick as she tries to swim away but I'm too fast, and I slide my hands around her waist and pull her beneath the surface. Her eyes are open and startled, and for a second I think I have taken it too far and have scared her, but then she reaches out and wraps her hands around my neck and we burst back above the water together, laughing.

'Not fair,' she exclaims. 'You're like a dolphin in the water.'

I shrug, acutely aware of the close proximity of our bodies. 'I warned you.'

Up close I can see her green eyes are flecked with blue, like the ocean we are swimming in. I want to kiss her right then more than I've ever wanted anything in my life. Her fingers curl into my hair and she lifts her legs to wrap them around my waist. The intensity and recklessness in her eyes takes my breath away.

'Do it,' she dares, as our bodies rise and fall with the swell of the ocean.

I lean forward and kiss her. Lightly on the tip of her nose at first. She closes her eyes and moans softly. I kiss her eyelids, her cheeks, and finally her mouth. She is salty from the water and it is the most delicious thing I have ever tasted. Her lips part under my hunger and our tongues meet. Her body is tight against mine, like she doesn't want to let go.

She needn't worry though, because now that she's here in my arms, I have no intention of letting go either.

Maddy

I don't realise I've been asleep until I wake, the sound of the waves on the shore edging into my dreams. At first I think it is just a dream, then I shift and feel warm flesh against my side, flesh that is not my own. My eyes fly open.

Albert.

The beach.

Our kisses.

It all comes flooding back. He is asleep on the grass beside me and I carefully raise myself up on one elbow without waking him. My towel is half underneath me; I scooped it up on our way up here earlier, so I wriggle my butt to free it and drape it over myself gratefully. We are in the dunes underneath the shade of the same pohutukawa tree that was privy to my nakedness this morning. Once again it has protected my modesty, sheltering Albert and I as we made love in the tussocks. There is no one on the beach, the fisherman left while we were still in the water. Perhaps he was embarrassed by us, or thought we'd scare away all the fish. I wouldn't blame him, but I really don't care.

I can't believe I just made love outside, on a beach, to a guy I haven't known all that long. It's the wildest thing I've ever done, hands down. And I don't regret it at all.

'Hey,' he murmurs beside me and I turn my head to look down at him. By rights I should be embarrassed. God knows what he must think of me right now. 'So that was . . .' He pauses.

'Unexpected?'

'I was going to say fun. But that's not quite the word I'm looking for.'

'Just so you know,' I start to say but he holds up a finger to silence me.

'Wait, I know what you're going to say. You don't make a habit of this, right?'

I grimace. 'Right.'

'Good. I'd hate to think you peel off your bikini for just anyone.'

I clap my hands over my mouth as his words invoke a memory. I did that, didn't I, I actually pulled my bikini top off while we were in the water and simply let it go. It's probably half way to China right now.

He lifts his torso up off the ground and gently pushes me back down, dipping his head to nuzzle at my skin. 'You're beautiful, you know that?'

'You're not so bad-looking yourself.' I find it hard to breathe

151

when he's so close. His skin and hair smell of the sea and the sun.

'Why thanks. Maddy ...' He looks intensely into my eyes and I get the feeling he's about to say something deeply profound.

'Yes?'

'Are you ready for round two?'

I choke on a splutter. 'What?'

He laughs. 'You should see your face. I'm talking about another swim, what did you think I meant?'

'Jerk.' I sit up and push him away from me, pretending to be upset.

'Hey, I'm also up for that if you are?'

But I've been crazy enough for one day. I'm still trying to wrap my head around doing it the first time. Anyone could have turned up and seen us. Even though the beach is deserted we didn't exactly stop to make sure that was the case when we were busy going at it. I shudder when I realise that I could have been one of those idiots who gets caught in public and ends up on the internet.

'No,' I say firmly. 'Once was quite enough.'

'Shame. OK then, how about that swim.'

I check the sky to try to gauge how long we have been asleep. The sun is lower in the sky to the left than it was earlier.

'It's late afternoon,' Albert says, reading my mind. 'Just after four, to be precise.' He lifts his wrist up to show me the time on his black cuff watch.

'I'd better be getting back,' I say reluctantly. 'Sorry.'

'Hey, you never need to apologise to me about your responsibilities, OK? I completely understand.'

'OK.' I believe him. He is so sincere when he says it and I don't detect even a hint of jealousy from him about the other demands on my time. I pride myself on my bullshit radar, and it's staying silent around him. I wasn't testing him by having Bee accompany us on several of our dates, but if I was, he'd have passed.

He gets to his feet and pulls me up. My towel slips, exposing one breast, and he draws in his breath audibly.

'Sorry,' I say, restoring it.

'Don't be,' he says. 'In fact do it again if you like.'

We collect our things off the beach and he pauses to survey the ocean. I can sense melancholy from him that we are leaving, and I don't blame him. He's clearly in his element here.

'We'll come back again soon,' I say, even though I don't normally like to make promises I can't be sure I'll keep.

'I'll hold you to that.'

We make the trip back to the city in silence, listening to mellow music on the radio. I keep getting flashbacks that make me squeeze my eyes shut in disbelief at behaviour so far removed from who I normally am. It was like I had a whole bunch of pent-up crazy in me, just waiting for the opportunity to get out.

When we pull up outside my home and he cuts the engine I don't get out immediately. Inside the house I am needed. Out here I am wanted. I'm not ready to say goodbye to him just yet.

'So,' I say, my hand on the door handle.

'So.'

'I had a good day.'

'Me too. Sorry again about the whole surprise thing.'

'No, it's fine. I guess I can admit that *some* surprises aren't all that bad.'

'I'm glad I changed your mind.'

'Do you want to come in?' I ask quickly, before I can think too hard about it and chicken out. I'm not sure he's ready to meet my mother, but, on the other hand, if he's going to be put off by her it's better I find out sooner rather than later.

'I'd love to.' He smiles.

We shuffle up the garden path and I try hard not to look at it through his eyes. My mother and I aren't gardeners or handy people, but even if we were we don't have the luxury of time to get anything done. Any gardens that were here when we moved in have long since self-seeded back into patchy lawns, although every now and then a flower pops up randomly as if to guiltily remind us of what once was. The house is likewise in a state of disrepair, its orange brickwork chipped and cracking. The bottom step droops to an angle on the right that hints at drainage issues underneath the soil; issues we are choosing to ignore until we are left with no other option.

'How was the beach?' Mum calls from down the hallway as I usher Albert into the lounge. 'I hope you weren't mad at your friend for surprising you. I thought it was a wonderful thing to do.'

'It was fine, Mum.'

'I knew it. I knew you'd have a good time. Now tell me

154

everything. What's he like? Did he kiss you? Are you seeing him again?' She emerges from the hallway drying her hands and stops short when she sees the subject of her interrogation standing awkwardly in front of her.

'Oh,' she says. 'Hello. You must be Albert?'

'Al-*bear*, actually,' I smirk.

Mum's forehead creases in a frown as she mouths it. 'Bear? As in, koala bear? Teddy bear?'

Albert sighs and casts me a wounded look. 'It's the French pronunciation of Albert,' he says. 'Blame my mother.'

'Us mothers tend to get blamed for an awful lot.'

'Usually with good reason,' I say pointedly. 'What's for dinner? Is it OK if Albert stays?'

'Roast with all the trimmings, and of course he can. The more the merrier. You know my open door policy.'

'Only if there's enough . . . ?' Albert says politely.

'Oh yes there's plenty. I always do more than we girls can eat,' she titters as if we are fragile Shakespearean heroines. 'Do you like lamb?'

'Is there anyone who doesn't?'

She titters again and makes a face at me that I think I'm supposed to take as signifying her approval. Either that or she's just felt the urge for a painful bowel movement.

As she brushes past us on her way to the kitchen, she hisses in my ear, 'He's very good-looking isn't he!'

Of course he hears her because she's not exactly subtle, and his cheeks redden.

'Could you be any more embarrassing, Mum?' I complain.

'What?' she says innocently. 'I was just admiring your young man.'

'He's not "my" young man, and you're not old enough to talk like that. Now go away.'

'OK, OK, I can take a hint.' She disappears into the kitchen.

'Um, do you have a toilet I could use?' Albert asks.

'Down the end of the hall, last door on the right.'

'Thanks.'

'I'll be in the lounge when you're finished.'

'Which is?'

I point. 'Through there.'

'OK.'

I find Bee on the floor in front of the couch, intently watching something on her laptop.

'Hey, Bee, what are you watching?' At first I'm not sure exactly what it is that I'm looking at when I look at the screen. I'm expecting her to be watching *Postman Pat* or something similar, because she loves cartoons, but this looks nothing like any cartoon I've ever seen. I stare at it for a moment, puzzled, before Albert walks into the lounge and distracts me. He has a smirk on his face.

'Something funny?'

'No, nothing. I was just admiring the poster in your toilet.'

I cringe. Dammit. I'd forgotten about that. 'Shut up.'

'It's a stunner. Collectable is it?'

'I wouldn't know. It's not mine.'

'Not yours? I find that a little hard to believe considering it's your namesake.'

His eyes are alight with mischief as he waits for my reaction. 'I can always revoke the dinner invitation,' I warn. 'Send you on your merry way out into the cold dark night to fend for yourself.'

He checks his watch. 'First of all, it's just gone five, so hardly night. And it's fairly mild out there, on account of it being summer and all, so I think I'd survive.' He sees me start to open my mouth and raises a hand. 'Tut tut, don't interrupt, I haven't finished.'

I'm too astounded at being tutted at to say anything, and he takes the advantage to carry on.

'*However*,' he continues, 'I'd quite like the pleasure of your company for as long as possible, so consider me warned. I won't say another word about it.' He makes a zipping motion across his lips.

'Another word about what?' Mum has come into the lounge so quietly I don't realise she's standing behind me until she speaks.

'Nothing.'

'I was just admiring the poster on your toilet door,' Albert says. 'Is that Madonna's actual signature?'

Now he's done it. I give him a look to say he's just opened a can of worms, but his faux innocent smile tells me he's already well aware of that fact, and he's not sorry either.

'It sure is,' Mum answers proudly.

'Wow.'

'Isn't she just fab,' Mum says breathily like the star-struck fan she is. 'That woman sure knows how to age gracefully.'

'I think you're confusing the definition, Mum.' I roll my eyes. 'And if you start flashing your bits around in public when you're in your fifties I'll disown you, seriously.'

Mum pokes her tongue out at me. 'Yeah, yeah, so you keep saying.'

'I mean it.'

'Have you always been a fan?' Albert asks.

'Oh yes, always. In fact, I got that poster after one of her concerts you know,' she says proudly. 'Of course that's not all I got.'

She sees my warning look and shuts up.

'It's a great poster,' Albert tells her.

'It's not in as good a condition as it used to be unfortunately.' She looks at me accusingly when she says this, but I don't feel guilty, as she well knows.

'It's not?' He looks from Mum to me.

'Notice the orange stain by her crotch?' I say.

'Yeah, I think so.'

'Spaghetti sauce. Leftovers in the wheelie bin I threw it in.'

'Oh.'

'And the brown smudge under her left armpit?'

'Chocolate?'

'Mud. From over the neighbour's fence.'

Mum sighs heavily.

'At least we hope it's mud,' I continue. 'They do own a dog.'

'So wait. You mean to say that you threw it away? On purpose? Wow. That's sacrilege, surely.'

Mum nods vigorously in agreement.

'Not just once, several times.' I say unashamedly. 'It's like a boomerang though, keeps coming back.'

Albert laughs.

'It's not funny.'

'It kind of is.'

'Well, of course you'd think that, Al-*bear*.'

'Exactly. I know how you feel when it comes to crappy names. And, in my humble experience, there's not much you can do except laugh about it.'

'Madonna is not a crappy name,' my mother protests. 'It's unique. Original. Well, not original obviously, but you know what I mean.'

'It is crappy, Mum. And then you went and trumped it by saddling Bee with a name like Beyoncé.'

Mum purses her lips. 'OK, that one wasn't my finest moment, I'll admit. But I couldn't imagine her being anything else now. Could you?'

We all watch my sister. As if she feels the weight of our eyes on her, she looks up.

'Oh the twins have been busy,' she says. 'You little monkeys.'

'Is that ...' Albert leans forward to peer at Bee's screen. 'Is she watching men paint lines on tarmac?'

We all peer at it.

'Yes,' Mum sighs. 'She finds these videos on YouTube and can watch them for hours. God only knows why. Maybe she finds it soothing. The other day I found her watching a tutorial on "how to make a mini lathe".'

'It would be so interesting to see inside her head,' Albert says.

Mum shakes her head. 'You are preaching to the converted. I'd give anything to know what goes on under these curls.' She wraps her arms around my sister and nuzzles into her hair.

A buzzer sounds from the kitchen and snaps Mum from her melancholy. 'Time to add the carrots. Dinner won't be far away now.'

'Anything I can do to help?' Albert asks.

'Thank you, that's a sweet offer, but you're our guest. You guys just hang out in here while I finish up.'

She rubs her hands together and smiles rosily like some 1950s housewife.

'You could listen to some music,' she suggests.

'We'll be fine, Mum.'

When she's gone I grimace at Albert. 'Sorry about that. She's not used to me bringing company back to the house.'

'Should I be honoured or afraid?'

I shrug. 'Maybe a little bit of both.'

With a wary glance towards the door to make sure my mother isn't still within eyesight, he snuggles closer to me on the couch and drapes an arm over my shoulders, pulling me into his side. His lips graze my forehead lightly, sending shock waves through my body.

'Does this mean you haven't liked another boy enough to share him with your family before?'

I rest a hand on his thigh, feeling his muscle tense underneath my fingers. I will never get tired of that feeling. 'Maybe,' I tease. 'Or maybe I just didn't want to subject anyone to the horror that is my family. Maybe you're the first one who I thought could handle it.'

He gives a deep sigh, and I feel the ripples fan out through his body to vibrate against my ribs. 'Your family are not horrible.'

'I wasn't meaning Bee.'

'Even your mum. She's nice. You want a horror story you wait till you meet mine.' He shakes his head. 'You guys are like the bloody Partridge family compared to my lot.'

I tilt my head to the side and look up at him, admiring the light freckles on his beautiful, sun-stained skin. He still smells of the sea and I'm tempted to lick him to remind myself of our day. I don't though. Bee is sat right next to me, for one. And my mother being in the next room is also a bit of a passion killer.

'So are you going to introduce me to them?' I ask.

He winces. 'One day. Maybe. Far, *far* in the future. I don't want them to scare you off.'

'Nothing could do that,' I reassure him, my cheeks blushing as I say the words. I'm unaccustomed to declarations of affection. I have a weird kind of floating feeling, like I'm outside of my body looking down. When I remember the beach and what we did, it all feels unreal, like a dream. In a way I almost wish dinner was over already so I could climb into my bed and digest the day. But then he would be gone, and I'm not in a rush for that to happen.

Albert

Every moment we're apart, I find myself plotting how to be with her again. Planning our next escapade. I spend so much time looking at my phone to see if she's texted that Francine hauls me into the office and kindly asks me to please leave my phone at home, or at least switch it off when I'm at work.

'Now that you're on a contract,' she says pointedly. 'We expect your attention to be here with us.'

'Of course,' I apologise. 'I'll turn it off.' And I do. Well, I turn the sound off but leave it on vibrate in my back pocket so I'll still feel if Maddy texts. I can't help it. Love has made me reckless.

I thought what Kate and I had was love, and it was, but it was nothing like this. The feelings I had for her were like damp fireworks compared to the explosions of colour and light I feel when I see Maddy. Or think about her. The cynic in me knows that everyone feels like this when they first start a relationship.

But the romantic in me feels that no one, *ever in the history of love*, has ever felt anything like this. I can't get enough of her. She makes me feel like I could do anything. Like the world is just sitting there, waiting for us to do what we want with it. I have more dreams than I can keep up with. Things I want to experience. Places I want to go. Before Maddy, I was stuck in limbo but not aware of it. Now, I'm tensed, on a springboard, ready to take her hand and catapult ourselves out into the universe. The world really is our oyster, and I plan on salting that squishy little bastard and downing it in one.

I know as soon as she steps out of the car at the riding stables that something is wrong. Her face is drawn together in annoyance, anger, and she snaps at Bee when she takes too long putting on her boots, something I've never heard her do before. She apologises straight away and Bee is none the wiser, but it's out of character for her to lose her patience with her sister like that.

'Morning, you two beautiful ladies,' I say loudly when they come through the gate, Maddy leading Bee by the hand. I've been loitering beside the stables, pretending to be doing something vitally important but really just looking at things and nodding and walking back and forth a bit, even though only Matt is anywhere near and he couldn't give a fuck whether I work or not, as long as I don't dob him in for the million and one illegal smoke breaks he takes daily. Then I ask a little quieter. 'You OK?'

'Hey.' She smiles. 'Yeah, I'm fine. Well, sort of. Just angry.'

'At me?'

'Horse riding,' says Bee.

'No. Why? Have you done something I should be angry about?'

'No.'

'Then that was a bit of a stupid question.'

'Horse riding,' Bee says.

'Sorry.'

She sighs. 'No, I'm sorry. I shouldn't take my bad mood out on you.'

'Anything I can do to help?'

'No. Not unless you have friends in high places.'

I point up to the sky. 'You mean like . . . ?'

Her eyes follow the direction of my finger. 'God? No. If he even exists. No, I meant like politicians, someone who can tell the stupid pencil pushers sitting behind desks in the benefit office to take their pencils out of their fat lazy butts and stop being power-tripping dicks.'

'Oh.'

She sighs again. 'It's complicated.'

'It sounds it.'

'Horse riding,' says Bee.

Someone clears their throat behind me and Maddy looks over my shoulder.

'Sorry, Ann,' she says. 'We got a little held up.'

'It's OK,' Ann says warmly. 'But we really do need to get started.' Ann comes forward and takes Bee's hand. 'Good morning, Bee,' she says cheerfully.

Bee ignores her, although she smiles.

164

'Say good morning, Bee,' Maddy prompts her.

'Say good morning Bee,' Bee says.

'How are you today?' Ann asks her.

'Horse riding,' Bee says.

She's a lovely lady, Ann, a motherly sort. She's in her fifties I would guess, from the grey hair, but after the Francine fiasco I'm keeping all guesses to myself. She's the kind of lady who brings a chocolate cake to work in a Tupperware container when it's someone's birthday and does a whip-round collecting money if someone needs help. I'm usually dubious of people like her, sensing that nobody can be that genuinely good-natured all the time. But in her case I think it's the truth. She's just a nice person.

'Come along, Teddy is all ready and waiting patiently for you.'

She leads Bee towards the arena and I put a hand on Maddy's arm to hold her back. 'What's happened?'

With Bee gone she drops her guard and kicks at a stone on the ground angrily. 'Bee normally gets a weekly disability living allowance but they've stopped paying it. They are saying we missed a medical appointment.'

'What sort of medical appointment?'

'That's the thing. It's so fucked up. They wanted us to see a government-appointed doctor to make sure she still needs 24-hour care. Only we never got the letter so we missed the appointment. But she only saw someone last year and it's not like anything has changed. Now they've stopped paying her benefit and we really need that money.'

'That's lousy.'

We walk to the arena entrance and stop. Ann is holding Bee's hand and is helping her stroke the length of Teddy's nose. We hear Bee giggle and she leans forward to kiss Teddy's mane.

'It's like they think she might have magically woken up one morning and been cured.' Maddy says. 'If only.'

'That's stupid.'

'I know. Any normal person can see that. But these people aren't normal. I swear they just like making us jump through hoops for their own sick enjoyment.'

'Anything I can do?'

'No. I mean I know that there are people who rip the system off. I get that, I really do. But how can they think that someone like Bee, with all her illnesses, is out to scam them?'

'I'm sure they don't think that.'

'Maybe not, but making her take a medical to prove it when they have her entire medical history already on file is just pathetic.'

'I one hundred per cent agree.'

Ann flashes us a smile. 'Are you ready, Maddy?'

'Absolutely,' Maddy calls back. She wraps her arms around my waist quickly and gives me a tight squeeze. 'Thanks for listening.'

'What are boyfriends for?'

She flashes me a wicked look and tiptoes up to whisper in my ear. 'I can think of one or two other, more exciting uses.' She bites my lower ear lobe gently and I moan.

'Thanks. Now I'm going to be walking around work with a raging great boner.'

She laughs and shrugs. 'Sorry.'

'No you're not.'

I watch as she walks over to join Bee and Ann. She coaxes Bee up on to the mounting block she stands on to climb on to Teddy's back but Bee misjudges it and face plants into Teddy's neck before awkwardly sitting back up. Ann takes the ladder away and then picks up the reins to lead her around the ring.

'It's a nice day, why don't we go outside, Bee?' Ann asks.

I open the gate for them to pass through.

'Call you tonight?' I ask Maddy.

'You better.'

I don't though, in the end. When I get home from work just before six and walk through the back door I can immediately sense an unpleasant vibe in the air. Mum is in the kitchen, frying sausages while a pot of spuds boils merrily on the stove. She gives me a look that I fail to interpret, and I'm just about to ask her what's up when my father walks in from the lounge with an empty beer bottle in his hands. He sees me and his face darkens. My heart drops and I feel a part of me shut down as my coping mechanism kicks in. I know that look. He's had a shit day at work and he's spoiling for a fight.

'Here he is, the useless lump himself,' he growls.

'I'll be in my room,' I say, desperate to escape before whatever he's angry about erupts out of him like some molten, furious volcano and oozes everywhere leaving hurtful words that can never be taken back. I've had more than enough of those words from him to last a lifetime. They are stamped inside every part of me.

My mother shakes her head ever so slightly and gives me an imploring look. I don't blame her though. I never have.

'My room, don't you mean,' Dad says. 'After all, I pay the mortgage.'

Bitter experience tells me there is nothing I can say that will diffuse the situation, especially when I don't yet know the cause for it. My father, once started, must finish. I say nothing and instead think about the day I will walk out of this house and out from under his thumb, while he goes off on a rant. It can't come soon enough. During moments like this I think I should just leave with what I already have saved, but if I'm moving back to the coast I'm going to need money for somewhere to live and to keep me going until I can find a new job. I've been bearing the brunt of my father's disappointment and frustration for nineteen years. I can take it a bit longer if it means I don't ever have to come back.

'And do I ask for much in return? Eh?' he carries on. 'I don't think I'm unreasonable, am I love?'

My mother doesn't answer, concentrating on the tongs she is using to turn the sausages.

'I put a roof over your head, food in your belly, and you can't even repay me by mowing a goddamn lawn when I ask you to.'

So that's it.

'I was going to do them this week.'

'Yeah right. You're just saying that because I've reminded you.' He slams the bottle down on the bench and my mother jumps. 'Jesus, Albert, when are you going to grow up and start acting like an adult, eh?'

'I'm sorry. I'll mow them now.'

'You're goddamn right you'll mow them now. And you'll do a proper job of it too. I'm sick of our house looking like the shit heap of the street because you won't pull your weight and help out around here. I shouldn't have to keep asking you.'

'No. Sorry.'

'You're *sorry*,' he sneers. 'I'll tell you what you are; you're useless and a disappointment, fawning about over some girl instead of getting a real job and trying to make something of yourself.'

I hold his gaze levelly, trying not to show any spark of defiance in my eyes. If I do, it will escalate. If I don't, he'll grow bored and move on to something else. I must do a good enough job because he scowls at me once more and then turns to open the fridge for another beer.

I mow the lawns, and then I drop the lawnmower down a level and I mow them again. Anything to avoid going back inside. I mow while the sun sinks behind the hills and the lights come on in the houses around me. I can see the TV blinking through the net curtains of Mrs Dansie's house across the street. When I'm finished and I know I have done them well enough to satisfy him, I put the lawnmower away, making sure I have filled it back up with petrol so he doesn't have another thing to complain about, and lock the shed. Then I sit on the front steps, the concrete cool underneath me, and I dream about being somewhere, anywhere, else.

Maddy

'Are you sure you don't mind?' I ask again, for the twentieth time. Mum rolls her eyes.

'Of course not.'

'You guys will be OK?'

'We'll be fine. I do know what I'm doing you know, despite what you might sometimes think.'

'I know. Sorry.'

'Relax. Enjoy yourself. You haven't spent a night away from us since your Year Six camp.'

'That's not helpful. I'm nervous.'

'You'll be fine. You'll be more than fine. I wonder where he's taking you? Ooh, maybe a flash hotel.'

'I have no idea. He wouldn't give me any clues.'

I drop the kitchen blind, which I have been nervously looking out of on and off for the last hour, and unzip my bag on the countertop again to check the contents.

'How did you know what to pack then?' Mum asks. She's sitting at the breakfast bar with Bee, colouring in some of Bee's tape covers. Bee is pointing to what she wants Mum to write, and after Mum writes it on the covers Bee colours it in with felt pen. She's a talented artist, my sister, and we have a few of her framed drawings up on the wall.

'I didn't. I've just tried to cover a few bases. Jeans, a nice top, a T-shirt, shorts, togs, a dress and some sandals.'

'Should be OK then.'

'I hope so.' I'm seized by a fresh set of nerves. 'What if I've forgotten something important though?'

'You haven't. It's not like you're going away for a week.'

Beep, beep.

I jump when we hear a deep horn sound out front and lift the blind.

'Is it him?' Mum asks.

'I have no idea.' There's a large black truck outside our house. The kind with a cab and a flatbed deck. I've never seen it before. A hand comes out from the driver's side and waves, then the door opens and Albert steps out and grins at me.

Mum follows me outside and stands on the doorstep, leaning against the wall with her arms crossed as I walk self-consciously up the garden path lugging my bag.

'Hey.' He smiles.

'Hey. Nice truck.'

He steps back and surveys it proudly. 'She's a beauty, eh?'

'As far as trucks go sure. Whose is it?'

'Mine.'

'Seriously?'

A bubble of excited laughter escapes him. 'Yes, seriously. I can hardly believe it myself, but I've just signed the paperwork.'

'Wow.'

'I know.'

'You bought a car.'

'I did.'

'Wow.'

'I know.'

'Seriously?'

'Seriously.'

'Expensive?'

'Not too bad. Second-hand, of course. I should just about be able to afford the monthly repayments and still treat my girl to the odd night out.' He takes my bag from my hand and throws it on to the back of the truck in one smooth move. Then he freezes. 'There wasn't anything breakable in there was there?'

'Luckily for you, no.'

'You're ready?'

'As I'll ever be.'

He holds out a hand. 'Then your chariot awaits, madam, to take you on your next adventure.'

I put my hand in his and run my eyes over his face. It's only been a few days since we last saw each other but when I see him again I am hit with the intensity of how much I have missed him. 'Still no clues as to our destination?'

He shakes his head and pulls me into his embrace. 'No. But

you'll like it. At least, I hope you will.' He dips his head down until the tips of our noses are touching and I'm swept away by the emotion in his eyes.

'As long as I'm with you how can I not?' I breathe, feeling the heat from his lips only millimetres from mine.

'Christ, get a room you two,' Mum hollers, ruining the moment. I'd forgotten she was there. 'Stop putting on a floor show for the neighbours.'

Albert laughs, his breath warm on my face.

'This from the woman wearing tartan tights,' I call back over my shoulder.

'What's wrong with my tights?'

'If you have to ask, there's no hope for you.'

'Ach away with you,' Mum laughs, putting on a fake Scottish accent.

Albert opens the passenger door and I hesitate, one hand on the roof. I turn my head to look at Mum. 'Are you sure you guys will be OK?'

Mum sighs and looks at Albert. 'Do you see what I have to put up with?' She looks at me. 'For the last time, we will be absolutely fine. Now go and enjoy yourself.'

Albert looks at his watch. 'Yeah, we need to get going or we'll miss part of the surprise.'

The truck has a black interior, tidy. It has an odd smell like it once belonged to a cigarette smoker, but time and a little strawberry-shaped air freshener dangling from the rear-view mirror have erased most of the offensiveness.

'Do you like it?' Albert asks hopefully, proudly.

'I do.'

He pats the dashboard lovingly. 'I can't believe it's all mine.'

'Me neither. It's a very grown-up thing to do, buying your first car.'

'I know right?' He grins. 'Although I had to ask my mother to sign as guarantor.'

'Maybe don't tell your friends that part. Kind of ruins your street cred.'

It's Friday night and, as we cruise through town, I can see people in bars enjoying the happy hour after work, or sat at tables outside restaurants enjoying a combination of good food, conversation and a balmy evening. Normal things that people do. Most people anyway. People with less worries or responsibilities. I feel a little pang of sadness inside and squash it. I am not going to feel sad, not tonight.

I notice Albert take the same turn out of town as he did a few weeks before, the last time we escaped together.

'We're going to the beach?' I ask, puzzled.

'You did promise me we'd go back someday.'

I nod. 'Yes, I did. I just figured it would be during the day.'

He flicks a sideways glance at me. 'Have you ever watched the sun set from a beach?'

I don't even need to think about it. 'No.'

'Then I can't wait to share it with you.'

The steady rhythm of the wheels on the road lulls me into a dozing state, until the sound changes when we crunch on to the gravel and I sit up, rubbing my eyes. The sky has darkened, but the sun is still above the horizon.

'Hey, sleepy head,' he says, reaching over to squeeze my leg. 'Been a long week?'

'Not any longer than normal.' I yawn. 'Just a few rough nights with Bee. She had another fit, and I always find it hard to sleep after that.'

'Yeah, I bet,' he agrees sympathetically.

'We're here?'

'We are,' he confirms, coasting to a stop and turning the engine off. 'Come on, I don't want to miss it.' He lifts a picnic basket out of the back seat of the truck and, taking my hand, leads me down the same path as last time. He picks a spot near the high tide mark and opens the basket, pulling out a blanket.

'Sit,' he says. 'I'll be back in a tick.'

I do as I'm told and watch as he jogs down the beach a hundred metres or so, stopping every now and then to pick up bits of driftwood. When he's satisfied he has enough he jogs back, dropping them to a pile on the sand in front of me. He fishes in a pocket and pulls out a few tissues and some matches, then he drops to one knee and in almost no time at all we have a little fire crackling away in front of us.

'Where'd you learn how to do that?' I ask, impressed.

'Boy Scouts.' He grins. 'All those Tuesday nights away from the telly weren't a complete waste.'

He blows on it a few more times to make sure it's well established then he sits beside me and pulls me close. 'I hope you're not disappointed.'

'About what?'

'That I've brought you back here instead of whisking you off to some five-star hotel for a spa night.'

I snuggle in against him. 'Of course I'm not disappointed.'

We sit in silence, admiring the sky stretched out in front of us. Everything around us – the sand, the sea and our skin – is bathed in a cosy, golden glow. There's a sense of anticipation in the air, a feeling of freedom.

It's not cold, but I shiver.

'Are you cold?' Albert asks, concern in his voice.

'No. Just happy.'

'Good.' He smiles. 'Good.'

He pulls a bottle of fizzy wine and two plastic cups out of his picnic basket and we make a toast to the end of the day and welcome the night. I am already heady with the freedom of being here with him, so it doesn't take much for the wine to go to my head.

'God, this is just amazing.' I close my eyes and breathe in the smell of the ocean and woodsmoke. 'Tell me we can stay here for ever.'

'We can stay here for ever.'

I open my eyes. 'I wish that were true.'

'What's stopping us? Apart from money, I suppose. And I guess eventually we'd run out of food. And wine. And clean underwear. Then again do we really need underwear?' He winks at me suggestively.

'I can't leave my sister.'

'Well sure, not now. But you'll have to eventually. Unless you're planning on living at home for the rest for your life.'

When I don't answer he pulls back so he can see my face. 'You're serious?'

'I don't see any other option. Bee needs me.'

He frowns. 'Sure, but she has your mum too.'

'Who works, and needs help.'

'Isn't there some kind of government help available?'

I snort derisively. '"The government" has no idea what caring for someone twenty-four hours a day entails. Sure, there's respite care available, but we're not keen on that. The care homes charge massive payments but only pay their workers a minimum wage, which means they pretty much do the minimum expected of them. Not everyone is like that, of course, but enough for us to feel uneasy leaving her there. Bee can't tell us if someone manhandles her or does something they shouldn't. We'd never forgive ourselves if anything happened.'

'What about your mum? What does she have to say about it?'

'We've never actually discussed it. It's more of an understanding. I can't leave her to deal with Bee on her own. It's too much for one person.'

I look down and burrow my toes deeper into the sand. The sun is low in the sky now and the first stars are making themselves known. The horizon is streaked a beautiful rose pink, that deepens into mauve and then violet as the darkness deepens. There is no sound apart from the waves gently sweeping the shore, their white caps a beautiful phosphorescent blue.

'Anyway,' I say firmly, my tone brokering no argument,

'that's enough talk of that. I thought you brought me here to relax and forget about everything back home.'

'You're absolutely right. Here.' He reaches for the bottle and tops up my glass. 'Drink up and relax, *ma chérie*, whilst I prepare you a feast.'

'A feast?'

'Yes, a feast.'

'You can cook?'

'Why do you ask like that?'

'Like what?

'Like you have doubts.'

'Well, you know.' I look him up and down.

He sighs theatrically and places a hand on his chest, pulling a wounded face. 'Always I am judged by my good looks alone.'

I have to laugh. He is pulling a fake outraged face but it just makes him look cuter.

Half an hour later I am eating my words. Not only them, but the most delicious and juicy piece of salmon I have ever eaten in my life. After fetching a small cooler bag from the truck, Albert proceeded to smugly drizzle salmon steaks with olive oil, a generous sprinkling of salt and pepper and some lemon slices before wrapping them in foil. Then he put them in a heavy soot-stained cast iron pan with a long handle and held them over the fire. The smell when he opened the foil to check if they were cooked made me groan with anticipation. Something about the seaside air has kicked my appetite into gear and I'm starving.

'Who says one can't eat gourmet food at the beach,' he said

triumphantly as he handed me a plastic plate with the piece of salmon and a side of coleslaw that he'd bought pre-made from a supermarket.

'I stopped quickly for supplies before I picked you up,' he explained. 'We also have another bottle of wine, and marshmallows, because let's face it, you can't have a beach campfire without marshmallows.'

We eat with our fingers as the juices run down our arms, and we toast each other with wine that tastes of summer nights. I breathe in the deliciousness that is the seaside, and delight in the heady intoxication of his company.

Albert

She is incredible.

In the flickering flames from the fire, her face comes alive and her eyes shine, like some enchanted princess brought back to life with a kiss. My kiss. Or kisses, I should say, because I bestow her with about a thousand of them while we eat and drink until she protests that her lips are becoming numb under the onslaught.

'I'm sorry,' I say sheepishly. 'I'll stop.'

'Don't you dare,' she says. 'I was merely observing, not complaining.'

I don't know what to think about the bombshell she just dropped. Is she seriously planning on living at home for the rest of her life? Surely her mother doesn't expect her to make that much of a sacrifice? I'm grateful she didn't ask about my own plans, because I'm not sure I could have answered truthfully if put on the spot. If I told her I'm leaving town as soon as I get enough money saved, she'd back right off. And she'd have every right to. Of course, my savings have taken a hit from buying the truck, but the way I see it, it's more than just a chariot for Maddy and I to spend time together, it's also my ticket out of here. Buying the truck gives me independence and now I can leave whenever I'm ready. If I was honourable I'd tell her so she could make her own decision, but I can't. I can't risk losing her, not now.

I've never met anyone like her. Not our age, anyway. She's so selfless, the way she cares for Bee. I try to imagine how I'd feel if it were Louis that needed my help but I can't. I know we're not typical brothers and that he pretty much can't stand the sight of me. I don't know when it all went wrong for us or why, but as it's always been this way I can't imagine it any different.

'Penny for your thoughts?' Maddy asks.

I don't tell her what I'm thinking about though. It would only bring down her mood again and I brought her here to forget all that.

'I'm just remembering how good you looked in that pink bikini,' I say instead.

She groans and slaps a hand over her eyes. 'Don't,' she says. 'That was mortifying.'

I laugh. She's as sexy as hell but without being aware of it. I may not have known her all that long, but already I can't imagine my life without her. I never want to stop seeing her smile, or hear her laugh.

She is addictive.

I can't get enough of her.

If this is addiction, I hope I'm never cured.

Maddy

'OK, your turn,' I giggle, a little drunkenly. 'Truth or dare.' I am feeling wild and free of responsibility, and it feels sensational.

He narrows his eyes while he pretends to think about it. 'You already know everything about me there is to know, so I guess it will have to be a dare. But please, be gentle with me, it's my first time.'

'I don't believe you.'

'It's true.'

'OK, dare.' I cast my eyes around in the dark for inspiration. I hear it rather than see it. 'Well there's really only one option available.'

'I'm a little scared.'

'You should be.' I take another swig of wine from my cup. I am feeling tipsy enough to be merry, to lower my usual inhibitions. But not drunk, not by a long shot. The cool sea air and

Albert's close presence and the way he keeps looking at me keep me sober. His eyes reflect the flames from the campfire, the orange giving him a fiery, wicked look.

'Do you know how beautiful you are?' he asks huskily.

He is so close I can feel his intensity. It comes off him like heat waves, and I wonder if he is feeling it just as much as I am. He leans in and I realise he is going to kiss me.

'Do you know how cold the water is?' I whisper when he is only millimetres away.

He blinks, swayed from his course. 'Cold?'

'Yes, cold. Despite you trying to change the subject, I *dare* you to find out. Now.'

'Seriously?'

'Yes.'

'You want me to swim?'

'No. I want you to skinny-dip.'

His eyes flicker with amusement. He pushes a strand of hair away from my face, his fingers lingering on my cheek. 'And if I refuse?'

'Then I'll have to think of some form of punishment.'

His eyes drop to my mouth and the longing in them is raw and unashamed. He wants me. I know this as sure as I know I want him just as much. I have never felt a level of lust for someone the way I do for him. It's almost all-consuming.

'Would I like this punishment?'

'I guess it's a risk you'll have to take.'

He is torn, I can see it in his eyes, but the daredevil in him can't refuse a challenge. He stands up and grins down at me, then lifts his T-shirt and jersey over his head in one smooth movement. His shoulders are broad and his waist is slender. He is defined but not muscular, athletic yet not in an obvious way. He is delicious.

'You sure you're ready for this?' he teases, and I squeal and cover my eyes as he drops his pants. Only when I hear his footsteps on the sand heading away from me do I risk peeking between my fingers. His bum flashes white in the night as he runs down to the water and without hesitation he plunges in. It's his turn to squeal.

'Shit, it's cold,' he shouts. 'Shit, shit, shit.' He cups his hands in the water and splashes his hair in an effort to acclimatise. Then he wades until he is waist deep and dives smoothly under.

I stand and walk quickly down to the water's edge, laughter shaking my shoulders in a way it hasn't for so long. *This* is what life should be all about. The light from a half moon is reflected in the smooth surface of the water. I watch as he surfaces, water streaming from his head. He shakes it off and smiles at me.

'Come on in, the water is lovely,' he calls.

'Yeah right.' I give him a dubious look and let the lapping water embrace my toes. It is *not* lovely. I step back quickly. He does a dolphin dive.

'No seriously,' he says, remerging. 'Once you're in it's OK, refreshing even.'

He takes advantage of my hesitation to swim in closer, stealthily, and before I realise what he's up to he is standing, taking large strides towards me. I have no time to run before his arms have scooped me up and he is pulling me into the water with him.

It is even colder than I thought it would be, and the shock of it takes my breath away. He drops down while still holding me until the water is around my shoulders.

'This wasn't part of the dare,' I say between gasps.

His face in the moon is all shadows and contours, but there's no mistaking the intent in his eyes.

'So punish me,' he says, and then he lowers his head and kisses me.

I have never been kissed like this. So urgently, like we have been desperately searching for each other. I weave my hands behind his neck and hold on like my life depends on it. He starts moving out of the water quickly and we stumble up the beach, kissing, only pausing to lift my sodden jersey over my head, followed by the rest of my clothes, leaving a trail behind us.

The air is cold but I couldn't care less. The heat from his skin is keeping me warm, and no matter how I try, I can't get close enough to him. We reach the fire and break apart, breathless. I realise I am fully topless, and automatically my arms go to cover myself.

'Don't,' he says. 'You're so beautiful.'

I have never felt more beautiful than I do standing there with his eyes drinking in the sight of me. We stand on opposite sides of the picnic blanket, a metre apart, staring at each other, breathing heavily.

'I don't normally do this,' I say.

'Me neither.'

We meet in the middle of the rug and I fall/am lowered down, Albert on top of me. My legs go around his waist, we move to meet and I can't help it, I let out a primeval, guttural moan. It feels so fantastically, unbelievably *good*, and I squeeze my thighs around his waist tighter, my hands in his hair as he kisses my forehead and my cheeks before grinding his lips on to mine with an urgency I thought only existed in movies.

Afterwards, we lie panting, breathless, our sweat mingling as we stare into each other's eyes and marvel at this wonderful thing we have just done together, as if we are the only people clever enough to have to have done it so perfectly before.

'That's twice we've made love alfresco on this beach,' I murmur, tracing my fingers along the curves of his chest. 'Anyone would think we couldn't afford a motel room.'

He nuzzles into my hair, his lips sending shivers down my body. 'Would you rather be in a motel room, or out here?'

'Do you even need to ask?'

We make love twice more under the vast Milky Way until neither of us has any strength left, and then we fall asleep entwined together, his clothes laid haphazardly over us for warmth. When I wake a few hours later the horizon is pink; dawn is almost upon us. The fire has gone out and I shiver, which wakes him. He opens his eyes, the most perfectly beautiful thing I have ever seen, and smiles up at me.

'Morning, beautiful.'

'Good morning.'

He pulls me in close and together we watch the birth of a new day, brilliant and gentle in its beauty. Like the day, I feel like I have been awakened, and I wonder how I am supposed to go back to my normal life after an experience such as this.

'Are you OK?' he asks when I sigh.

'I'm fine,' I smile, reassuring him. 'Just wishing this didn't have to end, I guess.'

'We'll have more nights like this, I promise,' he says fervently. 'This is just the beginning.'

I can't shake my melancholy though. He's given me a taste of what life can and should be like. What I've never dared let myself believe I could have. But I meant everything I said to him the night before. I *can't* leave my mother to look after my sister all on her own. I just can't. So where does that leave us?

'Come on,' he says, standing and pulling me to my feet. 'There's bound to be fishermen along shortly.'

My jeans have been stolen by the tide so I'm grateful I packed extra clothes. I lean my forehead against the cool glass and watch the world flash by. Everything feels different. I am different.

And yet everything is still just the same.

Albert

My euphoric mood from our night at the beach lasts approximately three days, before my father destroys it with his usual cruel efficiency.

At first when I get home from work and see him sat at the dining table with paperwork spread out in front of him and a steely expression I think Mum and I have been rumbled and he knows she's gone guarantor for me on the truck. Even though it was her idea, we'd rather hoped to keep it between ourselves. I'm not worried for myself; after all I'm used to disappointing him. But I don't want him to be mad at Mum.

'Albert, have a seat,' he says sternly.

'Before you go off on one, I can explain.'

'Sit.'

I do as I'm told and am about to launch into a prepared speech about how it was all my idea and I'd bullied her into it when I catch sight of the letterhead on the paperwork. I'd know that logo anywhere; after all I'd grown up seeing it stitched on to the shirt on my father's chest every morning when he'd head out to work.

'I've called in some favours,' he says.

'What sort of favours,' I ask cautiously.

'You've got an interview on the twenty-third of next month. Provided you don't say anything too stupid and you pass the physical and medical, you're in.'

'In?'

'Well, there's the formality of training college, of course. But even you should manage not to stuff that up.'

'College?'

He sighs, and rubs his temples wearily. 'Jesus, Albert, you act this gormless in the interview and all my bloody arse-kissing will have been a waste of time. I've talked you up, boy, so don't let me down. It's not just you who'll look stupid if you stuff this opportunity up.'

'What opportunity? I have no idea what you're even talking about.'

He pushes the paper across the table towards me, at the same time rotating it so I can read what it says on the top.

'APPLICATION'.

The penny drops and so does my stomach.

'Not interested,' I say flatly.

'I don't care if you're interested or not. You think people join the police force because they're interested?'

'Yeah.'

'Some maybe,' he admits. 'The rest of us understand that it's

189

a steady pay cheque, and a pretty good one at that. Pension at the end. And yes, there's the chance to make a difference and save lives blah, blah, blah. But it's job security, Albert. Time goes on we get more crime, not less. They're never going to lay off cops.'

'Maybe not, but I'm still not interested.'

He pushes his chair back angrily and gets to his feet, leaning forward to point a finger in my face. 'Are you planning on working at the stables for the rest of your life? Earning peanuts?'

I don't of course, but I'm not telling him that. If he knew what I had planned, I'd never hear the end of it. So I just shrug.

'I don't know,' I say impassively.

He snorts. 'You don't know. Of course you don't know. God forbid you actually plan for the future.'

'I'm nineteen, Dad. Plenty of time for that.'

'Time? Do you know what I was doing at nineteen?'

'Yeah, you might have mentioned it once or twice.'

He narrows his eyes. 'Always the smart-arse. That's your problem right there. Wendy!'

The laundry door opens and my mother comes out. He turns to her and she flinches under his red and angry gaze.

'Tell him,' he says, agitated. I see spittle fly out of his mouth and land on her cheek. 'Tell him he's being an idiot. *You* molly-coddled him growing up and made him the way he is. Now *you* fix it.'

He storms off outside, slamming the door shut behind him. My mother raises a hand to her face and ever so softly wipes her cheek. It's a gentle gesture, a simple one, and it breaks my heart. She doesn't deserve this life. Why does she put up with him?

She sits down at the table and picks up the application form.

'I'm not doing it,' I say, fully expecting her to be on my side like she always is. I'm thrown when she doesn't answer; instead she sighs and looks at me sadly.

'What?' I ask.

'Would it really be so bad?'

'Are you serious?' I can't believe what I'm hearing.

'It's not like you'd be signing the rest of your life away, honey. If you don't like it, you can always look at something else down the track. But for now this might be a good thing. You'd finally be earning some good money, you could get your own place.'

'You want me to move out?'

'No.' She shakes her head but then it turns into a nod. 'And yes. You need to move away from him, Albert. You two have always clashed, that's never going to change. I hate seeing him hurt you. If you stay I'm scared he'll permanently break your spirit.'

'So you want me to join the police force so I can end up just like him?'

'You're nothing like him. You never could be. Becoming a policeman won't change that.'

'I can't believe you're agreeing with him.'

'I just don't think it's his worst idea for once.'

'Come on, can you really see me in the same uniform as him? Doing what he does?'

'It takes all sorts to make the world work.'

'That's corny crap, Mum.'

'I know. But it's true. You can be the yin to his yang. You wouldn't be working with him anyway. You could get posted anywhere in the country.'

Immediately my thoughts turn to Maddy, and my face clearly betrays this.

'I know you really like her,' Mum says. 'But there's no reason why you still can't see her. If you guys are serious, there's long distance while you train and then maybe she'll move wherever you go. It's not like her job is holding her here.'

'No.'

Her job might not be, but something else is. Bee. I don't tell Mum this though. Irrationally, I'm feeling let down and a little betrayed. I thought my mother understood me better than this. The thought of being a policeman like my father fills me with dread. Not just because of him, but because it's not me. I'm naturally non-confrontational.

'Please, love,' Mum says. 'Just think about it. That's all I'm asking.'

'I have to go.'

'Don't be angry with me.'

She sounds so sad that any anger I feel deflates instantly. 'I'm not angry with you.'

She stands and holds out her arms hopefully. 'Cuddle?'

'As long as you don't tell anyone,' I say.

It's our little joke and it's always cheered me up but today it doesn't work. I can't help but feel as if things have changed.

It's an odd world when my mother agrees with my father, and it gives me an uneasy feeling.

I pick up a box of beer and go to Connor's. We drink and watch some action movie where apparently guns never run out of ammunition and the good guy never gets hit, despite everything around him being blown to smithereens. It's mindless enough I don't have to concentrate on it, but not enough to distract me from my thoughts.

Maddy

It's D-day, according to the calendar.

'It can't be,' I say, staring at the big black 'D' scrawled on today's date, circled twice for emphasis.

'Hmm?' Mum says, a piece of toast clenched between her teeth while she attempts to run a brush through my sister's violent curls, not helped by the fact my sister is wearing her headphones and is watching *The Simpsons* on her MP3 player. She keeps dropping her head down and Mum has to pull it back up.

'Do you like children?' Bee says. 'What do you mean all the time even when they are nuts? Oh yes, yes I do. Well done, Simpson.'

'The calendar reckons Bee has a dentist appointment today.' I drain the dregs of my morning coffee, wishing the cup was twice as big but making a half-arsed effort to cut down on my caffeine consumption. 'It can't have been six months since the last check-up though, surely?'

'Oh yes, I forgot about that. Time goes quick when you're having fun, eh?'

'Yeah. So much fun.'

Mum stops brushing to look at me shrewdly. 'You OK?'

'Fine.'

'You sure? You and Albert aren't having problems, are you?'

'No. We're fine.'

I haven't seen him since the beach. We've spoken on the phone a few times but our schedules keep clashing. Vague plans to catch up this weekend are in place, and it can't get here soon enough.

Mum clears her throat. 'Are you seeing him tonight?'

'No. Why?'

'No reason.'

There is a reason and we both know it. She wants to do something, most probably go out but she doesn't want to ask because she feels bad. It's a familiar routine.

'Just say it, Mum.'

She puts down the brush and pulls my sister's hair back in a chunky ponytail. 'We really need to get this thinned out and trimmed again.'

'Fine. I'm not going to force it out of you.' I shrug.

'Sonia and Kelly are going out for a few drinks tonight after our shift and I thought, maybe, if you weren't busy with Albert, I could go along for one. Just one. Probably water.'

'Mum, it's fine. Go. Enjoy yourself. Have a wine. We're not so broke you can't have a drink with your friends.'

'Speaking of, we've had a letter from the social welfare

department yesterday. They've reinstated Bee's disability allowance and backdated it. No apology for their stupidity though.'

'Of course not. Didn't expect one. But that's a relief, at least we can clear a few bills.'

Mum puts her arms around Bee and pulls her in against her chest. She looks at me sadly. 'This isn't the life I wanted for you girls, you know. I'm sorry it's such a struggle.'

I hate when she talks like this. It falls on me to talk her out of her low mood, and sometimes I just don't have the tolerance for it. Other times I try to put myself in her shoes and I have more patience for her. 'It is what it is, Mum. And no one is blaming you so stop saying sorry. Everyone has their own problems; we're better off than some.'

'I know.' She sniffs audibly and I look at her alarmed. The last thing I feel like dealing with is her tears, not when I already have Bee and the dentist visit looming.

'Do it. Drinks. Go. Have fun.'

'Are you sure, love?'

'Yes. Bee and I will be fine.'

She sniffs again but it's quieter, crisis averted. 'If you're sure?'

'Yes.'

She gets to her feet and starts hunting for her keys. I pick them up from the fruit bowl and hold them out for her. She takes them gratefully and gives me a sad little smile.

'What would I do without you, love.'

I smile tightly but don't answer.

'Let me know how you get on at the dentist.' She turns to Bee. 'Be a good girl for Maddy.'

As soon as we pull into the dentist's car park Bee starts getting anxious.

'No thank you,' she says, shaking her head. 'White car, Mummy's house.'

Our car is white. This is her way of saying 'take me home, please'. I would love to, but my sister has a smaller palate than most due to her disabilities. She also has an overcrowded mouth and a high pain threshold, so if she has a rotten tooth, for instance, she couldn't tell us. Problem is, she's not a fan of doctors or medical clinicians of any kind.

'White car, Mummy's house,' she says over and over in the waiting room. She won't sit down and paces, flapping her hands near her head. The receptionist comes out to offer Bee some water but she shakes her head. 'No thank you, white car, Mummy's house.'

'I'll just leave it here for her.' The lady smiles, indicating towards a table with a pile of ratty magazines that look like they've been there for the last ten years. As soon as she bends to put the plastic cup down I see what Bee is about to do but I'm too far away to be able to stop her. Still, I try.

'Bee, no,' I call out.

Slap!

Bee smacks the receptionist hard on her bum and the woman's eyes nearly pop out of her head. She lurches forward and grabs on to the table to stop herself from toppling over.

Bee laughs and jumps up and down.

'Sorry,' I say.

Luckily, this is a special dentist, used to dealing with

children and adults like Bee. It is probably not the first time she has had her personal boundaries invaded. She stands up and gives a little laugh and turns to shake a finger at Bee.

'Naughty girl,' she says. 'You caught me unawares then.'

'I'm sorry,' I say meekly. 'She just doesn't know any better.'

'No need to apologise or explain. It's fine, honestly.'

Thankfully, the dentist calls us in then and I lead Bee down the long white hallway. Her anxiety grows the closer we get to his room. She clearly remembers being here and knows what's to come.

'Hello, Bee,' the dentist, a cheerful man named Harold, says. He is thin, too thin, and it makes his head look like a skull on a stick. He has no hair on the top of his head, just a few tufts above his ears and around the back, and he wears glasses that magnify his eyes. I don't blame Bee for being scared of him. With his white lab coat and in this sterile environment with the tools of his trade laid out on a tray a bit like torture instruments, he looks like a villain in one of the cartoons she watches.

'No thank you, white car, Mummy's house.' She shakes her head, refusing to look him in the eye. He closes the door and flicks the lock and immediately she starts pacing around the room like a caged animal.

'It's OK, Bee, he's just going to look inside your mouth,' I reassure her, like I have so many times before.

'No thank you, white car, Mummy's house.'

I hate seeing her like this. I know he's not going to hurt her, and I know that this has to be done for her own sake, but it's hard to see the fearful look on her face.

I sit on the chair. 'Look, Bee, it's easy. Just open your mouth so he can look inside. It won't take long.'

I open my mouth and Harold peers inside. It is a stage show we have perfected over many visits.

'No thank you, white car, Mummy's house.'

'We're not leaving until you let the dentist look in your mouth, Bee.'

She stops in front of the window and prises open the blinds to look outside. Construction is happening somewhere nearby and we can hear the sound of loud hammering and drills. It adds to her anxiety and she flaps her hands near her face vigorously.

'Bee.'

She lets go and the blinds snap shut again.

'Come on, Bee, open your mouth.'

She opens it for the briefest of moments. Harold quickly looks inside with his little mirror before she closes it again, almost trapping his finger.

'Finished now,' she says 'White car, Mummy's house.'

'No, Bee. Not finished. Open your mouth, please.'

It takes about ten minutes. Ten minutes of pacing and coaxing and brief glimpses before Harold is satisfied that everything is OK, at least as OK as it can be. I am relieved because when Bee needs dental work we have to go through the local hospital and they have to put her to sleep. We have just bought ourselves another six-month reprieve.

I fish a ready-made pizza out of the freezer and heat it up for our dinner. Then while Bee watches *Barney & Friends* on her laptop I call Albert. He's distracted, I can hear it in his voice and we have a weird conversation like we are strangers instead of people who have been as intimate as they can possibly be with each other. I tell him about the dentist and he doesn't laugh when I tell him about Bee smacking the receptionist, even though it is funny.

'Guess you had to be there,' I say.

'Mm.'

'OK come on, spill. What's wrong?'

'Nothing.'

'I don't believe you.'

'Nothing you need to worry about anyway.'

'Well now see, that just *makes* me worry.' I try to say it in a light-hearted joking manner to break the tension but he just sighs.

'Just family stuff.'

'Oh. Right.' I'm still waiting for Albert to open up to me about his family. Having met his father, I'm aware that theirs is not an easy relationship, but I'm not going to push him into confiding in me. I'd prefer he does it when he's ready.

'Super-dee-duper!' Bee says, pushing me aside to try to talk into the phone.

'Hey, Bee,' Albert says.

'Has anyone seen my blankey?'

'Watch *Barney*, Bee,' I tell her, trying to push her away.

'You're busy, I'll let you go,' says Albert.

'No it's OK. I can talk if you want to.'

'It's fine. I'll ring you tomorrow. '

200

'Are you sure you're OK?'

'Positive.'

He doesn't sound at all like himself though. I shower Bee and dress her in her PJs. She lies in Mum's bed with me and refuses to sleep, no matter how much I ignore her or how many times I tell her to close her eyes. She is in a playful mood, and keeps touching me, pinching my nose shut, stroking my hair, wrapping her legs around mine. She recites nursery rhymes and scripts from shows, jumping between them so quickly I struggle to catch up.

Finally, she drifts off, just before twelve. I am just falling asleep myself when I hear the front door open. Sliding gently out of the bed so as not to wake Bee, I walk softly out to the kitchen where my mother is trying to pour herself a glass of water. She is having difficulty because she is twisting the tap the wrong way.

'Big night I take it,' I say dryly.

'Nooo,' she slurs. 'Not at all. Nooooo. Just a couple of drinks. Don't be mad.'

'I'm not mad. I'm glad you had a good time. Come on, you'd better sleep in my bed. I'll sleep with Bee.'

She snores loudly after a few drinks, my mother, and if she wakes Bee there's a high chance none of us will get any sleep tonight. I lead her down the hallway, where she bounces off a couple of walls and into my room. She sits on the edge of my bed while I take her shoes off and when I look up she is crying, but without making a sound.

'Go to sleep, Mum. You'll feel better in the morning.'

She lies down, her eyes closing immediately. Thinking she's asleep, I cover her with the blankets. Just as I'm tiptoeing out of the room she speaks.

'You're just like him, you know.'

'Go to sleep, Mum.'

'He was kind and caring too. You get that from him.'

I pause, my hand on the doorknob. 'Who?'

'Your father. You remind me of him so much sometimes. Night, baby girl.'

She rolls over on to her side facing the wall and sighs softly. Within seconds she is snoring.

I stand there for a couple of minutes in the darkness listening to her breathe, confused. As far as I know she barely knew my father. Couldn't even recall his face, let alone remember pertinent details of his personality. Do I wake her? Ask her what she meant? I'm a step towards the bed when through the wall I hear Bee say something. She has woken up and realised I am not there. If I go to her immediately I have a chance of resettling her without too much hassle.

My questions will have to wait until morning.

Albert

One thing in particular from the conversation with my mother has stuck in my head, and I've been mulling it over for days.

You need to move away from him, Albert.

She's right. Of course she is. And I plan on doing just that as soon as I have enough money saved. I just haven't told her that yet. I feel like I'm abandoning her, leaving her alone with *him*.

I feel guilty enough about that, but now I have Maddy guilt thrown in as well. I'm falling for her, and I'm pretty sure she's feeling the same way. Until she dropped her bombshell at the beach, the easiest would have been to ask her to come with me. And I'm still hoping that's a possibility, just maybe further down the track than I had planned. I lie awake at night, going over scenarios in my head, trying to figure out how we can make it work. But in the end it boils down to this: she won't leave Bee. And I can't ask her to.

For about two seconds I fantasise about asking Maddy if she wants to find a place together here. Set up home together like other couples do. It's a nice fantasy; one where I come home from work and she's waiting for me wearing next to nothing and we spend our nights making love and our weekends at the beach with the lovable scruffy dog that we pick out together from the local shelter riding in the back of the truck. So carried away do I get with the fantasy that I name him (Buddy) and hold an internal debate over whether Maddy is a character or modern house kind of girl. Character, I decide, with adorable quirks just like her.

Then reality crashes back in and I realise that she probably can't afford to leave home either, even if she *were* able to move away from Bee, which she's made perfectly clear she can't. Which leaves me to find somewhere for myself.

I do some asking around to gauge the current state of the rental property market anyway, do some figures, and realise that even using every cent I earn, I still couldn't afford to pay rent on my own place as well as utilities and food/truck payments.

'You could move in with us if you want,' Matt suggests when I mention my dilemma at work. He's leaning against a tree smoking, leg cocked against the trunk like he thinks he's some kind of James Dean. I'm shovelling manure into buckets that we'll try to sell on the roadside as fertiliser. Every penny counts, according to Francine.

'Who's us?'

'Me, of course, plus my brothers Derek and Johnny.'

I do a quick memory search and come up blank. 'Do I know them? Did they go to my high school?'

'Nah they didn't spend much time at school. Not really their scene. Don't suppose you've done time at Juvie?'

'Juvie?'

'Juvenile Detention.'

'Um, no. I haven't done time at Juvie.'

'Then you probably don't know them. 'Course they're adults now. Derek's in the big house down Palmerston ways. That's why his room's empty. I'm happy to sublet it till he gets out.'

'They sound like great guys.'

'Are you having a go at my brothers?' He pushes off the tree and drops the cigarette on the ground, grinding it into the dirt with his boot, and scowls at me. Intriguingly, I can actually see a bit of James Dean in him when he does that.

'Not at all.'

'Good. Because only I can talk shit about them, not you or anybody else. Understood?'

'Yes.'

'Good. You interested in the room or not?'

I pretend to think about it. I think he's on to something in that flatting with others is probably my only available option. But I'd rather it not be with him. Working together is bad enough. If I flat, I'd be splitting the cost with others. Surely I can afford that? 'Thanks, but no. I really need something more long term.'

'He's not due out for another year or so.'

'Still, he might be well behaved and get out sooner and then I'd be back to square one.'

He laughs. 'Derek? Good behaviour? Not going to happen.'

'Answer's still no, but thanks.'

'If you change your mind let me know. Be quick though, I might have other interested parties.'

'Sure.'

We hear tyres crunching on gravel and turn to see Francine's car pull into the car park. Matt picks up a shovel and applies himself enthusiastically to scooping up manure. For about a minute. As soon as she disappears into the office, he leans on the shovel and starts rolling himself another cigarette.

'Just out of curiosity,' I say, 'what exactly is Derek inside for?'

'This time? Oh it was nothing, a misunderstanding. He borrowed a car to go see his kids and some asshole reported it stolen.'

'Some asshole?'

'Yeah, this old guy up the street.'

'So was it? Stolen?'

'Well yeah, *technically*,' he admits, putting the cigarette in his mouth and lighting the end. 'But he would have dumped it somewhere so the guy would have got it back. My brother's not one of those losers who torches the cars he nicks.'

'I'm sure his victims are grateful.'

The day is hot as hell and I work up a huge sweat, thanks to Matt not pulling his weight, so when I get home and see Louis's car in the driveway I decide I'll have a quick shower and then head out, go see Maddy or Connor if she's busy.

Mum has other ideas.

'Albert,' she says as soon as I walk through the door. 'Could you fire up the barbecue, please? Your brother and family are here for dinner and your father was supposed to cook the steak and sausages for me but he's been caught up at work.'

This is welcome news. Since our last meeting where my father 'suggested' I join the police force I have managed to evade being caught in his presence via a complicated system of 'sneaking in once he's in bed' and 'hiding in my room until he's left'. It's helped that he's on long shifts at the moment thanks to an increase in burglaries. I make a mental note to thank Matt and his brothers for keeping my father off my case and on theirs.

Mum sniffs the air and stops grating cheese for a salad to turn around and look at me.

'Maybe shower first,' she suggests.

'I was planning to. Why can't Louis do the barbecue?' I ask, aware I sound like a resentful four-year-old.

'Because he's watching the news.'

'He can still watch it from the deck with the doors open.'

'He's our guest.'

'So?'

She sighs. 'Please?'

I sigh too, for effect. 'Fine.' I grab a beer from the fridge and drink it in the shower, taking my time. When I get out, Louis has fired up the barbecue and is standing there watching the news while holding the tongs in one hand and a beer in the other.

'Jeez, you took your time,' he says. 'S'pose when you've got girly hair like yours it takes longer to make yourself pretty.' He grins, pleased with his insult.

'At least I've got hair.' I walk away from him back towards the kitchen.

'What does he mean by that?' I hear him ask Miranda in a puzzled voice.

'No idea,' she lies.

In recent years my brother has developed what I refer to as a crop circle on the top back of his head, in a place he can't see unless he were to hold a mirror behind his head while looking into another mirror. It has slowly thinned out leaving a perfect little circle of almost baldness, of which he is completely unaware. How he doesn't feel it when he shampoos I have no idea, but Miranda quietly asked us all not to mention it to avoid upsetting him. It gives me petty pleasure every time I see it.

'Why are they here?' I ask Mum.

'Does there have to be a reason? It's what families do.'

'Yeah, other families maybe.'

'Good point,' she concedes.

I'm just reaching into the fridge for another beer when the front door opens and Dad walks in.

'I hope that's not one of mine,' are the first words out of his mouth.

'Hi, love! How was your day, love, oh fine thanks, love, thanks for asking,' Mum mumbles under her breath.

'Relax, Dad,' I say, 'I paid for these.'

'Relax? Damn straight I'm going to relax. If you'd had a day like I have you'd want to relax too. Of course coming home to a house full of freeloaders doesn't help.'

Mum goes into the laundry and slams the door shut.

'I didn't mean *you*, love,' Dad calls after her. Then he glares at me. 'See what you've done now? You've upset your mother.'

I don't even bother arguing. There's no point.

'Hey, Dad.' Louis wanders into the kitchen and helps himself to one of my beers. 'Steak is nearly ready.'

'Still pink inside?'

'Of course. What do you take me for, a philistine?'

They both laugh uproariously. I am struck once again by how different their shared sense of humour is to my own.

'Good lad,' Dad says approvingly. 'I'll have a quick splash first. Keep an eye on that steak, remember it keeps cooking while it rests.'

Louis nods.

Dad turns to me and narrows his eyes. 'And you, fix this.' He thumbs towards the laundry door.

When he's disappeared off up the hallway and Louis has gone out to monitor the meat, I knock gently on the laundry door.

'Mum?'

'Who is it?'

'Albert.'

'Just you?'

I check over both shoulders. 'Just me.'

The door opens a crack and a big green eye peers through, as if to confirm I am telling the truth. She relaxes when she sees it *is* just me, and opens the door the rest of the way.

'Come in,' she says.

I sidle in sideways and she closes the door behind me. I notice a new pot plant on the windowsill, a big leafy fern thing. There's also a new white cane chair placed underneath it and I imagine her sitting in it, watching the clouds roll by.

'Sorry if I upset you,' I say.

She sighs. 'You didn't.'

We both know who did, and it remains unspoken between us.

'I've been thinking about what you said,' I say.

Mum sits in the chair and takes a sip from her glass of wine. 'Refresh my memory.'

'About moving out.'

Her eyes light up and she sits up properly, leaning forward. 'Seriously? You're going to do it?'

'Yeah, I reckon it's about time.'

She relaxes back again and her face undergoes a serene transformation. 'That's the best news I've heard in a long time.'

'Thought you'd be happy.'

'You know it's not because I want you to go, right? I'm only thinking about what's best for you. I just want you to be happy.'

'I know.'

'Where will you go? Have you lined something up?'

I shake my head. 'Not sure yet. I'm going to check out the flatmate wanted adverts.'

She sniffs. 'My baby is fleeing the nest.'

'I wouldn't exactly call it "fleeing". I still have to find somewhere first. But yeah, soon hopefully.'

She sighs deeply, her expression serious again. 'I'm sorry,' she says.

'For?'

'You know what for.'

And I *do* know. I can read it on her face. She is apologising for him. But she doesn't need to.

'Don't,' I say firmly. 'You have nothing to apologise for.'

'I often wonder,' she says softly, caught up in thought. 'What life would have been like if I'd chosen you a different father? But of course if I'd married someone else I wouldn't have had you, and that doesn't bear thinking about. It hasn't all been bad, has it?'

'No, it hasn't.' And it's true. My father may have been overly strict but he took us places. We 'did things' as a family; he was good at that, so I have happy memories from my childhood too. The door opens and Miranda sticks her head in. She looks pale and washed out, like the baby is draining the very life from her.

'The meat is ready,' she says. 'Do you want me to start putting out the salads?'

'No it's OK, love, you sit down and rest. I'll do it.' Mum gets to her feet and kisses me on the cheek as she walks past. 'Best news in a long time,' she echoes softly.

Maddy

There's something wrong with the paving stones that lead the way across the lawn to his front door. They keep moving. I try to put my left foot on the next one but topple over, landing on the soft grass with an *oompf!* I giggle, then giggle at the sound of myself giggling. I'm not much of a giggler and the sound is hilarious.

Bang, bang on the door, my fist goes when I finally make it.

Bang, bang it goes again when the door fails to open. It feels like an hour has passed, but maybe it's only ten seconds. I'm lifting my fist to bang again when it opens.

Albert's mum is standing there. This will be the third time I've met her, if you count the time at the grocery store and the time I stopped by with Albert to pick up his surfboard and she came out to the car to meet me. Now that I think about it, why did he tell me to wait in the car? Is he ashamed of me? Bastard.

The smell of food wafts out of the warm, lit space around

her and my stomach growls audibly. When was the last time I ate? I can't remember. It smells like the most sensational thing I've ever smelt in my life.

'Ish Al-*bear* here?' I say. The words come out thick, like I'm speaking through syrup.

She gives me a knowing look. 'Maddy,' she says. 'How lovely to see you again. Would you like to come in?'

I lower my voice furtively. 'Are you sure I'm allowed?'

She frowns, confused. 'Allowed?'

'Yesh. See, way I figure is, either Al-*bear* is ashamed of *me*, or *you*. I'm not sure which.'

She steps back to call out to someone I can't see. 'Albert? Can you come here, please?'

Hearing her call him, I am suddenly filled with panic. What am I doing, why did I come? Shit. I step backwards, holding a finger to my lips to shush her and tell her I've changed my mind, but I forget I'm at the top of three stairs and my foot meets air. I land heavily on the ground, my head connecting solidly with the concrete.

I lie there, looking up at the stars and I say, 'Fuck. That's going to leave a bump.'

'Maddy, are you OK?'

Albert's concerned face swims into view and as soon as I see it the panic flees, replaced by warm fuzzy feelings and all the sadness that drove me to walk here in the first place. After the conversation with my mother he was the first person I thought of, and I needed to see him more than I've ever needed another person in my life. I reach up a hand to touch his cheek.

'Al-*bear*,' I say.

'Should I call an ambulance?' his mum asks from out of view.

'I missed you,' I tell him reproachfully, slapping my fingers against his cheek softly. 'I needed you. Why are you avoiding me?'

'No, I think she's OK. Help me get her up,' Albert says.

Together, they manage to pull me to an upright position. Stars immediately fill my vision and I hold an exploring hand out to try to catch them.

'Woah. Pretty,' I say.

'I think I should call an ambulance.'

'Let's just get her inside and decide from there.'

'No, I really shouldn't intrude,' I say.

'Maddy, you're not leaving here in this state. At least come in for a drink of water.'

'Oh go on then.'

They pull me upright and use their shoulders under my armpits to lead me up the steps and into the warm, delicious-smelling house. Six pairs of eyes seated around a dining table regard me thoughtfully.

'Ooh wine.' I spy an open bottle on the table and, without waiting for an invitation, I wander over and plonk myself down on an empty seat next to a couple of children. The one nearest shuffles his seat away like I'm contagious. Maybe I am.

'Don't worry, I won't bite,' I say to him convivially.

'She stinks,' he complains to a woman across the table who I assume has the pleasure of being his mother.

'Brad,' she scolds.

'It's OK,' I reassure her. 'He's probably right. I've just come from the pub and before that I was drinking at the park.'

Colin's face creases disapprovingly. 'The park has a liquor ban. You shouldn't have been drinking anywhere near it.'

'Does it? Oh dear. Sorry.'

'I'll pretend I didn't hear anything this time,' he says. I haven't seen Albert's father since that day he pulled us over on the way to the beach. There is something cold about his eyes. The way he is looking at me makes my skin crawl. 'Albert, fetch your guest a plate,' he says.

'And a glass,' I say, before spying an empty one in front of the pale, insipid-looking woman who is looking at me with eyes like saucers. 'Never mind, I'll just use this one.'

'I think you've already had enough,' Colin says disapprovingly.

'Enough wine? Actually – fun fact – I haven't had any,' I say truthfully. 'I've had a few beers, and a whiskey or two, but no wine.' I pour myself a glass and take a large gulp. It is horrendously sweet and I nearly gag, not sure how anyone can drink it, but I take another mouthful anyway. I know I'm being rude but I can't seem to stop myself. After my mother's confession, nothing seemed to make sense any more. I'd always thought I was unflappable, that I could cope with the unexpected, but this went beyond anything I'd had to deal with before. It was deceit, a betrayal of the worst kind, and from the person I least expected it from.

'You must be Al-*bear*'s brother,' I say to the big hulking man on the other side of the table who is watching me, amused. He has a steak the size of his head on his plate and is chewing on a piece, unaware the bloody juices are running down his chin. It turns my stomach.

'You have a little something . . .' I gesture.

He wipes it on the back of his hand. 'Louis,' he says, holding out the same hand.

'Do you mind if I don't?' I say, looking at it.

He shrugs. I sense immediately he has supreme confidence in himself, enough for a small country. I could insult him and it would bounce right off. He looks nothing like my sweet, gentle Al-*bert*, who has pulled a stool over from the breakfast bar and has squeezed it in beside me. He looks down at me, worried.

'Can I get you some water?' he asks softly.

'You can. I probably won't drink it though.'

'I think you should.'

'And I think you should call someone back when you see you have twelve missed calls,' I try to say it quietly but my drunken voice has other plans.

'Huh?'

'I've been calling you all night.'

'Oh. Sorry.' He stands and feels his back pockets. 'I must have left my phone in the truck. Is something wrong?'

I blink back tears that have suddenly sprung up and nod. 'You could say that.'

'*Whippesh*.' Louis makes a whipping sound. 'She's got you whipped.'

'*She* happens to be right here. And *she* has a name,' I say frowning. The tears rapidly dissipate. I am confused as to why he's being such a jerk, and I seize the opportunity to have something to focus my anger on, misplaced as it is.

Colin smirks. 'Oh that's right, Madonna.'

I turn to Albert, outraged. 'You told him?'

'No.' He shakes his head. 'I didn't. I told Mum.'

'I didn't realise it was a secret,' she says bewildered. 'What's wrong with Madonna? I think it's a lovely name.'

'I agree,' the insipid lady says.

Louis scowls at her and she drops her head to her plate. Instantly, I realise: he's a bully. Like father like son. I understand why Albert hasn't wanted me to meet them before. He needn't have worried though because I'm not scared of bullies. And I don't give a shit what other people think about me. Growing up with a sister like Bee has given me a thick skin and no qualms about challenging authority, or people who perceive themselves to be important. We all put our knickers on the same way at the end of the day.

'All the same, I prefer to be called Maddy.'

'What brings you here tonight, *Maddy*?' Colin asks. Then a thought occurs to him and he puts on his stern policeman's voice. 'I hope you didn't drive.'

'I needed to see Albert. And no, I didn't. I'm not that stupid.' The bang to the head and the chilly reception from Albert's father has had a sobering effect and I start to regret my decision to come here. I don't want this, to be around these people, and they certainly haven't done anything to deserve the agony that is my company at the moment.

Louis snorts. Considering he doesn't know me, I can only hazard a guess that he's some kind of sexist wanker.

'I apologise for gatecrashing your family dinner,' I continue, although the word comes out sounding more like 'apogigise'.

'I really think you should have some water,' Albert says. 'You might be concussed.'

'I don't want water. And I'm getting tired of people deciding what's good for me.'

'Ooh, she's a firecracker,' Louis says. 'Better watch yourself, Albert. She'll have your balls off if you're not careful.'

'Shut up, Louis,' Albert says.

'Of course, even steaming drunk, she's still way out of your league.'

I stare at him. 'What's that supposed to mean.'

'Oh come on, don't get all feminist. It's a compliment.' He gestures to Albert and then me. 'You're hot and he's, well, he's Albert.'

'Not that looks have anything to do with anything,' I retort. 'But girls much prefer Albert's clean and healthy outdoor surf boy look to your meathead beefiness.'

He chokes on the piece of steak he's just shoved in his mouth. 'What did you say?'

'You heard me.'

'Just eat your dinner, Louis,' Albert says. 'She's drunk.'

'I am not drunk,' I retort. 'But even if I was, you shouldn't let your bonehead of a brother talk to you like this.'

'Who are you calling a bonehead?' Louis drops his knife and it hits his plate with a clang. I see his wife put a hand on his arm and all I feel is pity for her. Imagine living with someone with such a trigger-happy temper and bullshit views on women. Louis's face darkens. 'You might look all right but underneath you're a mouthy tart just like that slut you were named after.'

'That's enough, Louis,' Albert's mum says. 'Maddy is our guest.'

'Guests are normally invited,' Colin says pointedly. 'But thank you, Albert, for ruining yet another family dinner.'

I push back my chair. 'Don't worry, I'm going.'

'I'm coming with you,' Albert says.

'You don't need to.'

'I'm not letting you walk home alone in this state.'

'Fine.'

Outside the air is brisk and it has the effect of deflating any bravado the alcohol had temporarily gifted me. Oh God, I can't believe I just did that. I cover my face with my hands and moan softly.

'It's OK,' Albert says softly, trying to put his arms around me.

I push him away, even though right now I want nothing more than to hide in his arms and forget the awful scene I just made in front of his family. But something holds me back and I realise it's anger, not only at myself but with him, for not defending me to his awful brother. Worse than that, though, I'm angry that he didn't defend himself.

Albert

The sharp coldness of the night-time air seems to sober her up more than any glass of water ever could. I reach for her hand as we walk up the path but she pulls it away with a sharp intake of breath.

I don't know what's wrong with her, what I've done or haven't done. I've never seen her drunk before so I'm unsure what my approach should be.

'You OK?' I ask cautiously.

She stops on the footpath under the circle of the street light and stares at her feet.

'Maddy?'

I hear it then. A sigh so gentle it's like a wispy summer breeze, so quiet you think you could be mistaken for hearing it. She's crying.

'Oh, Maddy.'

'I'm sorry,' she says, lifting her face. Tears on her cheeks reflect the yellow of the light and the anguish I see in her eyes rips my heart in two.

'What is it? What's happened?' I step forward and pull her into my embrace, holding her as tight as I can; her head nestled under my chin. If I hold her tight enough maybe I can protect her from whatever it is that has caused her this much pain. 'Is Bee ok?' I ask fearfully.

She nods into my chest, sniffing noisily. 'Bee is fine.'

'Your mother?'

'She's fine,' she says, but her voice turns bitter at the mention of her.

'I want to help you, if you'll let me.'

'You can't.' She pushes me away then, putting an arm's length between us. 'I wish you could.'

Whatever it is that has upset her she is reticent to talk about it. I'm at a loss, and I feel useless.

'You're scaring me,' I say.

'Sorry. I shouldn't have come here.'

'Of course you should. I'm here for you any time. I'm sorry I didn't answer your calls.'

She shrugs. 'It's OK. You had a family thing going on.'

'Yeah. Family.' It's my turn to sound bitter.

'Why do you let them talk to you like that?' she asks.

'Who?' I know full well who she means.

'You know who. Your father and your brother. They're horrible. The way they treat you and your mother.'

It's my turn to shrug. 'It's just the way they are.'

'Yeah, a right pair of assholes.'

'I'm not arguing.'

'So why don't you stand up for yourself?'

'It's complicated.'

She holds my gaze levelly for a moment and I try not to look as pathetic as I fear I must look in her eyes. 'Let's get out of here,' she says.

'Now?'

'Yes now.'

'And go where?'

'I don't care. Anywhere.'

Does she mean run away for good? She sees me hesitate and senses my confusion.

'Just for the night,' she says. 'I need to get away for the night.'

'OK.' I nod. 'Come on.'

When I turn the key in the ignition I have no plan, but instinct leads me to turn on the road to the beach. She is silent for the whole journey, her face turned away, her forehead against the glass of the passenger window. I wonder if she is asleep. I hope she is.

We pull into the car park and I cut the engine, the headlights blinking off and plunging us into darkness. Immediately, I hear the ocean and my breath exhales in one long breath. I'm home.

She hasn't stirred so when her voice cuts through the dark a few minutes later I jump, startled.

'She lied,' she says quietly.

'Who?'

'My mother.'

'About what?'

She doesn't answer though, instead I hear her pull the handle on her door and she is out of the truck in a moment, slamming it shut behind her. I follow, and catch up just as she reaches the beach. She walks fast, her path lit by the moon and the stars, her anger palpable.

'Maddy, what's going on? Please tell me.'

She doesn't stop at the water's edge; instead she kicks off her shoes and plunges in. The breakers swirl their foamy tips around her knees and for a terrible moment I think she is going to just keep walking, out into the ocean and out of this life, but she stops.

'All my life my mother told me she didn't know who my father was,' she says. 'That he was some drunken guy that she had a quick shag with in a back alley. Today I found out that it's all been a lie.'

I don't know what to say so I wade out into the cold, familiar water and stand beside her, waiting for her to tell me.

'She said something last night, when she was drunk. It didn't make any sense so this morning I had her up about it. It's like keeping the secret for all these years has been building up inside her because she just caved straight away and it all came pouring out. She told me everything. He was her boss, years ago. He was married but they fell in love and had an affair.'

'Woah.'

She laughs bitterly. 'My mother, God this is such a cliché. She actually believed he would leave his wife for her.'

'I take it he didn't.'

She shakes her head. 'No. He didn't. My mother was pregnant with me when she found out his wife was also pregnant.'

'Shit.'

'Yeah. She gave him an ultimatum. He chose to stay with his wife.' She shrugs her shoulders. 'She quit.'

'Does he know about you?'

'Yes. Apparently he doesn't care though, because she said he's never contacted her about meeting me, never sent a birthday card or any money towards my upbringing. The last she heard they moved to Australia. He obviously would prefer to believe that I don't exist.'

'That's his loss, not yours.' I understand her anger now. Why she turned up at my house drunk and why my family upset her so much.

'You'd think so, but it doesn't feel that way.'

'You could always look him up and confront him?'

'No.' She shakes her head angrily. 'No point. Why would I bother to look for someone who clearly wants nothing to do with me? He can go fuck himself.'

She turns to me, her eyes large in the moonlight. Her skin is luminescent. She is beautiful. 'But you know what that's like, don't you,' she says softly. I almost don't hear her over the water.

'What do you mean?'

'We both have fathers who couldn't give a stuff about us.'

Her words hit home, but they confuse me. I always thought my father cared too much, which is why he inevitably ended

224

up disappointed in me. Surely if he didn't care my failings wouldn't bother him? But maybe she's right and it's the opposite. I don't know. I'm not sure I'll ever know.

She shudders, whether from the cold or her emotions I'm not sure, but I reach out and put my arms around her.

'Come on,' I say. 'Let's get you warm.'

I lead her by the hand up to the truck and open the tailgate so she can climb up on to the flat deck. The blankets from the last time we came are still on board and I make a little nest with them for us to lie down on. We lie there, she in my arms with her head resting on my shoulder, listening to the sounds of the ocean and forest at night. They are like nature's lullaby and I feel the tension leave my body. I don't know what to say to make her feel better, I wish I did.

'Shooting star, make a wish,' she murmurs.

'You first.'

'Already done.'

I nuzzle my face into her hair. It smells like something fruity and sweet. 'What did you wish for?'

'I can't tell you or it won't come true.'

'Are you sure about that?'

'I'm not willing to risk it.'

'Fair enough.'

'Look, another one. Make a wish but don't tell me.'

I watch the brilliant light streak across the sky and I know exactly what to wish for.

I wish that every night could be spent just like this, with the girl I love.

The realisation hits like a slap to the face. I love her. I'm not going anywhere. This changes everything.

The star burns out to nothing.

Maddy

Surprisingly, I sleep deeply and I wake, feeling happier than the night before, in Albert's arms. This lasts about thirty seconds till I try to turn my head and the hangover hits like a hammer right between the eyes.

'Ugh,' I groan.

Albert stretches beside me and wakes. 'You OK?' he asks, his eyes still closed.

'If by OK you mean not feeling like my head is full of concrete and someone sandpapered my eyeballs, then yeah, I feel great.'

'Self-inflicted so no sympathy,' he says, but he says it affectionately.

'I'll remember that.'

I sit up, pulling a blanket around my shoulders. It's a crisp morning. The sky is a gentle riot of colour, streaks of orange and pink and yellow.

Albert sits up suddenly. 'Shit,' he says. 'What time is it?'

I pull my phone out of my pocket and check. 'Just after seven.'

He shakes the sleep away reluctantly. 'We'd better get going soon. I have to be at work at eight-thirty.'

'Call in sick.'

'I can't.'

'Yes, you can. I will too. We'll stay here all day and you can surf.' I aim straight for his Achilles and watch, satisfied, as the torture of temptation contorts his face.

'So tempted,' he admits. 'But I can't afford to get fired. I need to save every penny I can if I'm going to move out of home.'

'You're moving out of home?'

'Yeah, it's time. Well, it's past due actually.'

'Where will you live?'

'That's the tricky part. I'm still working on it.'

'Oh.' I hug my knees and watch the colours fade away leaving a pale-blue day in their place.

'Hey, don't worry.' He rubs a hand up and down my back. 'Wherever I go there will always be room for you.'

I turn and look at him, studying his face to see if he means what I think he does. In this morning light he is even cuter than he's ever looked before, with his hair all messy and wearing nothing but jeans and a thick cable knit jersey.

'No pressure,' he says. 'I know you have commitments. But, whenever you're ready, I'll be waiting.'

I've fallen in love with him. The realisation hits like an ocean wave; overwhelming and knocking me off my feet, plunging me down into depths I am unfamiliar with, leaving me breathless and feeling out of control.

'I don't know what to say,' I whisper quietly.

He circles his arms around me, pulling me in close. 'It's OK, I understand.'

And he does, I'm sure of it. He's the first person in my life who has understood. All the friends I lost when I couldn't go to their house and play because I had to help look after my sister. The teachers who gave me bad marks on tests, assuming I didn't care enough to study, instead of understanding that I had been up half the night with a sister who didn't sleep or who'd had an epileptic fit. So many people in my life who didn't try to understand, and here was Albert who in just a few months understood me completely.

I feel adrift on the wave, buffeted by storms, completely vulnerable. And there is Albert, the lighthouse in my darkness. The beacon of hope that, despite *everything* I promised myself going into this, the shields I put up, I've now come to depend on more than I care to admit even to myself. How did I let this happen? How could I have let him into my heart so deeply that the thought now of ever going back to how my life was before him fills me with complete terror?

I twist around to kiss him, desperate to be as close to him as I can, and we make love on the back of his truck. It feels like all my wishes have come true.

Afterwards, we drive back to town and he drops me outside my house.

'Come around for dinner tonight?' I ask him, leaning in through the driver's window to steal a few more kisses.

'Yeah OK, sounds good.'

I kiss him until he breaks away, laughing. 'As much as I'd love nothing more than to spend the entire day kissing you, I have to go.'

'It's OK. I think my lips could do with a break anyway.'

His face turns serious. 'Are you going to be OK? With your mother? You know, after yesterday's news.'

'I'll be fine. I've got work. She's bringing Bee in for her riding lesson later. Please don't say anything about what I told you.'

'Of course not.'

'Thanks.'

'Call me if you need to OK? I promise I'll answer this time.'

I kiss him one last time and watch as he drives down the street and turns the corner. I miss him already.

Albert

'Jesus, you look rough, and that's saying something because you always look pretty shit,' Matt says when I get to work. He's standing under an oak tree out front, sneaking a last cigarette before we're called into our compulsory monthly staff meeting. The other guys are all standing around, avoiding eye contact, looking a bit like the walking dead from a zombie movie.

'Thanks.'

'Not a compliment.'

'Don't care.'

He eyes me suspiciously. 'What's up with you?'

'Nothing.' I take my jersey off and hang it on a hook, pulling a green apron off the stand by the door. We're supposed to wear them to distinguish ourselves as staff to any guests, but usually we tend to 'forget' about it. Not today. Not any more. I meant what I said to Maddy. This job is my ticket away from my father. As far as I'm concerned it's head down, bum up. I plan on being the most diligent employee Francine has ever had.

'Yes there is. Something's different.'

'I don't know what you're talking about.'

He looks me up and down, trying to figure it out. 'Are you, *happy*?'

'As a box of kittens.'

'A box of kittens isn't happy. The only reason you'll find kittens in a box is because someone's about to throw them off a bridge.'

'Oh. Fuck that's depressing.'

He shrugs. 'Depends if you're the kitten or the thrower.'

'I don't even want to know if you're speaking from experience.'

'We're not talking about me anyway. So what gives?'

'Nothing.'

'Don't give me that. It's that girl, isn't it? The one from the photo desk? You finally shagged her.'

'Shut up.'

'I knew it. What was it like?'

'Seriously, shut up, Matt. I'm not telling you anything.'

'So there is something to tell.' He grins dirtily and I feel like smacking him because he's trying to cheapen what Maddy and I have. Lucky for him we're interrupted by Deborah opening the front door and glaring at us all.

'Meeting time,' she announces. 'Try not to touch more than you have to.'

We file into the meeting room and listen while Francine

rattles off the usual business. Numbers are up but could be better. Don't park on the grass because the rain is turning it to sludge. A reminder that we are a 'non-smoking premises', so please refrain from sparking up until you have left at the end of the day. She looks directly at Matt when she says it and he pulls his best 'who me?' face.

She finishes up and I'm almost out the door when I hear her call my name, asking me to wait back so she can speak to me. Instantly, of course, I assume I've done something wrong.

Matt gives me a pitying look. 'Nice working with you,' he says.

I decide if Francine is going to fire me I will throw him and his filthy smoking under the bus, no hesitation. It's every man for himself. A nervous minute passes until finally everyone is gone and she tells me to sit.

'Please don't fire me,' I blurt out.

She looks surprised. 'I'm not firing you,' she says. 'What made you think I am?'

'No reason in particular.'

'Well anyway, I wanted to see what you thought about doing some training. I've had good feedback about you, from both the coaches and our clients. They're impressed.'

'Training?'

'We feel that your abilities aren't being fully utilised. How would you feel about working your way up to becoming a coach? A vacancy has come up and we'd prefer to fill it from inside the ranks before advertising. I've spoken to the other

233

coaches and Deborah and we all agree it's something that might suit you. You'd start as a sidewalker, then leader. If you enjoy that and do well, we can train you to become a therapist, working directly with the rider to work out goals and strategies. After that there is the opportunity to become a coach and plan and organise the sessions. It's completely up to you how far you'd like to take it, but we feel you have a natural affinity for both the horses and their riders that would be better served working with them directly.'

'Wow.' I sit back in seat, completely dumbfounded for a moment. 'Seriously?'

'Yes.'

'What would I have to do?'

'We would provide the onsite teaching. You would need to sit some papers and attend some courses but it's nothing I think you can't handle.'

I sit there, looking a bit gormless I'm sure, trying to think of something to say. It's the first time I can remember someone telling me I am good at something. That I could be even better, that they *believe* in me. It's an unfamiliar feeling.

'Do you really think I could do it?' I ask.

'Yes.'

It's not what I wanted or had planned but it's there on offer, like a lifeline in a storm. If I hadn't been with Maddy I'd have turned her down, but everything is different now. I'm not saying goodbye to the Bali plan for ever, just for a while. Until we can find a way that Maddy can come with me. The strange thing is I don't feel disappointed that my plans have

234

been forced to change. How can I when it means I can stay here, with her?

'Then yes, where do I sign?'

I leave the office beaming, I can't help it. Everything is falling into place. I have Maddy and now I've just been offered an opportunity to take something I really enjoy and go even further with it. Not only that, but people actually think I'm good at something.

'Albert,' Helen, one of the riding coaches calls. 'Could you help me out for a minute?'

I follow her into the barn and see Bee and her mother waiting. She looks at me warily, and I can guess that's she's trying to figure out how much Maddy has told me.

'Hi,' I say, trying to look as if I know nothing.

'Hi, Albert. Bee, say "Hi, Albert."'

'Bee say Hi Albert.'

'Francine has asked us to give you a little experience of what being a coach entails,' Helen says. 'So I was wondering if you would like to be Bee's sidewalker for this session.'

'I'd love to, but I'm not exactly sure what to do.'

She shrugs. 'You've watched some classes. See what you can remember and I'll help you fill in the rest. Every child is different anyway so we try and tailor it to their individual needs. You'll get to know them better the more you work with them. For example, Bee here prefers to ride outside, don't you, Bee.'

'Hello said Bump, Hello said the stranger,' says Bee.

'Where's Teddy?' I ask Helen, as she leads over Pegasus, one of our newer horses.

'He's not well, Francine's called the vet to come check him over.' She stops beside the mounting block Bee will use to climb on to his back. 'Hopefully it's just a cold but we always play it safe with the older horses. Up you get, Bee.'

What happens next is a blur. I hear a loud noise and I see the horse rear, his hooves arching dangerously close to Bee. I instinctively dive in front of her.

Everything goes black.

Maddy

Photo of the week, by unequivocal mutual agreement, is a perfectly timed close-up of a fantail sitting on a fence post, its tail open like a fan. The detail on each beautiful feather is crystal clear, as is the curious look in the eye it has aimed on the camera lens. The other eye is in shadow, and its fat little body appears poised for flight at the slightest hint of trouble.

'I love fantails,' Kyle says, as he pins it to the board for us to admire.

'They're pretty cute.'

'Although they do scare me a little too.'

I look at the innocuous little bird in the photo, his feet no bigger than my thumbnail. It looks about as scary as a slipper. 'Do you have some kind of bird phobia you've neglected to mention until now?'

He looks at me sideways. 'You do know what they symbolise, don't you?'

'No. I didn't know birds had to symbolise anything.'

He hunches closer to me, lowers his voice and adopts what I think *he thinks* is a spooky voice. 'DEATH.'

'Bullshit.'

'Fine. Disbelieve if you will.' He sniffs, back to his normal voice.

'If any bird were to symbolise death it would be like a—' I cast my mind for any knowledge of other feathered creatures '—like a black vulture or something. Or a hawk. Not a sweet little thing like that.' I gesture at the photo.

'It's true,' he insists. 'Maori culture believes if you see a fantail inside your house it means someone you know will shortly die.'

I look at the photo again. 'Well that's cheerful.'

He shrugs. 'I guess at least you have forewarning.'

'Yeah, but you don't know who's going to cark it.'

'True.'

We hear the muffled sound of a cell phone ringing inside a handbag.

'Aren't you going to answer it?' Kyle asks. 'That's like the fifth time it's rung.'

'No.'

'Not relationship issues with Albert already I hope.'

'No. Mother issues.'

'What's she done now?'

'It's long and complicated.'

'I love long and complicated. Long and complicated is my middle name.'

'So is "juicy" and "gossip".'

He pouts. 'You know anything you tell me in the sacred sanctuary of our office stays between us.'

I lean against his desk and sigh. 'I know. I don't want to talk about it though. I'm actually trying to forget it.'

'Well, if you change your mind I'm here.'

'Thanks.'

I see a lady approach the counter and push myself off his desk. 'Duty calls.'

I'm midway through taking the customers details when Kyle comes out.

'Excuse me,' he says to the customer. 'Maddy, you have a phone call out back.'

'I told you I'm not taking it. She can leave a message.'

'Not your cell phone, the office phone.'

I smile sweetly at the lady and then look askance at Kyle. 'Is it her?'

'Yes.'

'Then tell her I'll see her tonight and to stop calling.'

'I think you—'

'I'm working.'

'I know. Maddy—'

Something in his voice makes me stop and look at him properly. His expression makes my blood run cold and my heart plummet.

Bee.

I push past him and run to the phone.

'Mum?'

'Maddy, why aren't you answering your phone? I've tried to call you a dozen times.'

'What's wrong? Is Bee OK?' I squeeze my eyes shut while I wait what seems an eternity for her to answer.

'Bee is fine.'

I expel the breath I didn't realise I was holding. It whooshes into the phone piece and echoes back noisily.

'Maddy?'

'I'm here. Jesus, Mum, you gave me a fright.'

'Sorry.'

'You should be. I've never been so scared.'

'Maddy, I don't know how to say this.'

'You're sorry. I know. You've said it a thousand times. Quit hassling me when I'm at work or you'll get me fired.' I go to hang up the receiver.

'It's Albert.'

I think maybe I misheard. I lift the phone to my ear again. 'What?'

'Oh, honey. I'm so sorry. Albert has had an accident.'

My newly restored heart plummets again. 'What kind of accident? Where are you?'

Her words come out in a rush. 'At the stables. They gave Bee a new horse today and something got into her and she darted out in front of it, squealing and flapping her hands and she startled it and it reared. Oh, Maddy, Albert was so brave. He saw that the horse's feet were going to knock Bee so he jumped in front of her and pushed her out of the way.'

It's not making any sense to me. 'So Bee is OK?'

'Bee is fine.'

I almost can't ask the next question. 'Albert?'

She sighs. It turns to a shudder. I realise she has been crying. 'He took a kick to the head, Maddy.'

'Is he OK?' It's a stupid question. Who gets kicked in the head by a horse and comes out better off? But I'm clinging to hope.

'He's just gone to the hospital by ambulance. He's unconscious. It's all I know.'

He's alive.

That's all I need to hear.

He's alive. Albert will be fine; I know this like I know the sky is blue. He will fight and he will be fine. He's not leaving me. He wouldn't.

I hang up without waiting to hear any more and grab my bag. Kyle looks at me and I see pity in his eyes.

'Go,' he says simply.

Albert

Everything is black.
    Open your eyes, I tell myself. But I can't seem to do it.
    Voices.
    Sirens.
    Hands.
    Sharp pricks.
    Machines beeping.
    So many voices.
    My head hurts.

Maddy

At the hospital, the lady on the front desk frowns and tells me three times to 'take a breath and calm down' because she can't understand the garbled words coming out of my mouth at great speed. I want to lean over the desk, grab her cashmere green scarf and threaten to throttle her if she doesn't tell me where Albert is *right now*, but a security man lurks nearby and I can't risk being thrown out.

'My boyfriend,' I repeat. 'He's had an accident and he's here somewhere. I need to see him. Tell me where he is.'

'Mm,' she says, and taps away at her computer. 'Name?'

I tell her for what excruciatingly feels like the eighth time.

She taps again and peers over the top of her glasses at her screen. I feel like she's drawing it out unnecessarily and I want to scream, but finally her face softens and she gestures to the doors on my right. 'He's still in emergency. You can't go into the actual department though. Just take a seat in the waiting room through there and someone will let you know what's happening.'

I want to ask her what she's read on her screen that made her look at me with pity the way she just did, but I don't. I know she couldn't say for confidentiality reasons anyway, but even if she could I'm too scared to hear her answer. I push open the doors and am greeted with the sight of Wendy's ashen face. Colin is standing beside her. When he sees me he frowns and says something but I'm too far away to hear it. Wendy flashes him a look of annoyance.

'Hi,' I say when I reach her. 'What's happening? Have you heard anything? How is he?'

I hadn't noticed Louis sitting on the row of chairs directly behind Wendy but I hear him snort.

'How is he?' he repeats. 'Bit of a stupid question, isn't it? He got kicked in the head by a horse, how do you think he is?'

I ignore him and focus on Wendy's face, searching for clues. She shakes her head.

'We don't know much yet, just that he was brought in unconscious and they're doing everything they can.' She puts a hand over her mouth to stifle a sob.

'What does that mean, exactly?' I ask. I don't like the way I'm feeling – powerless. I need answers, something more solid to go on.

'It means we wait,' she says. 'We sit here and we wait, and we trust that the doctors will—' she pauses to break into fresh sobs '—that they will save his life.'

She gestures to the seat next to her and I sink into it, ignoring the glare Colin gives me.

I sit in that chair for hours. Slowly the chairs fill around me. Louis's wife and kids arrive and I watch, as if from afar, as she struggles to get her pregnant body comfortable on the hard plastic seat. Then people from the stables where Albert works, including Francine, the manager, and a guy with yellow teeth who tries to hit on me.

When a doctor finally comes out to give us an update, saying that they have managed to stop the bleeding and Albert is now in surgery to relieve some of the pressure off his brain and check the damage, the yellow-toothed guy rolls his eyes.

'Tell him to wake up, dude,' he says. 'He's just milking it now to get off work.'

He looks around expectantly for a laugh or two. He gets none, and shuffles off under the pretence of fetching coffee. He doesn't come back.

I sit there while the light outside the small window darkens and street lights flicker on. As the six o'clock news comes on over on the small TV mounted on the wall in the corner. All around me are the sounds of life as a busy hospital goes about its business. I feel zombie-like, as if it's all a dream, and I can't get the image of Albert being kicked out of my head. Did he feel pain? Was he scared?

'No! I will *not* leave it.'

Colin's angry voice breaks through my thoughts and I turn to see him snarling at his wife. He whirls back to face Francine, who cowers under his fury.

'What sort of a Mickey Mouse outfit are you running where this kind of thing can happen?' he demands. 'Don't you have safety procedures in place?'

'Unfortunately working with any animal comes with risk,' she says.

He scoffs. 'Did your lawyer tell you to say that? Save it for the cops. You can bet I'll be getting them involved.'

'There will of course be an investigation and we will answer all questions truthfully,' she says evenly. 'I can reassure you this was nothing but a terrible accident and we have nothing to hide. Right now, our only concern is for Albert.'

'I bet if it had happened to one of your *disabled* kids you'd be taking it more seriously,' he spits. 'This is all down to one of them anyway according to the paramedic. Is that true? One caused the horse to buck?'

'Yes, one of our clients got a little excited and startled the horse,' Francine admits. 'But you have to remember it was not intentional. These children have no idea of the consequences of their actions.'

I'm still fuming over the way he said 'disabled' and can stay silent no longer.

'It's not her fault,' I say to Colin. 'Leave her alone. This isn't helping Albert.'

'No one asked you,' he growls, barely flicking me a sideways glance. 'You shouldn't even be here.' But he turns away from Francine and storms to the desk to ask what is happening, like he has a million times already.

Francine gives me a grateful look. 'Is Bee OK?' she asks.

I nod. I texted my mother an hour ago and she'd replied to say that Bee was home and watching nursery rhymes, happily unaware of what she had done. I haven't allowed myself to dwell on the fact that Albert is fighting for his life because of her, it's too much for me right now. Then I notice Louis is watching our exchange, his eyes shrewd. I realise he is putting two and two together and silently beg Francine to drop it, but she doesn't.

'I hope this won't put her off from coming back,' she says. 'No one blames her.'

Louis leans forward, his eyes flashing. 'Wait, this was all her fault? Your sister's?'

I take a deep breath and let it out slowly. 'Yes, but she didn't know what she was doing.'

'You've got to be fuckin' kidding me,' he says, throwing his hands in the air. 'Your sister nearly kills my brother and you have the nerve to show up here?'

'It was an *accident*,' I reiterate.

'What's this?' Colin is back.

'It was her sister's fault,' Louis says, thumbing at me.

Colin turns. 'Is that true?'

They are forcing me to confront what I haven't been able to face. 'Yes. But you're acting like she did it on purpose. Bee is autistic. She had no idea what would happen. She most likely *still* doesn't understand what has happened.'

'She shouldn't be allowed around horses if she has no control,' he snaps. 'Now my son is paying the consequences.'

'And believe me, if Bee *could* understand that she would be incredibly sorry.'

'Sorry won't fix it.'

'I know.'

'You should go. He won't want to see you when he wakes up. You'll just remind him of what happened.'

I look at him, unable to believe he really is as heartless as he comes across. How could someone so cruel produce someone so amazing like Albert? My sweet, understanding, Albert. I shake my head.

'You're wrong. Albert won't blame her.' I say the words with one hundred per cent certainty. I know he won't, and neither do I.

'Of course he will.'

'No. He likes Bee. He is good with her and the other kids at the stables. He understands. He won't blame her.'

We stare at each other for twenty seconds or so, neither backing down. Finally, he narrows his eyes and shakes his head dismissively.

'We'll just have to wait and see,' he says.

Around half-seven, Louis and his wife go home to 'feed the kids and get them in bed'. Because there is 'not much we can do hanging around here'. He ignores me completely when he leaves, which suits me just fine.

I sit there while patients are stretchered in and then wheeled out again. While weary nurses clock off and fresh, new ones arrive ready for battle. I watch as they converse in muffled tones behind the desk, the nurse on her way out jerks her head in our direction; the new one grimaces sympathetically. I wonder how they do it. Come face to face with injury and death every day, lives cut short, families torn apart. Still, they slap on a smile every time a new wave of bleeding, desperate humanity limps through the door.

It is after midnight when they let his parents in to see him. He is stable, they say. Wendy and I almost collapse with the relief. But it is touch and go. He has sustained a massive head wound, the sharp edge of the horse's hoof splitting his head open as easily as if it were a ripe tomato. They've closed the wound itself and aren't overly worried about that. His brain is the main concern. They've put him in an induced coma to give it time to heal and for the swelling to go down.

'Unfortunately in these kinds of cases it's a waiting game. Only time will tell,' the doctor says.

What he can't say is how *much* time.

Albert

Voices.

Strange noises.

I try to open my mouth to tell them to be quiet, that I am trying to sleep, but I can't. I can't seem to open my eyes either. Panic starts to build, then nothing.

Maddy

'How's my favourite patient today,' the nurse says cheerfully.

I lift my head from the armrest of the chair I'm folded into and blink at her. It's Dot, my favourite.

Dot is short, like ridiculously so. Clearly there is no minimum height restriction to working in the medical profession, because surely she would have failed if there was. She has curly hair like the queen. I've wondered many times whether it's natural, or a perm, or whether she gets up an hour early every morning and sets it in rollers, but I haven't asked. It suits her, anyway. Not many people it would, but it does her. She is solid without being fat, and has a bust like a windowsill.

'Morning,' she says to me as she pulls back the curtains. Bright sunlight floods the room and I wince and close my eyes like I'm allergic to it.

'Good old vitamin D,' she says. 'You could do with some of that. Too many days cooped up in here isn't good for anyone.'

I look at Albert. 'No. It's not.'

She looks at me sympathetically. 'I know it's hard, seeing him in this condition. But it's the best thing for him right now. He needs the time to recover.'

'I know.'

She fiddles with the needle that goes into Albert's hand, checking to make sure it's still positioned correctly and hasn't popped out or blown a vein during the night, and then records his vitals.

'How is he?'

'The same as he was yesterday. He's doing great.'

I study his sleeping face. 'How much longer are they going to keep him in the coma for?'

She clicks her tongue. 'I can't answer that, sweetheart. It depends on a whole bunch of variables. The doctors will monitor his brain and when they decide the swelling has subsided enough then they'll make a decision.'

I uncurl my body wearily and pick up Albert's free hand. His long fingers drape limply in mine. He has dirt under his nails I notice, not for the first time.

'I know it's hard,' she says. 'You just have to remember that this is what's best for him right now. We need to give his brain time to recover.'

'It's just hard to see him like this. Not knowing . . .' My voice trails off and I blink back a tear. I take a deep breath. 'Not knowing what he'll be like when he wakes up. If he'll still be the same.'

She comes around the bed and puts a hand on my shoulder

and squeezes. 'Until we have something to worry about you need to think positive.'

'I know.'

'I'll see you later OK.' She leaves and I lower my face to Albert's hand, pressing my lips against it softly. As I do every time, I wait, holding my breath, to see if he will give me some sign that he knows I'm here. A wriggle of his fingers maybe. But there's nothing.

'Morning,' I say to him softly.

My phone beeps in my bag and I dig under the chair for it. My body is aching, a result of another night squeezed into a tiny blue armchair instead of a bed. How many nights now? I try to count them but lose track after eight. I can't remember what day it is. Tuesday, I think. Or maybe it's Wednesday.

It's a text from Mum.

How is he this morning?

I text back.

The same. How is Bee?

Bee is fine. She misses you though. Just about to drop her at school then off to work. Text me if you need anything.

I don't respond to the last one. I'm still upset with her but I don't have the energy to feed the upset right now. Besides, she did what she did. It's done. It's the past. There is literally nothing I can do to change it. Albert needs my focus right now. I drop my bag and kick it back under the chair out of the way.

'So it's another beautiful sunny day,' I tell him. 'You need to wake up so we can go to the beach. Wouldn't you rather be out on your board than lying here?'

I watch for signs of life hopefully. If anything will get through to him surely it's the thought of being out on the ocean. But again there's no indication from him that he's heard me.

'Why is she talking to him? He can't hear her.'

'Shush, Colin.'

I stiffen at the sound of their voices and turn. Albert's parents have arrived for their morning visit. Wendy goes immediately to Albert's side and starts fussing. Even though there's nothing really she can do she likes to try to do something, so she fluffs the pillow beside his head and straightens up his sheet, rolling the top down evenly on both sides and tucking it under his arms so it looks tidy.

'Good morning, my beautiful boy,' she says. Her face is pained but she attempts to keep it from her voice.

'I told you you're wasting your time. He can't hear you.' Colin has gone straight to the window like he always does and is looking out. His posture is rigid, like he's uncomfortable to be here.

Wendy ignores her husband.

'How was his night?' she asks me.

'It was fine,' I reassure her. 'No change.'

The first few nights Albert lay in this bed, Wendy slept here as well, but her body is older and less open to being punished, and after she woke one morning with horrible back pain both Colin and I convinced her she needed to sleep at home. I promised her that I would call immediately if anything changed, but she only agreed after the doctors reassured her that he wouldn't wake up until they let him.

The wound on the side of his head is covered with a bandage, but the purple and yellow bruise that blooms down the side of his face is starting to fade. Surely that's a good sign, we agree.

'Have the doctors been around this morning yet?' she asks.

'No. Just Dot.'

'I told you they do their rounds the same time every day,' Colin says irritably.

'I know what you said. I just didn't want to miss them.'

There is so much tension between them. An hour passes awkwardly. It's eased when Colin leaves to fetch coffees. We all know he goes the long way around the hospital corridors and sits and reads the paper in the café before he comes back, but we don't mention it. I hate that he seems uncomfortable around his son. That even when Albert is at his most vulnerable, his father still can't seem to muster up enough affection to care.

I hate him full stop.

Albert

Maddy is here.

She is always here.

Her presence is gentle and soothing and reassuring.

Sometimes I hear her. When I am awake. At least, I think I am awake. I don't remember sleeping.

I wish I could open my eyes. I want to see her.

Dad is here.

Everything is black but when he is here everything becomes blacker.

I feel anxious and tense.

I'm scared.

Why can't I open my eyes?

Maddy

Colin walks back into the room while the doctors are talking.

'What did I miss? You need to start again,' he orders them gruffly. The younger one, the one who is 'in training', rolls his eyes. He has not yet learnt the level of self-control he will need to deal with difficult patients and their families. Colin should be like the dummy model they use for training. The thought makes me smile.

'I was just explaining to your wife that we are pleased with Albert's progress.'

'Pleased? How can you be pleased? Nothing's changed.'

'Not externally, no.' This doctor, the older one, is more patient. He talks slowly as if Colin is an idiot. It will infuriate him, but in a way that he can't protest against. 'But the scans have shown that the swelling is greatly reduced.'

'Does that mean we can wake him up?' Wendy asks hopefully.

'Soon, yes. Not today. But perhaps in the next couple of

days. We will do it slowly. Reduce the medication that is keeping him in the coma and let him wake up gradually.'

'And will he be OK?' Wendy is fearful when she asks, and even though she doesn't use the words we all know what she is worried about.

Brain damage.

The doctor shrugs. 'I can't say, I'm sorry. We'll know more when he wakes up and we can run some tests. His brain's had quite a shock. There was tremendous swelling. We're doing everything we can.'

All words we've heard before, over and over.

They leave and Colin walks to stand behind his wife. He places his hands on her shoulders in an effort to be comforting. She winces at his touch.

'He'll be OK,' he tells her.

'You don't know that.'

'It's Albert. The boy has a head like a coconut. Take more than a kick from a horse to keep him down.'

It's neither funny nor reassuring.

'Why don't you go home, Maddy,' Wendy says.

'No.'

'Go on. Have a proper sleep. How many days is it since you had a shower?'

I can't remember. Now she's planted a seed. The thought of hot water on my aching body sounds good. Still, I waver.

'Go on,' she says. 'Colin has to go to work but I'm not going anywhere today. I'll be with him until you get back.'

'Are you sure?'

'Of course. You can't look after him if you don't look after yourself,' she says wisely.

'OK.' I stand up and scoop my bag off the floor. Not caring that Colin is still in the room and disapproves of me, I lean over the bed and kiss Albert on his beautiful forehead.

'I'll be back tonight,' I promise him.

I'd forgotten what fresh air tastes like compared to regurgitated air-conditioned crap, and I gulp it down thirstily. Dot was right, the sun feels good and I peel off my cardigan so my arms are exposed to its life-sustaining rays.

No one is home when I get there. Bee is at the specialist school she attends and Mum is at work. I eat two pieces of peanut butter on toast and drink three cups of coffee. I regret the coffee when I start shaking in the shower, but still, the water and the heat feel amazing and massage my body, removing some of the aches and pains. I close my eyes and lift my face up towards the nozzle. The water runs down my face, like tears. I am out of tears. I cried buckets of them in the first few hours after the accident.

I sigh and turn the shower off. As much as I'd love to stay in here all day I have things I need to do. I am exhausted through to my very bones, and mentally drained. I feel like I haven't stopped to breathe for weeks, torn between the hospital and home. My sister and my boyfriend. As it is I haven't seen Bee or Mum for two days and Mum has mentioned that Bee keeps asking for me. She doesn't understand where I am, why I have disappeared. I stay by his side because I am petrified that if I don't something will go wrong. He might wake and be upset that I'm not there, or worse, he might not wake up at all. I know this is irrational and that my being there has no influence on any outcome. But it is still hard to fight the fear.

Even though I want to believe that Albert needs me, he doesn't. Not really. Not right now. But my sister does so I decide I will spend a few hours with her until Mum gets home and then head back to Albert. I text Mum to tell her she doesn't need to rush home from work and she texts back that she will put in some overtime then, earn a little extra.

I do a few loads of washing and tidy up until I hear the school van pull into the drive.

Mary, the driver, waits until I am in position beside the side door of the van before she unlocks it. I help Bee out and we stand on the doorstep and wave goodbye to the van. At least I do. Bee is excited to see me and has started screeching excitedly. She starts jumping up and down and grabbing my hand to get me to join in.

I laugh. It is so good to see her. I have missed her.

'You don't blame her do you,' Mum had asked fearfully, the first time I'd come home from the hospital.

'Of course not. Why would I?'

'Because she startled the horse.'

I shake my head. 'She didn't know what she was doing.'

'Well, yes, we know that. But what about his parents? Do you think they blame her?'

'No,' I lie. Well it's really only half a lie. Wendy doesn't, I know that. And I really don't care whether Colin does or not. I know Albert won't, and that is the only thing that matters.

Albert

I'm dying.

Or I'm dead.

I can feel myself slipping further and further into the darkness.

Nightmares.

Black, faceless beings clawing at me. I run and I run and I run but I can't escape them.

I try to scream but no noise comes out.

Why can't I open my eyes?

Maddy

Muffled voices.

'Why is she always here?'

'Louis.' A warning tone.

'What? She's not family.'

'She's his girlfriend.'

'Barely. How long have they known each other? Two minutes?'

Seven months actually, I nearly say to him, but I don't bother. What's the point? He's an idiot. Idiots don't care what anyone else has to say about anything. They think I'm asleep. I keep my eyes firmly shut to keep up the pretence. It's preferable to making small talk.

'I'm just saying it should be family only.'

'And I'm telling you to drop it, OK? As far as I'm concerned she *is* family. Albert would want her here.'

'Whatever.'

Louis has been here three times. Three times in two weeks. He's stayed about an hour each time and each time it's been excruciating.

I don't understand it. I've tried and I've tried, but I can't figure it out. These people are Albert's family. Wonderful, kind, sweet, funny Albert. They should be *grateful* to have him in their lives.

His mother is. She adores him. We've spent hours together watching him sleep while she recounts childhood anecdotes and I fall more and more in love with him. She tells me how he insisted on holding her hand while crossing the street until he was nine, according to him more for her protection than his own. And how some nights, she'd go to check on him before she turned in only to find his bed empty. He'd slip quietly out his window and fall asleep on the trampoline, under his beloved stars.

'He was born deep in the night,' she said. 'And he's loved it ever since.'

She talks to Albert when she thinks I am asleep. About how proud she is of him. How much she loves him.

But his dad and his brother only visit when it's painfully obvious that if they don't it will look bad. They don't talk to Albert. They barely look at him.

I understand not everyone is the same. I know that different generations show affection differently, and that sometimes people just don't like other people, for whatever reason.

But this is Albert. He is their son, their brother.

What the hell is wrong with them?

Albert

Voices.

Strange, distorted voices.

I hear my name.

Maddy. She is here. I feel her presence; reassuring.

She has not left me.

Maddy

'Albert? Can you hear me?' I watch his face intently, hoping he will surprise me by opening his eyes and giving me that big beautiful smile of his and saying, 'Gotcha!'

He doesn't.

'I swear he squeezed my hand last night,' Wendy says.

'It's possible,' the doctor says, but his voice says otherwise. 'Although I think it's too soon for that. He will start to become more aware though now that we've reduced the medication.'

'When will he wake up?'

The doctor shrugs. 'Soon, hopefully.'

'What do you mean, "hopefully"?' Colin asks shrewdly.

'Unfortunately, as I've said before, it's a waiting game.'

'I'm sick of you and your vague answers.'

'Colin!'

'Well I am. Honestly, what's the point in medical school if

all you can say at the end of it is: maybe; hopefully; possibly. Any fool in a white coat could say that.'

'I apologise for my husband,' Wendy says to the doctor. 'He's just worried.'

The doctor smiles at her. 'It's understandable. Don't worry. I have a thick skin.'

'That's not all that's thick,' Colin mutters.

'Colin!'

He's so rude. I've stopped taking it personally because he speaks like this to everyone: doctors, nurses, the lady behind the counter in the café, Albert's friend Connor who has visited a few times. There doesn't seem to be anyone who Colin holds in as a high a regard as himself. Everyone else, it would seem, is stupid.

'There!' Wendy squeals excitedly and we all jump.

'What?'

'His eyelids flickered.'

We all stare intently at Albert's eyelids for a minute or two. They stay resolutely shut.

'Don't expect him to just wake up as one would from sleep,' the doctor warns. 'It's a process. He'll be a bit groggy and disorientated for a while too. Be gentle with him.'

'How long till we know if he's a vegetable or not?'

'Colin!'

'He is not in a vegetative state,' the doctor says. 'Tests show brain activity. We're just not sure of any long-term damage to his cognitive abilities. I'm afraid we just need to be patient.'

'That's easy for you to say,' Colin grumbles.

Albert

The light is getting brighter and the voices are getting louder and more frequent. Why do they keep waking me up?

I went for a walk today. Down a country road. It was gravel. There were cornfields on either side. A chicken followed me most of the way until he got tired, then he lay down and turned into dust. The sky was bright blue and the sun was up high in the corner.

I heard music, country. I wanted to dance but my feet wouldn't lift off the ground.

A pig came out of the cornfield and told me it was dinner time.

I don't like pigs, but I prefer them to the faceless black cawing things. So I told him I was coming, but after he left I was too tired so I lay down like the chicken and watched my feet dissolve to dust. I think I fell asleep, then.

Why does my head hurt?

Maddy

This morning, sixteen days after his accident, Albert woke up.

He opened his eyes and he looked around the room. When he saw me he smiled.

He mumbled something, it sounded like, 'I'm coming.'

Then he closed his eyes again and he drifted back off to sleep.

I wept then. All the fear and pent-up emotion that I had been holding on to since the day of his accident was released and I cried so hard and for so long that a nurse came scuttling into the room, alarmed by the strange noises emanating from within. When she saw it was just me she gave me a lopsided smile and retreated, diplomatically closing the door behind her.

Wendy was upset that she had missed the moment we have been waiting for, and stayed at his side, clutching his hand tightly, for the rest of the day hoping that he would wake again. I lied and told her he didn't seem to even recognise that I was in the room and so wouldn't have noticed her absence. She was slightly pacified by this.

Colin makes her leave around ten, but I stay, curled up in my chair beside his bed. Around three in the morning I hear a funny sound and look up, blinking away exhaustion to find him looking at me.

'Hey.' I uncurl quickly, picking up his hand and lifting it to my cheek. 'Welcome back you.'

He blinks at me.

'It's OK, don't try to speak.'

His eyes rotate, taking in his surroundings.

'Do you know why you're here?' I ask him.

He shakes his head and tries to lick his lips, which I can see are dry from the air conditioning. I pick up my bag and scrabble in the bottom until I find my tub of coconut lip balm, which I smear on his lips. His eyes never leave my face and I feel I might combust under the intensity in them. Until that moment, I hadn't allowed myself to give voice or dwell on my biggest fear, that Albert might wake and not remember who I am or how much in love we are. But the look in his eyes is unmistakable. He knows me, he loves me, and the relief is tremendous. I bend my head to rest it on his chest and I cry again. I feel his hand move to sit lightly on the back of my hair, comforting. He makes a gentle patting gesture as if I were a kitten.

'Don't cry,' he croaks, his voice weak from weeks of silence.

'I'm sorry,' I mumble into the sheets. 'It's just I was so scared.'

'What . . . happened?'

I lift my head and wipe the tears from my face, sniffing back my pain. I don't want to cry any more. I don't need to. Everything is going to be OK. I take his hand in mine and squeeze it reassuringly.

'You had an accident, at the stables. A horse got startled and kicked out and you were in the way.'

I watch his forehead furrow as he tried to remember but draws a blank. He shakes his head in frustration. 'Why don't I remember?'

'You had, *have*, an injury to your brain,' I explain carefully. He's only just woken up and I'm wary of causing him any setbacks with the truth. Sure enough, I see fear in his eyes.

'My brain?'

'The doctors expect you to make a full recovery but things might be a bit foggy for a while.'

He closes his eyes for a few minutes and the sound of his breathing settles. Believing he has drifted back off to sleep, I study his hand, noticing how long his nails have grown since the accident. Suddenly he squeezes my hand hard.

'Thank you,' he says, startling me.

I look at his face, his eyes are still closed. 'For what?'

'Being . . . here.'

I kiss the back of his hand, pressing my lips against it so firmly I hope I haven't hurt him.

'As if I'd be anywhere else,' I say.

Albert

Why does my father keep scowling at me? Have I forgotten to mow the lawns again?

Maddy

'A coma?'

'Yes, an induced one.'

Albert blinks at us. He has lost weight. Being fed through a tube will do that to you. His cheekbones are prominent in a way most girls would kill for.

'An accident?'

'At the stables. A horse kicked your head,' Wendy explains patiently for the tenth time today. Yesterday we told him twenty times. One day soon it will stick, that's what the doctors say.

'You're a hero,' I tell him, my voice breaking. 'Thanks to you Bee is still alive.'

'A bee?'

'No, Bee. My sister.'

'Oh.' He blinks. 'A coma?'

The doctors are pleased. They say he is making good

progress. As I have nothing to compare to, I can only take their word for it. He is very confused at first, and his short-term memory is unable to hold anything longer than a few minutes. To everyone's great relief his long-term memory, right up until the accident, seems unaffected.

He drifts in and out of sleep. Every time he wakes we have to remind him where he is and why he is there. Sometimes when he hears he has been in a coma he gets scared and believes great chunks of time have passed. One day he worked himself up into a frenzy believing he was now an old man and only settled when a mirror was found and he could see his reflection. He lifted his fingers to tentatively explore the bandage on his head and said, 'So that's why it hurts.' Then he went back to sleep.

'This guy at work said his uncle was in a coma after a car accident,' Louis told Albert one day on one of his token visits. 'And when he woke up he could speak a whole new language. Spanish, I think. Or Chinese. Can you speak a new language?'

Albert shook his head.

'Pity,' said Louis, disappointed. 'Would have been a good story for down the pub.'

'Tired,' said Albert.

'OK, I'll go.' Louis jumped to his feet, grateful for the excuse to leave.

Albert sleeps a lot, that first week. It's good, the doctors say, best thing for him. While he sleeps his body is repairing itself. The first thing he does when he wakes is look for me, and when he finds me he relaxes.

'You're here,' he says.

'Of course.'

It's hard. I need to be here for him, but Bee is missing me and I am conscious of upsetting her and the implications this could have on her health. She doesn't cope well with change, and my absence is a pretty big one. Sometimes I sneak out when Albert has just gone to sleep and go home to see her. She is happy and demands my full attention, which I happily give her. She sits on my lap, which is her own way of trying to stop me from leaving again. When I do have to leave, the sad look on her face is crushing. I feel like I have become a carer for two people and decide that the universe or whoever the hell gets to decide this stuff has a sick sense of humour.

Albert

She looks so peaceful when she sleeps. I was confused when I woke up and saw her on a mattress on the floor in the corner, but then I remembered.

I am in hospital. I had an accident.

I have been in a coma.

My head hurts, though not as bad as it did yesterday. That has to be a good thing.

I don't remember the accident. I only know what they've told me.

I feel a bit like you feel when you first wake up, but I feel like that all day. Groggy. Like I've had too much to drink and not enough sleep. I suppose it's the drugs they have me on. I don't care. I'm just grateful to be alive.

I remember the nightmares. I can still feel the terror I felt.

Maddy

'Doctor says you'll be able to go home soon.'

'When?'

'Soon.'

'When is soon?'

'Soon. Wait and see.'

'I don't want to wait and see.'

'Too bad.'

'You'd make a terrible nurse.'

I laugh and snuggle closer to him. 'Gee thanks.'

I am up on the bed beside him. Every day he comes back to us a little more. He remembers things, although still not the accident itself, just the days leading up to it. He has started to make jokes, bad ones of course. But he gets tired easily, and grumpy. It's understandable.

'Is it night or day?' he asks.

'Night.'

'I don't like the curtains closed. Open them.'

'No. They don't like me to open them.'

'Who?'

'The nurses.'

'How do you know?'

'Because you ask me every night. And when I open them they come in and growl.'

'Oh. Please?'

I sigh. 'OK. Just for a little while. But you're taking the heat if we get in trouble.'

'Deal.'

I push off the bed and walk in my socks over to the window to draw back the curtains. As soon as he sees the starry sky, he relaxes.

'I missed them, you know,' he says.

I flick the main light off so we have only the light from the small one by the door and then hop gently up on the bed beside him. He curls one arm around me.

'The stars?'

'Yes. I remember sometimes it was black and I wondered where the stars were.'

It's the first time he has mentioned the coma willingly and I stiffen, unsure if I want to hear this. It was hard enough to go through from this side, and I've been hoping for him it was easier, that he just slept and felt nothing . . .

'But other times,' he continues, his voice tense, 'it was white, like a waiting room. Nothing, just white all around me. I thought I was dead,' he says softly.

'Shush. Don't say that.'

'Imagine if I never saw you again?'

'You don't have to. Because you're still here, and so am I.'

'I love you, you know that right.'

'Yes.' I push up on one elbow, my hand on his chest, my face close to his. 'I love you too.'

I kiss him. Softly, because he is still recovering and I am wary of hurting him.

'So it was only the stars you missed then?' I joke, nuzzling his lips.

'Of course not.'

I smile.

'I missed the ocean too.'

He laughs when I pout, outraged. The sound of his laughter is music to my ears. I had thought at one point I might never hear that sound again. It would have been unbearable.

'And you of course,' he says. 'Desperately you.'

We kiss again. I pull away.

'Are you sure this isn't too much for you?'

'Too much?' he murmurs, reaching up a hand to stroke the side of my face. 'It will never be enough.'

Albert

Louis visits with Mum. Well, when I say he visits, he sits in the chair in the corner and wears an expression that says he'd rather be anywhere else but here. He looks out the window, reads all the posters on the wall and inspects the floor. He yawns, stretches, and taps his foot to a tune I can't quite pinpoint. When he's bored with that, he gets his keys out and dangles them so they clunk together. The noise is loud in the room.

What he doesn't do is speak.

At least nothing beyond the normal greetings and standard pleasantries.

It is so painfully awkward I almost wish I was back in the coma just to avoid having to look at him. It's obvious that he's been dragged here under duress. I listen to Mum prattle on about the neighbours, and what happened on *Ellen* yesterday, and I wonder, are we the only brothers in the world who can't stand to be in the same room together?

'Do you know the one I'm talking about? The one with the orange curls? Tall? Speaks funny?'

Mum's voice breaks through my thoughts and I realise she is waiting for me to answer. I try to recall any of her previous words but draw a blank.

'Sorry?' I ask sheepishly.

She sighs. 'I knew you weren't listening. That's OK, it's probably hard for you to concentrate right now.'

She fusses with my pillow like she always does. It's annoying, but I understand her need to feel useful.

'So what was it like?' Louis finally says.

'What was what like?'

He rolls his eyes. 'Duh, the coma. Did you see any bright white lights or anything? Could you hear us?'

'I can't remember,' I say, even though I do occasionally get flashbacks. They are more feelings than visions.

'Boring. What a cop out,' he says.

'That's enough of that,' Mum warns him. 'He's been through enough of an ordeal.'

'Fine.' Louis shuffles his seat, barely hiding his desire to be somewhere else. 'So when are you getting out?' he asks.

'Soon, hopefully. Going a bit crazy stuck in here.'

'Yeah, I bet.'

'You'll leave when you're one hundred per cent recovered and the doctors say you can leave,' Mum declares sternly. 'And not a minute before.'

'Yes, Mum.'

'And you're not going back to work around horses either,' she says.

This makes me sit up. 'Of course I am.'

'You can't,' she frets. 'What if the same thing happens again? Horses are brutes, unpredictable. No, you'd be safer going back to office work. You may have survived this time but who's to say you would survive another knock?'

'Mum,' I say firmly. 'It's was a freak accident.'

'I know that, but you do hear stories about lightning striking the same spot twice.'

'That's no way to live, Mum.' I shake my head. 'In fear. I love my job and I can't wait to get back to it.'

Louis snorts.

'What?' I ask him.

'Well, it's not exactly a real job, is it?' He puts on a girly voice. 'Brushing the horses' hair and tails. Do you braid it too? Put bows in it?'

'Fuck off, Louis. There's more to it than that.'

Mum clucks her tongue when I swear but I don't care. I feel like my accident has made me see things more clearly. Why do I bother trying to impress my brother and father? They clearly don't like or have much respect for me. Isn't life too short to spend with people whose beliefs and morals are pretty much the polar opposite of my own? But, on the other hand, they're family. And family sticks together. Or so I've heard.

'With pleasure.' He shrugs, getting up off the chair and scratching his head. 'You coming?' He directs the last question at Mum. She is torn, I can tell, but if she doesn't go with him then she will need to call my father to come and get her, and we both know how well that will go down.

'It's OK,' I tell her. 'I'm tired anyway so I'll probably sleep.'

'Are you sure?'

'Positive. Maddy will be up later.'

'OK.' She leans over the bed and kisses my forehead. Over her shoulder I can see Louis roll his eyes, and I realise I have never seen her kiss him like she does me. Not since we were both young anyway. Maybe his resentment stems from jealousy?

Maddy

'Busted.' Albert grins at me when I walk into his room and find him out of bed, stuffing his clothes into his blue duffel bag.

'What do you think you're doing?'

'Packing.'

'Why? They haven't said you can go, have they?'

'No,' he says. 'But I want to be ready for when they do.'

He notices Bee behind me and his face cracks into a wide smile. 'Hey, Bee, good to see you again.'

'Bee, say "Hi, Albert."'

'Bert, Bert, Oh Ernie, go to sleep.'

I shrug. 'That's about as good as you're going to get, sorry.'

He walks over and wraps his arms around me. 'It's perfect,' he says. 'I'm just so glad to see you both.'

'You might not be saying that soon,' I warn. 'She's on fine form tonight. It's taken me half an hour to get to your room from the front door of the hospital.'

Bee starts bouncing around the room like a kangaroo while I help Albert back up on to his bed. She knocks his bedside table and a plastic cup with water falls off.

'Bee, careful,' I say.

'It's OK.' Albert smiles. 'It's really nice to see her again.'

'I had to bring her,' I apologise, pulling a few paper towels from the dispenser on the wall and getting down on the floor to mop up the water. 'Mum had a late shift. I couldn't bear the thought of not seeing you so figured this was the lesser of two evils. I'm slightly regretting that choice now. She's so hyper.'

'Does she remember the accident?'

'I would say yes, because she has such an amazing memory. But what she made of it is anyone's guess. She's not upset, if that's what you're worried about. In fact, she was more upset about missing out on her ride and spent the rest of the day asking for it. Bee tends to be indifferent to anyone but herself. It's not personal.'

'Good. I'd just hate for her to think it was her fault, you know? I could never blame her for what happened.'

Even though I suspected this was the case, hearing him outright absolve my sister of blame is such a huge rush of relief. I tiptoe up and kiss him hard on the lips. 'And that,' I say breathily, 'is why I love you so much.'

'And here was me thinking it was because of my insanely good looks.' He smirks.

I kiss him again. 'Well that too, obviously.'

'Obviously.'

'But mostly it's because you are who you are. Kind, sweet and caring. I feel you're almost too good to be true.'

He nods in joking agreement. 'I know. I'm pretty perfect. I do have one, teensy tiny fault though.'

'Oh yeah? What's that?'

'Impatience. When are they going to let me out of here? Seriously, I miss being outside. I could kill for a surf.'

'Oh no you don't.' I poke him in the chest until he backs up against the bed and climbs on with a sigh. 'You're not doing anything that exerts yourself until you're given the all-clear. Understood?'

He sighs. 'Yes, ma'am.'

I'm on my hands and knees mopping the water up when I see under the bed a pair of feet enter the room. Before I can get up Bee is gone, straight to the doctor.

'Bee, wait,' I call, scrambling to my feet but she has a head start and before the startled doctor can react Bee has grabbed his dangling stethoscope and is pulling it, jerking the poor man's head forward.

'Bee, stop,' I growl, hurrying around the bed and prising her hands off it. 'Sorry,' I say to the doctor.

'It's OK.' he smiles, rubbing the back of his neck. 'That was quite a welcome. She's very strong, eh?'

Bee is breathing heavy and starts to say 'All better now,' over and over.

'You have no idea,' I tell him.

I make Bee sit in the corner chair while the doctor does his checks on Albert. She immediately holds her hand as if her arm is in a sling and adopts a hangdog expression.

'Oh my hand, what about my letters,' she says morosely.

The doctor stops what he's doing to look at me questioningly.

'*Postman Pat*,' I say, as if that explains it all.

'Well you can't work today, you'll have to rest it,' Bee continues.

The doctor smiles at Bee. 'Yes, rest is definitely the best thing for a broken arm.'

She ignores him, but I appreciate his effort.

'You're doing well,' the doctor tells Albert when he's finished his checks. 'A model patient.'

'You wouldn't have said that five minutes ago,' I say. 'I caught him out of bed packing his bags.'

Albert shoots me an outraged look. 'You snitch.'

I hold my hands up, palm facing outwards in a conciliatory gesture. 'Sorry, but I'm not sorry. You won't listen to me, maybe you'll listen to him.'

The doctor puts his hands on his hips and adopts a stern expression. 'Is this true?' he asks Albert.

Albert flushes guiltily. 'Maybe.'

The doctor clicks his tongue in disapproval. 'Do you *want* to set back your recovery?'

Albert looks from the doctor to me and back again. 'Is that a trick question?'

'Look,' the doctor sighs. 'Rest. Take it easy. Please don't push yourself or you could make things worse. You've been through an ordeal; give your body the time it needs to heal. OK?'

'OK. Sorry.'

'Don't be. I understand. Cabin fever is a real thing,

especially in someone your age. These walls can be confining. But just trust us when we say you're not ready to go yet. You're almost there, you just need to be patient a little longer.'

'Thanks, Doc.'

'Yes, thanks, Doctor,' I agree. 'He won't listen to me.'

'Don't worry.' Albert grins. 'The doctor has got through my thick skull.'

'Hey, that thick skull is what kept you alive,' I remind him. 'I happen to be very fond of that thick skull.'

We smile so dopily at each other that I don't even notice when the doctor leaves the room.

Albert

'So when can I go home?'

The nurse changing the bandage on the side of my head clucks. 'Stay still. You've made it loose again.'

'Sorry.'

'I don't know when you can go home. You'll have to ask the doctor.'

'He doesn't know either.'

'Well, there you go then.'

'So who does?'

'What? Stay still.'

'Who knows?'

'Albert, as much as we're all extremely fond of you, you're starting to drive us mad with the constant questions.'

'Sorry.'

She sighs. 'I'm sure it won't be much longer. You're doing well, although ...' She frowns, using her hand to tilt my chin

288

sideways so she can see my head in the light. 'Have you been exerting yourself? Your wound has started to bleed again on the corner. It's a little inflamed.'

'Is that bad?'

'Well, it's not good.' She gives me a stern look. 'No, it's OK. It's minor in the grand scheme of things. But I'll get the doctor to prescribe some antibiotics, just to be on the safe side.'

'Then can I go home?'

She rolls her eyes. 'You don't give up, do you?'

'Never.'

'Good. That's a good attitude to have. Now sit still while I finish wrapping this. When is Maddy due back?'

'Not till tomorrow,' I say forlornly.

'Good. That girl needs a break. She has barely left your side in weeks.' She finishes what she's doing and starts wheeling her trolley away. 'I'd hang on to that girl if I was you.'

'I plan to,' I call after her.

I miss her. Even though I saw her this morning, I hate when she is not here. The time passes so much more slowly. I literally sit and watch the minute hand click over on the clock until she returns. But I understand why she had to go. Her mother has been working and looking after Bee so that Maddy can be with me, but now she has a head cold and Maddy is giving her a break. I have to share her, and I hate that, but I understand.

I'm asleep when I feel someone adjusting my blankets. It could be a nurse but my instinct tells me it's not. When I was in the coma I could *sense* when Maddy was in the room. Not consciously, just on some deeper level.

I still can.

I open my eyes and blink at her sleepily. The light from the hallway gives her dark hair a halo. She looks like an angel.

'Hey, you.' She smiles.

'I thought you weren't coming back until tomorrow?'

'I wasn't. But I've dosed Mum up on Lemsip and she's feeling better. She and Bee are asleep but I couldn't sleep, so here I am.'

'I'm glad you came.'

'Good. Now go back to sleep. I'll be on the floor if you need me.'

'Sleep up here with me.'

'After the last time? I'm not supposed to remember, that nurse was *not* happy.'

We laugh at the memory of being scolded like naughty teenagers.

'Don't be so chicken.'

'Who are you calling chicken?' she demands.

'You.' I try to make a chicken noise. It sounds like someone punctured a balloon.

'Move over then,' she says.

I pull her close and breathe in the smell of her.

'Maddy?'

'Mm.'

'I don't think you should come in tomorrow.'

She pushes herself up on one elbow to look down at me, frowning. 'Why not?'

'You've been spending so much time here with me and as

much as I appreciate it and, believe me, I really do appreciate it, I just think you need to spend some time with Bee. I thought you could do this.' I reach over to the bedside table and pick up a newspaper, opening to a page I folded down earlier. 'Look.'

She scans the black and white words. SENSORY MOVIE DAY, the headline says. She gives me a 'look'.

'I know.' I grin. 'I'm the perfect boyfriend right?'

I watch as she reads the article I found that morning. One of the cinemas in town is holding a sensory movie day for autistic children. The fact that they are screening the new *Beauty and the Beast* movie got me excited, because Maddy has mentioned before that it is Bee's favourite film. She loves the cartoon version and, according to Maddy, knows all the words off by heart.

'I thought she might enjoy it,' I say.

'She'll love it.' She stares at me for a minute, silent.

'What?'

She sighs. 'Once again I'm blown away by how much you understand my life when so many have never taken the time.'

'I know how much Bee needs you too. It's selfish of me to keep you here all the time.'

'You didn't ask me to be here. I'm here because I want to be.'

'Are you always this stubborn?'

'Are you always this annoyingly sensible and understanding?'

I shrug. 'It's one of my weaknesses, yes.'

She leans down and kisses me on the tip of my nose. 'If that's your weakness I'd hate to think what your strengths are,' she says.

291

I reach up and lightly pull her head down so that our faces are only millimetres apart.

'*You* give me strength,' I say. 'I can do anything with you by my side.'

Maddy

Springing things suddenly on my sister is not a good idea. Spontaneity became a thing of the past when she was born, replaced by careful preparation. There are certain things that must be done when going somewhere new in order to not upset her. Wherever possible anyway.

'Bee, look,' I say, pointing to the laptop I have open on the table. It takes me calling her three times before she looks at me.

'Bee, sit.' I point.

She sits on one of the dining room chairs and I lift the headphones off her ears so she can hear the laptop audio, which I have turned right up. Emma Watson twirling in a huge yellow ball dress fills the screen.

'Look, Bee, *Beauty and the Beast*, Bee. You love *Beauty and the Beast*.'

'Falls down a hole!' she shouts.

'Yes, Bee, that's right,' I say. 'Gaston falls down a hole.'

She knows the cartoon movie off by heart as it's one of her favourites. She can, and does, recite it word for word, complete with fierce facial expressions when she's re-enacting the part of the Beast. Of course she doesn't look fierce, she looks cute. Achingly so.

'Would you like to go and see *Beauty and the Beast* at the movies today, Bee?'

'*Ma chère, Mademoiselle*,' she starts to sing. It is the opening line of the 'Be Our Guest' song.

'I'll take that as a yes.'

I play the trailer of the film for her so that she understands what we're going to see. She puts it on repeat and watches it over and over. This is a good sign, it mean's she's interested. While she's watching it I text Albert.

> Thanks for the idea, we're heading to the theatre soon xx

He texts back.

> Have a wonderful time.

A text conversation kicks off.

> Are you ok?

> I'm great :) Stop worrying about me.

Can't help it, you have a habit of doing heroic, dangerous things.

I'm blushing. You think I'm a hero?

Don't get a big head, but yes.

That's totally made my day.

Good.

Go. Enjoy your time with Bee.
I have plans for you later.

Sounds intriguing. Clue?

Nope. You'll have to wait and see.

The movie trailer finishes and before Bee can lose attention and start watching something else I quickly bring up the cinema's webpage and show her what it looks like, inside and out. If she has some kind of an idea where we're going she won't get so frazzled once we're there.

When we get there, I see other autistic children and their families milling around. There are children of all ages and even autistic adults. It's nice to see kind, acknowledging glances from people who understand, instead of the judgement we often face in public. I can't control Bee's actions any more than I can control my mother's. She is her own person, with her own behavioural traits. If she wants to start twerking in someone's face she will.

With a sinking feeling, I realise I forgot to go to the toilet before we left the house. Toilet trips in public aren't desirable even under normal circumstances. Throw my sister into the mix and they become fraught with difficulty.

'Toilet, Bee,' I say. She diligently follows me. There is no way I can leave Bee outside the cubicle while I pee, plus I want to make sure she also goes before we go into the theatre so I lead her into the disabled toilet and lock the door. She goes first, and after I do her pants up and help her wash her hands I give her my sternest look.

'Wait, Bee. Don't touch the door.'

She giggles as if she understands, but I know she hasn't.

I pull my jeans and knickers down and sit on the toilet, all the while keeping a wary eye on her. She fixates on a movie poster on the back of the toilet door and I think I'm safe. It lasts two seconds. While I'm still peeing she starts fiddling with the lock.

'No, Bee.' I hold up a warning finger.

She doesn't stop, and I hear the ominous sound of the lock click.

'Bee, NO.'

Too late. She opens the door and I am greeted by the startled faces of a couple of ladies at the handbasins.

'Close the door, Bee,' I urge quietly, squeezing my knees together and smiling apologetically. 'Close the door, now.'

She doesn't of course. Instead, she wanders out and smiles at the ladies, who have finished washing a little quicker than probably they intended, and quickly scurry out of the bathroom.

'Sorry,' I call after them. Then I add when they're out of earshot, 'You could have bloody shut the door though.'

I sigh at my sister who looks as if she hasn't a care in the world. 'Thanks, Bee,' I say. 'I can always count on you to keep my heart racing.'

The cinema is kindly allowing attendees to the special screening to bring in their own food and drinks, recognising that so many autistic children have very clear likes and dislikes. I have brought Bee's favourite snacks with us, but decide I will treat myself to a ridiculously priced Coke and a choc-top ice cream. Bee won't touch either of them. The Coke is too fizzy and the ice cream too cold for her. While we wait in the queue I try to remember the last time I was here. For most families a trip to the movies is a fun day out. For autistic children though it can be too much: too much noise, too dark, and too many strange people. It can make them anxious.

I have never been to the cinema with my sister. In fact, I haven't been since I was a child full stop. The theatre still has that familiar smell from my childhood memories of popcorn and excitement. Or maybe it's just pee from too many excited children. I'm not sure. There are certainly suspicious stains on some of the seats.

Bee starts to get excited at being around people. She is wide-eyed and starts vocalising loudly, flapping her hands and grinning. She leans forward in her seat and fake coughs on the person sitting in front of us. Right on the back of their head, loudly, parting their hair with the force, and then she taps them on the shoulder.

'Hello,' she says. 'Hello.'

The lady turns and smiles. 'Hi.'

I smile at her gratefully. So many people don't know how to react around Bee. I know some are just scared of doing or saying the wrong thing, and I know there is a stigma that autistic children can be violent or aggressive. But that's like saying all certain breeds of dogs are savage. It's pigeonholing. And it pisses me off.

As promised in the newspaper article, the lights dim but stay on, and the movie comes on at a volume slightly lower than it normally would. Still, some of the children immediately rise from their seats and start wandering around the theatre, pacing up and down, spinning and tiptoeing. It is interesting to see some of the methods they use for stimming. There are a few theories as to why autistic children stim, but the main one, and the one I think relevant when it comes to Bee, is that it's a way to self-calm when they are facing a sensory overload. Bee flaps her hands and fingers near her face. I see one boy who taps his ears repetitively. Quite a few start rocking in their seats. A few start to express themselves audibly, scripting phrases from movies and TV shows, or squealing and making other strange sound effects. Normally, as a family member, that would be our cue to remove them from the situation, but that's more for the benefit of the people around. It avoids the tuts and the stares that we get. I always feel like telling them that autism doesn't come with a remote control, we can't just push a mute or pause button.

Not today. We are all in the same boat today. We all know what it's like, we all understand, and no one bats an eyelid at anyone else.

It's incredibly refreshing.

I revel in the fact that Bee seems to be enjoying herself. She still wears her headphones because they are like a security blanket, but she can hear the movie and she knows every single word. I marvel once again at her memory, but I also feel the usual sadness that she knows all these words, and can recite an entire movie, but she cannot have even the simplest of conversations with me.

She sings along. Occasionally the words are slightly different to the cartoon version Bee knows off by heart but it doesn't faze her. She just grins and picks it back up again when she can. When her favourite song, 'Be Our Guest', comes on, she climbs on to my lap and sings at the top of her voice. She smiles broadly at me, and I feel like my heart might explode with my love for her.

Albert

'Where's Maddy?' Mum asks, fussing with my sheets as usual even though they are perfectly fine, she just needs to feel useful.

'At home. I told her to spend some time with Bee.'

Mum makes an 'aww' sound. 'She's such a good girl, looking after her sister like she does.'

'Maddy says that's just what you do for family.'

'Wouldn't the world be a better place if everyone felt like that?'

'Mm.'

'Are you OK?'

'Yes.'

'You look a little flushed.'

'It's hot. They turn the heat up so high at night it's like a sauna.'

'It is rather hot,' she agrees, looking up at the ventilation hole in the roof where the hot air pipes out from. She feels my forehead. 'It's warm,' is her verdict.

'Good. That means I'm alive.'

She gives me a soppy look. 'Don't joke. Oh my boy, you gave me such a scare. When I got that phone call it felt like my world stopped turning.'

'Sorry.'

'You should be. You've given me more grey hairs.'

'Where's Dad?'

She turns her attention on to a bouquet of flowers on the table beside my bed, fussing over them. 'Oh look at these poor things, they're wilting in this heat.'

'He's avoiding me, isn't he?'

She pulls the flowers out of the vase and sniffs inside. 'Thought so. Only a smidgeon of water and it's gone rank. I know it's not the nurses' job to replace the water, but still, these aren't cheap flowers by the look of it. Who were these from again?'

'Uncle Fred and Aunt Marge.'

'That was nice of them.'

'It was.'

She sighs. 'It's not that your father is avoiding you, it's just he doesn't like hospitals. He has a lot of dealings up here with his job, and none of them usually any good.'

'It's OK. Doesn't bother me.'

We both know this isn't true.

If I'd thought my coming close to death might shock my father into realising how much he's actually, *deep down*, fond

301

of me, I was mistaken. I'm fairly sure he visits only because it's expected of him and, when here, sits in the corner reading his paper until an acceptable length of time has passed and he can leave again.

'Can you open the curtains?' I ask quietly. 'I like to see the stars.'

She opens them and switches the big light off, leaving the room dim.

'You can get going if you like,' I say.

'Not yet.'

'You're not in a hurry to get home to him, are you?'

She gives me a wry smile and changes the subject. 'Is Maddy coming up later?'

'I'm not sure. Can you pass my phone? I might check on her.'

She opens the drawer on the bedside cabinet and lifts out my phone. 'You care about her a lot, don't you?'

'I love her,' I state simply, shrugging my shoulders lightly.

'And she loves you too, I can tell that by how she looks after you. I think it's wonderful, what you two have.'

'Yeah, I'm thinking about asking her to marry me.'

I say it so casually it takes her a moment to register what I've said and then she splutters. 'Marry? Don't you think you're a bit young for that?'

I laugh. 'Yeah. Probably. But it was funny to see your face.'

She smacks my arm playfully. 'You just concentrate on getting better.'

'Yes, Mum.'

'Good boy.'

'There is something I've been thinking about asking her though.'

'Oh?'

'She'll probably say no. And even if she did say yes we'd have to ask her mother. It might be too weird for her.'

'What might be weird?'

'Well, if Maddy can't leave her sister, which I completely understand, then I was thinking maybe I move in there. With them.'

She thinks about it. 'You don't think it might be a bit soon for that?'

'Maybe,' I concede. 'But I love Maddy. I want to help her, and her mother. And Bee is great, she really is. If I can help them out with looking after her *and* be with Maddy at the same time it's a win-win as far as I can see.'

'You're not just doing it to get away from home, are you?' she asks. 'Because that wouldn't be fair on Maddy.'

'I'm not going to lie and say it's not part of the reason. But it's only a small part. I just want to be with her as much as I can. And I want to help her. She's had it tough, Mum, although she'd never admit it. I promise you my motives are good.'

She nods. 'I just had to make sure.'

Being stuck in this hospital room going out of my mind with boredom has given me a lot of time to think. Mostly, I think about Maddy, of course. About how lucky I am to have met her and how grateful I am that she let down her guard long enough for me to elbow my way into her affections. But at night sometimes, when I am alone and can't sleep, I think about what might have been. I can't help it. I don't remember the accident itself, but from what I've been told it only took a split second. A split second where my life could have been changed, or worse, wiped out, for ever. It's a terrifying thought and I try not to dwell on it but it's hard not to. It's not something I'd ever given a thought to before, but now the knowledge is there, niggling away. Life can be taken so quickly, without warning. I'm determined not to waste a minute of it. For the first time in my life, I am clear on what I want. I want to take the job Francine offered and work my way up through the ranks. I want to help kids like Bee, and make a difference in their lives. But I also want adventure, to travel and experience what this world has to offer. I know I can have both. And I want to do it all with Maddy by my side.

'Oh, love.' She tilts her head and looks at me with a mixture of pride and affection. 'When did you get so grown up? You have to be sure though. It's a big thing, looking after someone with disabilities. I'd hate for Maddy to say yes and then in a month or two you decide you don't want to do it any more or it's too hard, because I'm sure it has its difficult moments. It wouldn't be fair on them. You have to be sure it's what you really want.'

I look at the stars stretched across the sky. So endless and magnificent.

'I'm sure.'

Maddy

Bee is not herself. She is pale and quiet. Mum also looks tired.

'She had so much fun today,' Mum says. 'So I don't want you to feel guilty for taking her. But I think maybe the excitement was a bit much. She's been missing you, so having you back to herself and seeing her favourite movie on a big screen all on the same day has probably just left her more tired than normal.'

'Yeah, I think you might be right. Why didn't you tell me how much she was missing me?'

'Sore head,' says Bee.

'I didn't want to worry you, but she's not been sleeping well and she keeps looking for you at the window.'

It's the first time in her life that I haven't been here, so of course she's noticed. It doesn't take much of a change in routine to upset Bee, and my absence is a pretty big change. I'm flooded with guilt when I see her, but at the same time I feel bad that

I'm not with Albert. They both need me. I'm being pulled both ways but I'm determined not to let either of them down, even at the expense of my own health and temporary sanity.

'Sorry, Bee,' I say, cuddling her. 'I was looking after Albert.'

'Oh, I go demented,' she says.

I look at Mum. It's a new one to me.

'Beatrix Potter, I think,' she shrugs.

We eat dinner. Bee shakes her head in refusal more than normal and I can barely get her to eat anything. Her face is fretful, and she won't let me out of her sight. She flaps her hands constantly and follows me everywhere, even when I go to the bathroom, so I go to the toilet with the door open.

'Sore head,' she says again sorrowfully. 'Ouch.'

I get a text from Albert asking if I'll be back in tonight. As much as I want to say yes, I can't. My sister needs me more than he does right now, so I text back and tell him Bee isn't well and I need to stay home, but I'll be up to see him in the morning.

I get a sad face emoticon back.

☹ I miss you

But I understand. Hope you guys had a good time
at the movies and that Bee is OK xx

We've all been in bed barely half an hour when I hear Mum yell out. I run to her room and she has the light on. Bee is convulsing on the bed, her lips blue and her eyes rolled back. She is jerking, her hands and wrists twisted like claws.

'It's a bad one,' Mum says.

'Call an ambulance?'

'Not yet. Let's give her a minute, see if she comes out of it.'

I drop to the floor beside the bed. It's the most awful, help-less feeling in the world to see my sister like this and to not be able to do anything to help.

'We're here, Bee,' I reassure her, trying to keep the panic from my voice. 'It's OK, baby girl, Mummy and Maddy are here.'

She continues to jerk, her body rigid. I hold her hair back from her face so I can watch to make sure she is breathing. Her tongue is lolling in her mouth and I worry as always that she will choke on it. She takes a sharp breath through her nose, then another one.

'That's a girl, Bee, keep breathing. Good girl. Mummy and Maddy are here.'

Mum rubs her back, frowning.

'How long has it been?' I ask.

'Not long, a minute maybe? Two? I called you as soon as it started.'

I feel completely powerless and I see it reflected on Mum's face. The person we love most in the world, her skin white, the tendons in her neck taut and stretching as her face cranes upwards, and there is nothing we can do to stop what she's going through. I wouldn't wish this on my worst enemy.

'It's OK, Bee, it's OK, girl. Mummy and Maddy are here.'

Another ten seconds pass but it feels like hours, then some-thing changes and she stops jerking. I register the moment she comes back to us as her eyes try to focus and she frowns and starts to whimper.

'Hey, Bee, it's OK, baby, we're here. Just breathe.'

She blinks rapidly and tries to get up, but we hold her down gently. She is always weak and disorientated after a fit. She takes short shallow breaths.

'Big breaths, Bee, come on. That's a girl,' Mum tells her.

She starts to moan and tries to speak but nothing that comes out of her mouth makes any sense. We straighten her body and roll her on to her side. Mum rubs her back while I gently rub her forehead. We reassure her that we are here and that she is OK.

It is all that we can do.

Mum calls work the next morning and tells them about Bee and they give her the day off. She is quiet and complaining of a sore head, but she is OK. Or at least she will be. Right now she is sad and understandably feeling sorry for herself.

'Go and see Albert,' Mum says after I finish clearing the breakfast dishes. She has intuitively guessed I am torn between my sister and Albert. She and Bee are snuggled up together on the couch, a blanket over them. Bee is watching *Noddy* on her MP3 player.

'Are you sure?'

She nods and pulls Bee in tighter, kissing her on the head. 'Yes. We're fine. Honestly.'

'I'll just go for a little while,' I say gratefully, grabbing my keys from the bowl. 'But I'll have my phone on so if you need me just call and I'll come home straight away.'

I am tired but I can't wait to see Albert, and I almost break into a run the closer I get to his room. It's been twenty-four hours since I've seen him, the longest since his accident.

'Miss me?' I ask loudly as I burst through his door frame.

He's not there. His room is completely cleaned out. No sign that he was ever there. Even his name has gone from the door. At first I get excited, thinking maybe they've discharged him. But then I realise that he would have let me know if that was the case. So I figure he's been moved, like they've mentioned might possibly happen as his condition has improved.

I go to the nurses' station. There is only one nurse I recognise and she's the one who growled at Albert and I for sharing a bed. She looks up at me when I cough nervously.

'Hi, Steph,' I say, smiling. 'Do you know where Albert has been moved to?'

She studies my face for a moment.

'Maddy, isn't it?'

'Yes.'

'Come with me.'

I follow her down the corridor and through a few doors. We turn left, then right, then right again. She stops outside a set of doors and pushes an intercom. It beeps and a voice echoes through it.

'Yes?'

'It's Steph. I have Albert's girlfriend with me.'

There is a buzzing sound and the door clicks unlocked. She pushes it open and gestures me through. I have no idea where we are. She leads me down a set of stairs and then points to an open door.

'There,' she says.

'Thanks.' I say, revising my earlier opinion of her. It was nice of her to show me the way in person instead of leaving me to get lost on own. I'm almost through the door when she calls my name.

'Maddy.'

I turn. 'Yes?'

'You have my condolences.' Then she turns and walks away.

I frown, not understanding. Then I hear a sob from within the room and I look inside. Albert's mum is sitting on a black faux leather couch. She has her head in her hands and the sobs are coming from her. Colin is standing in front of the window, his preferred position. His hands are laced together behind his back, his body stiff like he is at attention. Louis is leaning back in another chair, his feet crossed in front of him. He is kind of staring at the wall and doesn't seem to notice when I walk into the room. The atmosphere is cold. I feel my blood run cold too. Something isn't right.

'Wendy?'

She looks up, and I reel. Her face is puffy and red, her eyes glassy with tears. What I see in her eyes makes me recoil in horror. Grief, raw and weeping. She is in pain, so much pain.

'Oh, Maddy,' she wails. 'Where have you been?'

'At home. Where is Albert?'

At the mention of his name she starts to sob again. Proper, deep sobs, from the depths of her belly that shake her whole body violently. I start to panic. What the hell has happened in the last twenty-four hours? Where is he? Has he had a setback?

I whirl to Louis, demanding answers. 'Where is he?'

It takes him a moment to focus on my face and I see the instant he recognises me.

'You,' he says. '*Now* you decide to show up. Well, you're too late.'

I whirl from the room and grab the first blue uniformed arm I see. 'Where is Albert?' I demand, tugging at it.

The arm belongs to a doctor. He gently prises my fingers off. 'I'm sorry, are you family?'

'Yes. Kind of. I'm his girlfriend.'

He reads the panic in my face and exhales. 'I'm sorry but Albert passed away last night.'

I stagger away from him, my hands flying to my mouth. What is he talking about? 'No, he didn't. He was fine. You guys said he was fine.'

'They fuckin' lied.' Louis has followed me out and is standing in the doorway, glaring at the doctor. He looks furious, like he wants to hit something.

'What are you talking about?' I look madly from Louis to the doctor and back again. 'No one is making any sense.'

The doctor gestures to the room. 'Please. I will try and answer your questions.'

'I'm not moving until you tell me what the hell is going on and where Albert is.'

He nods. 'Very well. Although I'm afraid that it's all

guesswork at this stage. We won't know anything for sure until we have the autopsy results.'

Autopsy?

'We believe Albert suffered an infection in the brain, which last night developed into sepsis. As soon as we realised we started to treat him but he went downhill fast. The infection travelled very quickly into his major organs and he went into septic shock. It caused him to have a stroke, from which, I'm sorry to say, he did not recover.'

I can hear the words coming out of his mouth, and I know these words, I know what they mean, but in this context they just don't make any sense.

'You're wrong,' I tell him, shaking my head fervently. 'You've got him confused with someone else. Albert is doing great. You guys said so yourself.'

'I know. Once again, I'm very sorry for your loss, I am. But I'm afraid I can't comment any further until the autopsy and a standard internal investigation has taken place.'

'You mean while you scramble to try and cover your butts,' Louis growls.

The doctor winces. 'Excuse me, I need to be somewhere else, but if you need anything please let one of the nurses know.'

He walks off quickly, clearly keen to be somewhere that is anywhere but here. Louis turns and disappears back into the room. I feel like I'm in a different dimension. Nothing seems real, from the dark blue carpet to the bright, fluorescent lighting.

I'm dreaming?

A nightmare.

Where am I?

I feel like I am floating above my body, replaying the words over and over on repeat.

It caused him to have a stroke . . .

. . . *he did not recover.*

I hear a guttural wailing again, and I think it's Wendy. Then I realise it's me.

Maddy

Albert's funeral takes place on a Tuesday, a week after his death.

The funeral, like the week preceding it, is a blur.

A sea of black.

A sea of sorrow.

I sit beside his open casket in his lounge room while his friends and family, people I have never met, arrive to pay their respects.

Children peer ghoulishly into the coffin, their eyes wide.

I've heard people say that when someone dies and they are embalmed they look the same, just as if they are sleeping.

It's not true.

He looks like my Albert, yes. But a horrible version of himself. His skin looks like it's sliding off his face, like silly putty. They have left the bandage on his head to cover the wound and the fact that his beautiful hair had been shaven.

A girl my age comes and cries so much she leaves a wet circle of tears on his shirtsleeve. She strokes his hand and tells him she is sorry she hurt him. An ex-girlfriend, I decide. I can see that she loved him once, too. We regard each other, quietly acknowledging our common ground.

At night I go home and sleep on and off, tortured by nightmares and the knowledge that I let him down.

I wasn't there when he needed me the most.

We file into church at one-thirty on that Tuesday afternoon and I sit in the back seat with Mum and Bee, so that we can make a quick escape if she starts to get loud or try to grab people. Halfway through the service she starts to sing 'If You're Happy and You Know It'. People turn to look at us, so Mum ushers her outside with an apologetic smile.

'We'll be outside when you're ready,' she whispers to me.

It all feels like it's happening to someone else.

None of it feels like Albert. I look at the sea of black, and the dark mahogany coffin with its arrangement of white lilies on top, and none of it feels like him. The hymns, while solemn and suited to the occasion, do not suit *him*.

He wouldn't want any of this, I think.

I hold it together until the end, when the coffin starts to be lowered into the floor. I didn't know that was going to happen, and it catches me out. Until now, I have still had him with me, in my sights. Even after the coffin was sealed two days ago he was physically still here. But now the coffin is disappearing in front of my eyes, and I'm not ready for it. I'm not ready for that final goodbye. He is going somewhere without me, somewhere I'll never see him, or touch him again.

He's already gone, I know that.

But while his body was still here I could pretend he was here with me.

I lose it. I watch it disappear into the floor and be swallowed up, and I lose it. I weep for everything I have lost. Everything the world has lost. This beautiful, amazing, kind and wonderful man, who never did a damn thing to hurt anyone, where is the justice in this?

I stare at the spot he disappeared from while people file from the church. I hear talking, laughter, as if people have already started to move on with their lives. How can this be happening? Wendy touches my arm on her way out the door.

'You'll come to the house. For the wake,' she says, and it's more of a statement than a question.

'I wasn't planning on it.'

'Of course you will. You have to. I won't take no for an answer.'

'OK.' I nod. She is clogging up the aisle and Colin is frowning at me.

Mum and Bee drop me off, promising to pick me up again whenever I am ready, even if it's in five minutes. 'Just call when you're ready.'

Sitting at the table, hemmed in by elderly relatives who fill their plates with mini quiches and triangle sandwiches with the crusts cut off, I listen as they lament the fact they only see each other at 'weddings and funerals'. When I can't take any more of their small talk about the weather or the twenty pounds cousin Shirley has regained since her gastric bypass operation, I push to my feet. I need to get out of here, I can't breathe. Before I leave, I seek out Wendy, weaving my way through a room full of strangers, the odd face vaguely familiar. She is standing in the lounge, her back to the room, looking out over her garden. I stand just behind her and wait for her to feel my presence. Her face turns to the side, she is crying silently.

'Maddy.' She sniffs, turning to face me and taking my hands. 'Thank you for coming.'

'Of course.'

Her eyes roam about my face. 'You knew him better than anyone here, I think.'

'Apart from you.'

She gives a small, conceding smile.

'It went OK, today, don't you think?'

She seems to be seeking my approval and I nod, because it doesn't matter what I think, but she sees my hesitation and her shoulders droop.

'He wouldn't have liked any of it, would he,' she says quietly.

'No. But it doesn't matter.'

'It does. I wanted to make this day perfect for him but I ...' she trails off and glances over my shoulder. I follow her eyes and see Colin and Louis standing under the arch between the lounge and dining room. They are watching us.

I put out a hand and touch Wendy's arm reassuringly. 'It's OK. Albert would understand.'

Tears well in her eyes. 'I failed him.'

317

'No, of course not.'

'You don't understand. I don't mean just with the funeral.'

'I know. But please, don't do this. He loved you very much. He wouldn't want you torturing yourself with guilt.'

She takes a deep breath and exhales it heavily. 'I can see why he loved you.'

She uses the past tense and the words sting.

'I wish these people would go,' she says, looking around the room. 'These kind of things are more to benefit the people left behind than the one who has gone, don't you think?'

I nod. 'I'm going to get going now.'

'Oh, I wasn't meaning you,' she says, horrified to think I've taken it that way.

'I know,' I reassure her. 'But Mum and Bee are waiting.' The lie trips easily off my tongue.

'OK. But please stay in touch.'

'Sure.'

I think we both know I'm lying. I turn to go and she says my name one more time so I stop.

'I'll let you know when we have a date for burying the ashes,' she says. 'In case you'd like to come.'

I hadn't thought beyond today, what would happen with Albert's remains.

'Buried?'

She nods. 'Yes, on his grandparents' grave down in the Waiarapa. A little cemetery in Carterton.'

'You mean buried, as in, in the ground?'

She gives me a strange look. 'Of course. Why?'

My conversation with Albert, all those months ago at the Tree Trust, flashes into my head. 'No,' I say, shaking my head. 'That's not what he wants.'

'What do you mean?' Wendy looks puzzled. 'Did he say something?'

'Yes, he did. It was a few months ago when we—'

'You shouldn't be here,' Louis says, interrupting us. People close to us stop talking and eyes swivel to see who it is that he is talking to.

'Stop it, Louis,' Wendy says tiredly. 'This isn't the time or the place.'

'Well, she shouldn't,' he snaps. 'Crying and pretending like she cared about him.'

'I loved him,' I say. 'Not that I have to justify that to you.'

'Louis, please,' his mum begs.

'If you loved him why weren't you at the hospital? He wanted you, before he stroked and lost consciousness, he kept asking for you. Why weren't you there?'

'I didn't know,' I say, my voice breaking. He has just broken my heart all over again. I'd been hoping Albert hadn't known something was wrong, that he'd simply slipped away.

His face is red and mottled with his rage, but I see something else in his eyes too. Pain. It puzzles me. His anger is disproportionate, too venomous. He never wanted me around anyway, why does he care so much? Then I understand. He is directing his own guilt and anger towards me, his own failings as a brother. For the first time I realise that he did care for Albert, in his own, weird way.

319

'Dad tried to call you,' he continues 'He left you messages. And you just waltz in the next day and pretend you had no idea?'

'What are you talking about? I never got any messages.'

Wendy, a shadow of the woman she was a week ago, studies my face. She can see I am genuinely confused and she looks confused along with me. I see comprehension dawn. She turns to her husband.

'Did you call Maddy?' she asks levelly.

'What?' He looks shifty.

'In the hospital. That night. Did you call Maddy when I asked you to?'

'I don't know,' he brushes her off. 'I don't remember. There was a lot going on. My son was dying.'

'Oh no, Colin.' Her whole body sags. 'You didn't, did you?'

For a moment it looks like he's thinking about lying, then he stands up straight and his face turns defiant.

'No, I didn't call her. At a time like that he needed his family around him, not his latest crush.'

How easily he dismisses what Albert and I felt for each other.

Wendy puts her drink down on the counter and shakes her head at him.

'That was *not* your call to make,' she says, and walks out of the room.

Maddy

'Are you sure about this?' Mum asks quietly from the back seat.

I nod. 'More sure than I've ever been about anything in my entire life.'

'Then that's sure enough for me.'

'What's the plan?' Kyle asks. He is behind the steering wheel, and is taking this expedition seriously.

'Why are you dressed like that?' I ask him.

He is dressed head to toe in black, including a turtleneck jersey, despite the balmy afternoon outside.

'What? This is how all the getaway drivers dress,' he answers defensively. 'Haven't you seen any Bond films?'

I turn away from him and study Albert's house. Colin's car isn't in the drive. Wendy's is.

'Shop,' Bee demands. She is in the back seat beside Mum because we had nowhere to leave her and no one to leave her with. I'm glad she's here though; it feels right that she is. She is excited because she thinks we're going to the shop and that usually means her favourite biscuits. Mum passes her over her colouring book and pencils.

'No plan. I'm just going to wing it.' I reach for the door handle.

'OK,' Mum says. 'Do you want us to come in with you? For moral support?'

'Shop,' says Bee.

I think about it. It's tempting, but I need to do this on my own. 'Thanks, but I'm OK.'

'What if you can't convince her?'

I shake my head, unwilling to accept that's even a possibility. 'I don't know. I'll cross that bridge when I come to it.'

She smiles sadly and reaches out a hand to cup my cheek. 'Oh, darling. If I could take the hurt away I would, a thousand times over. We're here for you, me and Bee. We're the three Baxter girls, remember?'

'Ahem,' Kyle says.

'And Kyle,' Mum adds.

I flick Kyle a grateful look. He didn't have to come along, but had a day off and was bored and wanted to help. He's been a good friend to me while I've been locked in my own little world of grief. Unable to afford time off work but barely able to function while I'm there, he's been holding down the fort and covering for me so I don't find myself fired on top of everything else.

'Thank you,' I say to him. 'For this and everything.'

'You're welcome.' He smiles. 'But just so you know, if

anything happens and the cops get called we're out of here,' he says. 'No point all of us going down.'

'Shop,' says Bee.

'Oh shut up, Kyle,' Mum scolds. 'We'll be right here waiting when you come out.'

I take a deep breath and get out of the car.

When Wendy opens the door to my knock I try not to show how startled I am at her appearance. She has changed so much in such a short period. Her clothes are loose and her face gaunt. She blinks at the afternoon sun behind me before recognition dawns.

'Maddy,' she says. 'How lovely to see you.'

'Can I come in?'

'Of course.' She stands to the side and opens the door.

As soon as I'm inside I start looking, but there's no sign of it in the kitchen. Wendy goes to the bench and fills up the jug with water.

'Coffee?' she asks. 'Or tea?'

'Coffee, thanks.'

'How do you take it?'

'Milk but no sugar.'

'Biscuit?'

'No thanks.'

She flicks the switch and the low rumble of the water boiling fills the silence. Neither of us speaks while she pours the water and stirs the cups. Then she passes me mine and gestures towards the arch that leads to the lounge.

'Shall we?'

'After you.'

I see it as soon as I walk in. It is just sitting there in the centre of the coffee table. The sight of it takes my breath away.

'Is that . . . ?'

She follows the direction of my eyes. 'Yes.'

'May I?'

She nods.

I put my coffee down and sit on the couch. Hesitantly, I put out a hand and run it over the small grey container. It is cool to the touch, the opposite of the man whose ashes it contains. His name is inscribed on the end of it.

'Still so hard to believe, isn't it?' she says, sitting down beside me.

'Yes.'

'I keep expecting him to walk through that door covered in horse muck.'

'I know what you mean. Every time my phone beeps there is a moment where I forget what's happened and I get excited, thinking it's a message from him, but then I remember. And every time it nearly kills me.'

She takes a deep breath and exhales it slowly. 'I guess it will get easier with time. At least that's what people keep telling me. I don't know how losing a child could ever stop hurting though.'

She puts her coffee down and holds out a hand. I take it.

'I'm so sorry about what my husband did,' she says. 'It was unforgivable.'

I look at my knees. I've been trying not to think about it, but this might be the only chance I get to have some answers.

'Did he know? That he was dying?'

She shakes her head. 'No, I don't think so.' She picks up her coffee again and blows on the top to cool it down. 'It all happened so fast. One minute we were chatting and then he said he was feeling dizzy. He started to say some weird things, things that didn't make any sense. I called the nurse and she said she'd get a doctor to look at him, but you know what hospitals are like. Their resources are thinly stretched and I don't think she thought he was a priority. By the time the doctor came I thought he was asleep, but he was unconscious.' She looks me in the eye and shrugs helplessly. 'He just never woke up.'

'Louis said he was asking for me.'

'No, well not in the literal sense. We were talking about you though, before it happened. He loved you so much you know.'

Her words rip the air right out of my lungs and I have to swallow hard to force breath back into them. It means a lot to me that she understands that what Albert and I had was real. It may not have been tangible, but it existed. I want to cry, but I have to be strong. 'I loved him too,' I tell her. 'I always will.'

'I know. I'm very grateful he had those last few months with you. You made him so happy.' She fusses with a cushion. 'I hadn't seen him that happy in a long time.'

I hear a clock chime in the hallway and it reminds me that Colin might be home at any moment.

'The reason I'm here,' I say, 'is that I've been thinking about what you said when we were here, after the funeral, about Albert's ashes.'

'Oh yes, I remember now, you started to say something, about a conversation?'

I take a deep breath and tell her about that day at the Tree Trust, back when Albert and I were just starting to get to know each other. It seems a lifetime ago, and so much has happened since then, but I can still hear his words and see his face when he shuddered at the very thought of being buried in the cold, dark earth.

'He hated the thought of his grandmother down there,' I finish. 'He said he never wanted to suffer the same fate.'

She collapses softly back against the couch when I am finished talking. 'I really should have guessed that for myself, you know. I remember when I used to take him there, he'd always be reluctant to get out of the car, and at her grave he'd stand well back, never saying a word. He couldn't wait to get back in the car and leave.'

'I'm glad you understand,' I say gratefully. 'And it's your decision, of course, ultimately, whatever you choose to do. But I have an idea for where you could put them, somewhere I know he'd feel at home. If you'd like to hear it?'

She leans forward again and nods.

I am just describing the place to her and seeing her face light up for the first time since I arrived, when we hear an angry snort that makes us both jump.

'How dare you.'

Both Wendy and I jump, startled by Colin's low, angry voice. Neither of us had heard him come in. He crosses the lounge quickly to stand beside his wife, placing a hand on her shoulder protectively.

'What are you doing here, upsetting my wife? Can't you see she's grieving? She has just lost her son.'

I stand up and face him. I will not be bullied by this man. 'I'm well aware of that.'

'You need to leave. Now.'

'It's OK, Colin,' Wendy says reassuringly. 'Maddy is here about Albert's ashes. I think you need to hear her out.'

He frowns. 'What about them?'

'Albert wouldn't want to be buried on his grandmother's grave,' she says. 'He would hate that. He told Maddy that himself, a few months ago.' She turns to me. 'Tell him, Maddy.'

I open my mouth but Colin raises one hand dismissively.

'I don't want to hear it. The gall of you, thinking you can turn up here and have any say in the matter.'

'That's not fair. She loved him as much as we did,' Wendy says. 'And he adored her. Just hear her out. Please. For my sake.'

'No.' He shakes his head. 'This has nothing to do with her.'

'Why are you being so stubborn?'

'Because *I* make the decisions around here, and I will not be dictated to by *her*.' He points a finger at me and shakes it angrily.

'What about me? Do I get any say in the matter?' Wendy's voice has grown in strength, and she is looking at Colin as if he is a stranger. Too late, Colin realises he is being dismissive of her feelings.

'Of course you do,' he says. 'And we'll discuss it later, in private.'

'No.' She shakes her head. 'There's nothing to discuss. It's very simple. We were thinking of what *we'd* like instead of what Albert would have wanted.'

Colin snorts. 'You know how fickle he was.'

Wendy steps back like he has slapped her. 'Even in death you can't resist having a go at him?'

'I didn't mean anything by it.'

'You never do.' She exhales slowly and then looks directly at me. 'Maddy, I think it's the perfect choice. And I'm grateful you had the courage to come here and stand up for Albert's wishes. Now if you'll just excuse me a moment, Colin and I need to have a discussion in private.'

I nod. 'OK, I'll go.'

'No,' she says quickly. 'Please wait here.'

I frown, puzzled. She seems to be trying to convey something to me with her eyes but whatever it is I'm not getting it.

'Colin.' Wendy gestures. 'The hallway, now, please.'

He makes an annoyed noise, but turns and stalks out of the room. I stand beside the couch as she follows him, unsure why she has asked me to stay. Then just as she reaches the doorway she turns, her voice quiet and urgent.

'Take them,' she hisses. 'Do it, Maddy, do it for Albert.'

'You want me to . . . ?' I point at the box, unsure.

She gives a little nod and then disappears from sight.

I hesitate for only a second, and then adrenaline kicks in and I scoop up the box of ashes, walking as quickly and as quietly as I can. The front door makes a creaking noise when I open it so I leave it open, taking the steps in one jump and running up the garden path to where Kyle is parked on the street.

'Go,' I pant, climbing in. 'Quickly.' I pray that this is not one of those times the car decides to play up on us.

'What's that?' Mum asks, looking over the seat at the box. 'Is that . . . ?'

'Go!'

Kyle turns the key. The car roars to life.

'Where are we going?' he asks.

'Shop,' says Bee.

I am watching the house. The door has just opened and Colin is at the top of the steps. He sees me and starts shouting something, his face red with rage.

'Just go, I'll tell you when to turn,' I yell at Kyle. He floors the pedal and we're off, just as Colin starts to run up the path. He's too late though and reaches the footpath as we pull away from the kerb.

'I'm sorry,' I mouth to him out the window as we drive past. I see Wendy standing at the bottom of the steps. She clasps her hands together in front of her mouth and smiles as we drive away.

I exhale my breath once we are around the corner, travelling fast, putting more and more space between us.

I whisper to the box on my lap, tears streaming from my eyes. 'I'm taking you home.'

Maddy

When we pull into the car park the sun is low on the horizon. The sky is a vibrant orange. It is breathtaking.

'Seaside,' Bee says. She loves to look at the ocean and listen to the waves, but she refuses to walk on sand barefoot. When we've tried in the past she curls her toes and tries to lift both feet up at the same time. It's been an epic fail, so we haven't brought her here in years.

But today she has her sneakers on and she is so excited by the sight of the water she willingly lets Mum lead her down the dunes and towards the water. I carry the box of ashes under my arm, breathing in the salt air and remembering the last time I was here. Tears spring up. It wasn't that long ago. I am assailed by memories. We were so happy.

'Is this where you two used to come?' Mum asks softly, looking around.

'Yes.'

'I can see why. It's beautiful.'

There is no one here. Just us and the empty ocean, the sky and the hills. It is incredibly peaceful, and exactly where Albert would like to be.

'He loved it here. You should have seen him on the water, it was like he was a part of it.'

Mum stands back with an arm around Bee as I walk down towards the water. Kyle stands behind her, his hands on Mum's shoulders.

Suddenly we hear the sound of tyres on the gravel road, travelling fast. The car pulls into the car park with a skid. I turn, curious, and as soon as I see it my stomach sinks.

It's Colin.

He gets out of the driver's door, Wendy following, but she is slower. I haven't come this far to let Albert down now though. I don't care if he arrests me and throws away the key, I'm doing this for the love of my life. I wipe the tears away angrily and run to the water.

'Stop,' he calls as he runs down the beach. 'Don't you dare open that box.'

I wade through the water until it is just above my knees. The waves swirl around me protectively, as if they sense why I am here.

'Don't come any closer,' I warn him.

Bee is picking up bits of driftwood and throwing them into the water. 'Splash,' she says, oblivious to anything that is happening.

He stops at the waterline. For the first time I see a look of

331

vulnerability flash across his face, but it's quickly replaced by anger, leaving me in doubt as to whether I saw it or not.

'You're in a lot of trouble,' he says, speaking slowly and clearly as if he is a hostage negotiator. 'But if you come out of the water now and give me back that box it'll go easier on you.'

'Go easier on me?' I call back to him. 'I'm not doing this to upset you or defy you, whatever you think. I'm doing this because it's the right thing to do.'

'Come out of the water,' he repeats.

I ignore him and look over my shoulder, out towards the open sea. 'Did you ever watch your son surf?'

He frowns. 'What's that got to do with anything?'

'Splash,' Bee says.

'You have no idea do you, what you've missed out on. What an amazing, *incredible* man your son was. But he was never good enough for you.'

'You don't know what you're talking about,' he says. '*If* I treated him harshly, it was only because I knew he could do better. Better than working in some stable for the rest of his life for stuff all money. And better than this.' He gestures to us all. 'You and your dysfunctional family. And I was right to be worried, he's dead because of you.'

My mother gasps. She reaches over and plucks a piece of driftwood from Bee's hand and hurls it at the back of Colin's head.

'What the hell,' he yelps as it connects. He reaches up a hand to feel for blood. 'Jesus, you're all crazy. That's assault on an officer.'

'Stuff you, pig!' my mother shouts.

I feel a bubble of inappropriate laughter pop up. I've never felt more connected to my mother as I do in that moment.

'You tell him,' Kyle yells out.

'Right, stuff this,' Colin says, starting to wade into the water. 'You asked for it.'

'Enough.'

Wendy says the word quietly but with enough emotive power to make us all freeze and look at her. Except Bee, of course, who says, 'Splash,' and throws another piece of wood. Because she has just seen my mother do it she aims it at Colin. Luckily for him she is a lousy shot and it misses.

'Wendy?' Colin pauses to look at her questioningly.

'I said, *that's enough*,' Wendy repeats. She walks down to where her husband stands and stops a foot in front of him.

'I can't let her get away with this,' he says.

'Can't? Or won't?'

He splutters. 'Does it matter?'

'I want a divorce,' Wendy says.

'What?'

'You heard me. I want a divorce.'

'You don't mean that.'

'I do.' She nods her head. 'I really do. I don't know why I stayed married to you as long as I have. But I'm done. I've had enough.'

'You're just grieving,' he says, then glares at me. 'And *this* isn't helping.'

'No. I mean, yes, of course I am. But this isn't because of that. This is me making the best decision I have made in a long time. If Albert's death has shown me anything, it's that life is too short to waste with an *asshole like you*.' She spits out the last three words bitterly.

He reels back as if she has slapped him, but fails to realise that his shoes have sunken into the sand while he's been standing there. He loses his balance and falls backwards, landing in the shallows.

Mum snorts with laughter.

I bite my lip.

Colin gapes up at Wendy, completely speechless. She turns to me.

'Thank you,' she says. 'For everything. I've been too scared to make changes for far too long. But not any more.' She shakes her head. 'You stood up for what you knew was right. The least I can do is the same.'

She looks around, her face serene as if she has suddenly gained inner peace and strength.

'Yes. You were absolutely right.' She nods. 'This is the perfect place. Let's do this.'

She bumps through the waves until she is at my side. The sea is green and choppy, and the waves kick up and splash us both. I smile through my tears, feeling like Albert is here with us.

'He loved riding the waves,' I tell her, my voice breaking. 'Now he can ride them for ever.'

'Yes.' She smiles through her tears. 'He would like that.'

I prise open the lid and she gently lifts out the plastic bag and its contents. Seeing them gives me a shock. How can one person be reduced to so little? A handful of dust is it?

All that is left of the boy I fell in love with?

'No,' Wendy says firmly, seeing the distraught expression on my face. 'This? This is not him. He is here, in our hearts.' She presses her free hand to her chest. 'And here, all around us.' She gestures to the sky and the ocean. 'As long as there are stars in the sky, he will always be with us.'

Then she rips open the bag and sprinkles Albert's ashes into the water, while a blazing sun sets over the horizon. After the last pieces fall and the swirling water takes them away, we stand arm in arm and watch, as the ocean currents carry them off on adventures unknown.

Maddy

The envelope itself, when it arrives on a sunny Friday morning three months after Albert's funeral, gives no indication as to the magnitude of its contents. So plain is it that it sits on the dining table all weekend until my mother finally asks, 'Did you not see you have mail?'

'It'll be a bill,' I say dismissively. 'Or a reminder that I'm due for my pap smear. It can wait.'

'It might say you've won the lottery,' Mum says.

'Yeah right. You have to buy tickets in order for that to happen.'

'Well, open it anyway. I'm curious even if you aren't.'

I am in the middle of helping Bee colour in a cassette cover so I just shrug. 'If you care that much, *you* open it.'

She doesn't need to be told twice and has a finger under the flap on the back before I can blink. She is silent for thirty seconds as she reads and then she gives a little gasp. 'Oh.'

I look up at her. 'What?'

'Oh Maddy.'

'What?'

She shakes her head and gives me a weird, emotional look that is halfway between a smile and a grimace.

'What?' I put down my felt pen and look at her. 'Is it bad news?'

She shakes her head. 'No, not at all. The opposite.'

'As usual you're not making any sense.'

She takes a deep breath and looks down at the paper again. '"Dear Madonna Baxter",' she reads. '"It gives us great pleasure to extend to you our congratulations for your winning entry in our inaugural photography competition."'

I frown, confused. 'What competition?'

Mum turns the paper around so I can see the letterhead. It means nothing to me.

'According to this it was run by our local council,' she explains. 'Don't you remember entering?'

'Of course I don't, because I *didn't*.' I get up off my chair and take the letter off her, frowning at it. 'They must be confused.'

'They don't sound it,' Mum says. 'It has your full name and address and everything. Look what you've won.'

I scan the rest of the letter. When I get to the bit about the prize, I give a sharp intake of breath.

'This can't be right,' I say, backing up till I feel the chair hit my legs.

'Five thousand dollars,' Mum squeals. 'Sounds about right to me.'

'An apprenticeship with Oliver Hapeta?' I sit down, feeling faint.

'Oh yes, and that too. Have you heard of him?'

I give her an incredulous look. 'Sorry? Have I ... are you serious? *Have I heard of him?*'

'I take it that's a yes.'

'He's only like, the most *amazing* photographer in the area. His stuff is just incredible. So innovative, he's a genius.'

'Oh well. You'll be able to tell him that when you start working with him.'

'I can't.'

'Why not?'

'Because he's brilliant.'

'So are you.' She taps the letter. 'And they clearly think so too. Believe it, Maddy, you won. I'm so thrilled for you. You deserve this.'

'But I don't understand.' I look at the back of the letter for clues. 'I didn't enter a competition. This has to be a mistake.'

She picks up the envelope and looks inside. 'There's something else in here.'

She passes it over to me. I tip it upside down and shake it a few times until something falls out on the floor.

'What is it?' she asks.

I pick it up and turn it over and instantly I freeze. All noise disappears into the background like a vacuum just sucked all the air out of the room.

I recognise the photo instantly. The same one hangs on the wall above my bed. Albert's face looks up at me. He is luminous, full of life, laughter dancing around his lips and in his eyes as he looks at the fern frond in his hand. It is the photo I took all those months ago at the Tree Trust.

'Well?' Mum cranes to look over my shoulder. 'Oh.'

'It must have been him,' I say as realisation dawns. 'I gave him a copy of this photo. He must have entered it.'

'He believed in you. Your talent.'

'More than I did myself.'

'And he was right. You won.' She bubbles up with excited laughter. 'Oh, Maddy this is perfect. You have to take this apprenticeship. It will be life-changing for you. *And* it says that Oliver Whatsit guy is local so you don't even have to leave home if that's what's worrying you. And I'll work my shifts around you, we can make this work.'

I trace my finger over Albert's face, feeling tears prick up. I miss him so much. It doesn't surprise me that he did this. It's perfectly him, thinking of others, pushing people to achieve their dreams. Something I read in the letter niggles at me and I pick it up to reread it. The theme of the competition.

Fresh Starts, New Beginnings.

The irony of it is almost painful. He obviously entered the photo because the budding fern frond fitted the theme. But, at the same time, he and I were on the threshold of a new beginning too. The start of our journey together. And now, here I am, teetering on the verge of another new beginning, all because of him.

I can't think under her hopeful gaze. 'I need to go out. Will you guys be OK without me for a few hours?'

'Of course. Where are you going?'

'I don't know.'

I do though. I need to go to the one place I can go where I'll feel closer to him.

There is only one other car parked on the grass in the shade of a pohutukawa tree when I pull into the car park. The late-afternoon sun is warming and reassuring. The beach is deserted, whoever the car belongs to is nowhere in sight.

It's the first time I've been back here since we released his ashes into the sea. I couldn't face it. Not the memories or the heartache they bring. I have days where I think I'm doing OK, and the pain is more like a dull background ache, present but bearable. Those days I see a way forward, difficult, at first, like a newborn foal learning to walk. But then there are the days when I wake up from dreaming about him and the pain is intense and breathtaking in its rawness and I weep hot tears into my pillow at the unfairness of it all. Those days I torture myself, remembering every detail of our time together. Every detail of *him*. The feel of his skin, the smell of him, the way he looked just before he kissed me. Those days I barely function, just go through the motions. Grief is a funny old thing. It ebbs and flows just like the water lapping the shore.

I kick off my shoes at the high-tide mark and walk slowly down towards the water, stopping just short. His final resting place. I know, of course, that his actual ashes are most likely far away by now, carried off by the currents to distant shores. But as long as there is water in the ocean I know he is here, somewhere. Riding the water just as he loved.

'I miss you,' I say softly, and the wind sighs.

I sit, just above the waterline, and I allow myself to openly cry for him. For us, and what we lost. When I have exhausted myself of tears, I bury my head on my knees and just sit, remembering.

'Maddy?'

The voice is unsure, quiet, almost snatched away by the breeze. I think I have imagined it. Then it comes again, louder.

'Maddy?'

I look up to see Wendy a few metres away. She looks different. The few other times I've seen her she has always been wearing trousers and shirts in dark navy or green. Today she is wearing a long flowing white dress, her hair is loose and wavy from the salt in the air and she is carrying a pair of strappy flat sandals. Bangles jingle on her wrist.

'I thought that was you,' she says, walking over to sit beside me. She notices my tear-stained cheeks and clucks her tongue.

'Oh, Maddy,' she says. 'Don't, or you'll start me off too.'

I wipe my tears away. 'Sorry.'

She sighs. 'No, I'm sorry. Of course you should cry. It's only natural. Telling someone who is suffering the way you are not to show it is something that Colin would have done. I have thirty years of bad habits to break.'

At the mention of his name I stiffen and peer behind us. 'He's not ... ?'

'Here? No.'

'Good.'

'As far as I know he doesn't come here, but then I haven't seen him for a while so I could be wrong on that.'

I stare at her. 'You mean, you really did it? You left him?'

She smiles and links an arm through mine. 'I did. Oh I should have done it years ago, I know that now. Still, better late than never.'

I can't say anything for a while. I'm too stunned by her news. 'Wow,' I say eventually. 'Albert would be proud of you.'

She closes her eyes for a moment at the mention of his name. 'Thank you,' she says when she opens them again. 'That means a lot.'

'So what are you doing here?'

'Same as you I suspect.'

I grimace. 'Seeking insight?'

She gives me a long look. 'Not so much insight, no. I come here because I feel close to him here. I like to walk up to the headland.' She points down along the beach to where the land extends out far in the distance. 'It's quite a walk but it gives me time to think.'

'Maybe I'll try that one day.'

'What are you seeking insight for, if you don't mind me asking?'

I tell her about the letter that arrived and Albert's part in it.

'I'm just not sure whether it's the right thing to do or not,' I finish by saying. 'I have so many other things to consider.'

She shakes her head with a smile. 'Even after he's gone that boy finds ways to make me proud. So what exactly are you worried about?'

I shrug. 'Failure. Not being good enough. Maybe that photo was a fluke and I'll disappoint everyone.'

'Oh, I doubt that,' she says. 'Albert clearly thought you had talent, and even though I may be ever so slightly biased, I can still say with absolute certainty that he had a good eye for that kind of stuff. He would never have entered you if he didn't think you had something special.'

'Maybe. That's not the only reason stopping me though.' I watch as a container ship slowly moves across the horizon.

'Look, Maddy. I hope I'm not speaking out of place here, but I do know a little about your situation. Albert mentioned your sense of responsibility towards your sister when he was in the hospital and I think it's admirable, I really do. But I also know that you can't put your life on hold because of her. You're young, you have so much ahead of you. If there is one thing you should take away from Albert's death, it's that we never know how long we're here for.'

I wince at the cliché.

'I know, I know—' she holds up her hands '—it's a cliché, yes. But it's oh so true. It's up to you to make the most of the time you have. Don't get to the end and look back with regrets.'

I sense bitterness in her tone with her last words and know she is talking about the years she has wasted in an unhappy marriage.

'But she needs me,' I say helplessly. 'They both do.'

'I have no doubt. But there are always, *always*, options. Please don't use them as an excuse.'

I start at her words, an angry retort rising to my lips. Then I stop as her words really connect. It knocks the air right out of my lungs. She's right. I *am* using them as an excuse, because I'm terrified of taking a chance and failing.

'I'll leave you to it,' she says, getting to her feet and dusting the sand off her dress. I look up at her, with the sun silhouetted behind her head, and I realise it's not just her wardrobe that has changed. She looks happier, at peace. Content and more self-assured. She looks radiant.

'It was nice to see you again,' I say. 'Thank you.'

'You're welcome. Don't be a stranger.' She smiles as she walks away.

I think about her words long after she's gone. While the sun sinks lower and bleeds orange into the ocean until they merge into one fiery show. My fingers itch to capture the moment on my camera but I didn't bring it. I think about spending every day doing something I love and for the first time I feel stirrings of excitement instead of fear.

'Should I do this?' I ask. '*Can* I really do this?'

The tide, even though it has been receding in front of my eyes, swells up with a small rogue wave that washes up the beach to bubble around my ankles. I laugh and cry at the same time as I jump to my feet and chase the water back down the beach till I am standing in it up to my knees.

'I'll take that as a yes.' I breathe in the scent that smells of my lover and let it fill my body with strength.

'Catch you on the next drift, Al-*bear*,' I whisper.

Acknowledgements

My tremendous thanks and gratitude to my husband, Karl, and our beautiful children: Holly, Willow, and Leo. Without your enduring patience and understanding this book would never have seen the light of day. Kids, your kisses and cuddles made the hours locked away from you in a room hammering at a keyboard all the more bearable. I did this to make you proud.

Thank you to my friends and family. Especially my wonderful dad, Tony Ryan, brother Rob Ryan and twin sister Kerrie Ryan, for all your encouragement and your unwavering belief that one day you'd be able to buy my books off a shelf in a shop. Well guess what, now you can (and you'd better!). Eternal thanks to my mum, Patrice Ryan, who is sadly no longer physically with us. She always knew I would be a published author (she was very clever like that). I miss you more than I have words for.

Also, thanks to my aunt, Jacqui Morrissey, for looking out for me after mum was gone.

Huge gratitude to Vicki Marsdon, my enthusiastic agent extraordinaire! Thanks for taking me on *even* after I made you cry. You're always there with encouragement and advice, and not just on writing either.

Thank you Emma Beswetherick and Anna Boatman at Piatkus for falling in love with Maddy and Albert's story and championing it to your colleagues and the Powers that Be. And to Kate Stevens and everyone else at Hachette Australia and New Zealand, for also believing in its potential. You have all been so friendly and welcoming, and you've made this publishing process an easy and enjoyable one. I am so fortunate to be in such good hands.

Thank you to the fabulous Tracy Fenton and the members of TBC (THE Book Club on Facebook). By far and large THE best online book club, you guys have been some of my biggest supporters. I can't wait to come to the UK to meet you all!

And lastly, I must acknowledge the wonder that is Lorraine Tipene, my first reader and treasured friend. Thank you for your honesty, advice, support and for just always being there.